WHAT GOES AROUND

JEN FAULKNER

Copyright © 2024 Jen Faulkner

The right of Jen Faulkner to be identified as the Author of the Work has been asserted by her in accordance with the Copyright, Designs and Patents Act 1988.

First published in 2024 by Bloodhound Books.

Apart from any use permitted under UK copyright law, this publication may only be reproduced, stored, or transmitted, in any form, or by any means, with prior permission in writing of the publisher or, in the case of reprographic production, in accordance with the terms of licences issued by the Copyright Licensing Agency.
All characters in this publication are fictitious and any resemblance to real persons, living or dead, is purely coincidental.

www.bloodhoundbooks.com

Print ISBN: 978-1-916978-24-9

For Alfie and Eddie xx

PROLOGUE

1997

Kicking doesn't work. Her arms thrash out, then her hands curve and paddle as though trying to pull her body up the rungs of a ladder.

Not long now, we'll save each other.

The breath in her lungs catches on fire and when her mouth reaches the sky, she gasps; the cool stormy air dousing the flames as lightning blazes across the clouds. Surprised to feel calm, she closes her eyes and lets the rough water drag her down, but only for a second.

Seaweed brushes against her leg and she flinches.

Where is she? I can't see her.

Panic sets in. Thudding in her chest. Ringing in her ears. The taste of saltwater on her tongue. Wave after wave pushes her up and pulls her down. Everything gets darker and darker, until the clouds and the sea blend into a swirling mass of grey and blue. The horizon is lost. The beach, and the two girls who stand there watching, swallowed whole.

She questions her motives for being here, for risking everything.

Why me? Not them? Never them.

But they'll learn. This can't be for nothing, however the day ends. Karma has to bite back. She chooses to believe this fact as all hope leaves her.

At least she tried.

Then a flash of red shimmers ahead. A glint of silver hides amongst the crimson ribbon. She's there. They've found each other.

Save her.

A surge of adrenaline propels her through the choppy sea, her legs full of power as though recharged. Her fingers stretch ahead, her arms long, her gaze fixed. They are close to the rocks. They can climb out of the sea instead of swimming to shore. Hope sneaks back in through the cracks of sunlight lighting up the waves and guiding the way.

But with every snatched glance the rocks appear smaller, as though she's looking through binoculars the wrong way round. The red is gone. She hears a scream, then a deep underwater thud. Then only the roar of the sea and the storm.

She can't move. Her battery is depleted. The sun vanishes behind a black cloud. Rain pelts down harder than before and she swallows water as though a desert has sucked her dry.

You tried. At least you tried.

The current carries her out to sea. The water wraps around her body like a net, capturing her, a lobster trapped in a pot.

Her last thought amidst the silence is comforting.

What goes around comes around. I promise.

ONE
BEX – 1997

My lips stung. An unpleasant sensation. More awkward than when Mum or Dad kissed me on the cheek, which rarely happened now I was a teenager. I rubbed my mouth as the tingle vanished, tasting an unfamiliar mix of beer and cigarettes that remained as I wiped.

Everyone was still, waiting for my reaction. Dance music, tinny, filled the space around us in the barn. All eyes on me, exactly how I liked them to be. Nicole and Mel glanced at each other and I sat back down, hiding the hammering of my heart behind a smirk. Damian laughed and moved back to his position on the opposite side of the circle, at the other end of the bottle in between us on the floor. He too massaged his lips, but with pressure as if to rub remnants of me deeper into him. He gripped the can of lager by his side, drew it towards him and gulped, before belching and blowing his stale breath in my direction, winking as he did so.

'Right.' Michael reached for the bottle. 'My turn.'

I looked around, all eyes now staring at the floor and no longer at me. Tempted to suggest I went again, wanting a better snog, I rose up, but Mel beat me to it, grabbing the bottle from his hands. I'd never seen her so bold before.

'I want to go first.' She placed the bottle on the floor in front of her.

Most of the boys in the circle curled their lips at the thought of kissing Mel, but none of them were brave enough to speak out. She twisted the bottle around before Michael could protest. His eyes glistened today and he'd styled his hair. He looked hot.

The boys jeered as the bottle slowed down and pointed at some spotty kid in the year above us. Laughter erupted as Mel's turn ended in a brief peck and a sulky expression on her face, before Michael grabbed the bottle.

I looked over at Nicole; her expression was fraught, as though she wanted to cry. Her arms were folded across her chest – a barrier between her and the bottle – willing the top to pass her by and pick someone else every time a boy spun the brown glass, drips of beer flinging out. Everyone knew this wasn't an ideal place to have a first kiss. Not romantic, not private. Not like I'd imagined, but being in the centre of the circle and the focus of everyone's attention felt amazing, so who cared about the other crap? Backing out wasn't an option. Nicole needed to suck her fear up. This needed to be done. A line needed to be crossed.

The bottle spun around, dizzy, deciding where to strike next, and Michael, now on his knees and leaning forward in anticipation, watched, eyes wide. We all knew he wanted to kiss Nicole; he'd made no secret of the fact. He was older than us, and friends with my brother, Grant.

I'd fancied him since I was thirteen and he used to come round our house after school for dinner. Grant wasn't here even though the party was at his mate's house. It was a miracle I was here. Nicole, Emily and I never got invited to parties. Secretly, I was glad he wasn't because he would've hated watching his little sister play spin the bottle with his mates. I was annoyed Michael had taken a fancy to Nicole as soon as he'd first seen her. At school he often tried to sit next to her; and at every party he'd seek her out somehow.

But she didn't like him back. I knew that. Instead, she was intimidated by his intense attention. In truth, Nicole was intimidated by everything, and I hated her for it. How stupid was she for not wanting a boy who was gorgeous and clearly throwing himself at her?

His aftershave – Lynx or whatever it was – smelt divine, manly almost, this evening. He rubbed his hands and the scent was propelled in my direction.

Then the bottle stopped. Nicole's silent plea had not been answered. The bottle had chosen her as its next victim. Deep cheering from the lads filled the room as though they were congratulating Michael on scoring a winning try. He licked his lips, nostrils flared, and moved towards Nicole whose cheeks flushed pink. Her arms remained folded as they kissed. I watched, touching my own lips again, as Michael's tongue lashed around the outside of Nicole's mouth, trying hard to penetrate the barrier. She pulled away, saliva glistening across her chin, marking Michael's trespass attempt. I felt sick. I'd seen Michael kiss other girls before, but this was different. Nicole was my mate and she knew how much I liked him.

I'd been so busy watching their kiss I hadn't noticed Mel leave the room, the gap she'd left in the circle big enough for two people. I didn't care where she'd gone. She was annoying. Plus, if I went to find her I would be leaving Nicole and Michael alone and I didn't want to give him any further opportunity to kiss her again.

The circle broke up and some of the lads went out the back to smoke, while others got more beer from the cool-boxes dotted around the room. The party was just getting started even though all of the parents had been told pick-up was at eleven on the dot and the time was now quarter to. Michael didn't have far to travel, this being his house. Having a home with a small barn attached came with the responsibility of hosting all the teenage parties, which he loved.

A sudden cheer alerted me to a new arrival to the room. Emily, fashionably late as always, not giving a crap about what anyone thought.

'Where have you been?' I whispered in her ear. 'You missed spin the bottle.'

'My aunt wouldn't let me come so I had to wait until she was asleep before I could sneak out.'

'Well, you missed Nicole kissing Michael.' I folded my arms and raised my eyebrows encouraging her to be outraged. I knew Michael was the one who had driven the kiss, but in my head she kissed him. 'She knows I like him. How dare she.'

Always the one who got the most attention, was Nicole. All the teachers at school loved her. She had nice parents too. Some bitches got all the luck. Although, there was some dark rumour about her uncle, something dodgy, but when I'd pushed her on what, she wouldn't elaborate.

Bright lines shone through the window – lighting up the bricks covered in cobwebs on the wall opposite – as a car pulled into the driveway. The beams settled on me as the car turned, making me a rabbit caught in headlights. My heart thudded in my chest. I knew who had arrived. And I knew why. Tears formed in my eyes. I wanted to run and hide.

Looking through the window at the number plate my suspicions were confirmed. My dad. He didn't care where I was most of the time, didn't even notice me, and yet now – the one time I didn't want to have a normal parent, one who turned up to make sure I got home safely – he was the first parent to arrive. I looked behind me and caught Michael leaning into his arm on the wall above Nicole's head, sipping his beer and leering over her. She glanced up at him, smiled as though she was a small child and he was a drunk uncle asking for a kiss on the cheek at Christmas. She wasn't encouraging him, but she wasn't pushing him away.

Why wasn't she talking to him about me? Telling him how amazing *I* was? Why was she getting all of his attention again?

My dad beeped the horn of his car, and before anyone realised I was the one whose stupid parent had turned up on time, I snuck out of the barn.

I climbed into the car and looked at my dad, wondering if he knew what we'd been up to in the small barn outside Michael's house. Did the furrow in his brow mean he was remembering what sixteen-year-old boys thought about and did with those thoughts? Was he anxious teenage boys now thought that way about his daughter? Although – if their actions and words were anything to go by tonight – the boys didn't lust after me at all, they only wanted Nicole.

We drove home in silence. Dad didn't even care enough to ask how the evening had gone. Tears welled in my eyes again. I needed a plan. A plan to make everyone notice me. A plan to give me the attention I deserved. A plan to make Michael realise he wanted me, not Nicole.

A smile spread across my lips, and I licked them, removing any trace of the kiss from earlier. The plan needed to be big. Something no one could fail to notice. Then everyone would be talking about me, me, me.

I'd show Nicole.

I'd show them all.

TWO
NICOLE - 2022

The world has a strange hovering and swirling mist when Nicole loses herself in her mind. The sky lowers around her. The ground softens and swallows her whole. Her senses dull until no smells, no sounds are left.

She is there.

She is here.

Except, she isn't.

Nicole is not here, nor there. She is trapped inside herself.

Sounds flow from Bryony's mouth as she stands and talks opposite Nicole. Her friend's lips move and Nicole laughs. But Nicole isn't listening. Yes, she nods as though she's heard. And every now and again she stretches her lips into a thin smile so Bryony thinks Nicole is present, engaged in their conversation. But she isn't.

Because she doesn't care.

Nicole has listened to Bryony whinge many times before and usually ignores her friend when she's like this. And today, she has no energy for Bryony's angst. Bryony's small mouth moves, her foundation cracking along the upper lip, every groove revealing her secret smoking habit.

Bryony thinks Nicole cares. She thinks Nicole wants to listen. She thinks everyone wants to listen.

But none of what Bryony is saying is important.

Today, Bryony isn't important.

'I have to go,' Nicole says. 'I've got the dentist.'

She doesn't have the dentist.

'Oh, okay. Drinks soon though, right?' Bryony moves to cuddle her.

Not again, Nicole thinks. The ghost of the horrendous hangover from the last time they drank cocktails together still lingers.

Then Nicole switches off. Without Bryony realising, she retreats into her head, with the dark skies and soft floors. A heavy weight claws at her neck and nestles in the base of her head and she takes a deep breath in.

'Thursday?' Bryony asks. 'How about Thursday?'

'I'll need to check my diary,' Nicole replies – even though she knows she's free because she has no job, no hobbies and her twin sons all but ignore her unless they want food – but now it's Bryony who isn't listening.

'Great.' Bryony claps. 'Thursday then. I'll tell Emily.'

You can tell her, Nicole thinks, *but she won't come.*

'I'll let you know, okay? Joe might be out.' Nicole steps backwards. Bryony knows her boys are old enough to stay at home alone, but Nicole is scrabbling for an excuse. Besides, Thursday is visiting day at the prison and she's never in the mood for a night out as the guilt of not visiting Uncle Tom with her mum is still too much for her to make peace with, even though her mum never questions why.

With a dismissive wave she turns and walks away. The waft of stale cigarettes released from Bryony follows her. The noises of the busy main road alongside the shops buffet her. The stench from the overflowing bin beside them makes her want to retch.

The mist has lifted.

Back at home Nicole makes dinner and puts a load of washing on while her teenage twin boys take themselves to their bedrooms. Kieran and Luke don't care if she isn't fully here. They are used to this half-Nicole, this almost all-right mother. They know they'll still be fed and watered, which is enough for any teenager.

'Mum,' they shout a little later. 'Mum!' They sigh, wave their hands in front of Nicole's face, and then she hears them tell each other, 'She's gone again.' They roll their eyes and leave her to dream. They know she'll be back when the buzzer goes and the sausages are done, even though they are at an age now where they could cook their own dinners as well as hers.

Standing by the back door to the garden, imagining smoking a cigarette even though she gave up twenty-five years ago, the memory of smelling them on Bryony still vivid, she waits for the buzzer on the oven to trill.

The neighbour's cat washes himself under the cherry tree in front of her. Short, sharp licks along his back legs. Sweet flicks over his ears. *Cats know how to do self-care right,* Nicole thinks. The cat looks at her and then licks himself clean again. Every last bit of her gaze lapped up and swallowed.

As she stands at the back door the blurry, calming mist she craves sneaks in through the tiny crack in the window. Waves roll away from her. The ceiling lowers. The floor dips, but she cannot get lost again. And then the smells start. The unwanted memories return.

Seaweed. Saltiness. Bracken and thistles. Smells she hates. Smells marking all of that horrible day from the start to the end. They creep up her nostrils and for a minute the stench is so powerful she retches into the darkness outside. But she isn't there, at the beach. She is here, safe, at home. And she's toed the line today. Nothing bad will happen.

Write her a letter, Nicole was once told by a counsellor. *Apologise.*

The letter remains unwritten. This way is easier. Ignorance works. Imagine the mist. Do the right thing.

Detach.

Avoid.

Behave.

Sleep.

Repeat.

Then she hears a sound. Loud. Insistent.

In the lounge the phone rings.

No one ever rings the landline.

'Hello,' Nicole gasps, out of breath having run from outside, knowing neither of the children would think to answer. Knowing the only reason this phone rings is because someone wants to deliver bad news. *He's gone down again. Fifteen years this time.* The sudden lurch back to reality making her heart race and her hands tremble.

'Nicole,' the deep, comforting and familiar voice says, 'it's me. They think she's going soon. Please come. Say you'll come. They are asking for you.'

She scrunches her eyes to stop the tears. 'I'm on my way.'

The phone clicks as the call ends. She watches as the mist rolls around the lounge door. Silver threads wind towards her from everywhere. Down the stairs. Through the kitchen archway. The ends of the threads look like fingers reaching out towards her. They grab hold of her clothes. Her hair.

She's going soon.

Nicole has run out of time. *She* couldn't read a letter now.

She hadn't been able to since that day on the beach. And besides, Nicole is convinced telling everyone the truth will only make everyone hurt more. The guilt she feels is here to stay. And she deserves to be overwhelmed by every little bit.

A hand is placed on her shoulder.

'Joe?' Nicole's husband is beside her in the lounge. When had he got home? How had he known?

'I'll drive you,' he says and holds out his hand when she tells him what is happening. He is patient. Even though he has always known her like this, he doesn't know the real truth as to why. He thinks she's this way because of her uncle. But that's not even close to the truth.

Joe's waited a long time for Nicole to be fully present. For this to end.

But then, what next?

Downstairs in the house where her friend grew up, Nicole is escorted into the back room. The one where the family ate and laughed, but now houses *her*. A scent Nicole can't place makes her stop. Not the sterile smell of hospitals in this makeshift hospice room, but warmer. Comforting.

Three people gather around her hospital bed in the centre of the room, the one their last fundraising escapade paid for. Walking one hundred miles across the Pennine Way, the South West Coastal Path too close to the sea for them to even contemplate ambling alongside it. Too near the waves that caused the accident and irreversible brain damage, paralysing their daughter.

She lies here, motionless, her eyes closed. Her breathing is slow, the beeping of the machines even slower. Her skin is translucent, as though dissolving as she dies.

The patient's mother turns to face Nicole, tears in her eyes, and beckons her over. Nicole embraces her, holding back tears of her own, then touches her sleeping friend's cold hand, not sure what to expect, but surprised when the fingers don't squeeze back like they used to.

A nurse in the far corner writes on a chart, looking as though she is only pretending to do this to give them all some much-needed space.

'How long?' Nicole winces at her own insensitivity.

The mother shakes her head, the father murmurs, 'We don't know, but soon.'

Nicole leans over her friend, bends down to her face and whispers, 'Goodbye' in her ear. She cannot say the other word, the one she came to say, not here, not now, not in front of everyone. They don't know and they mustn't find out. She cannot believe Bex Williams is dying after all these years. In an alternate universe she's married to Michael with four children and a huge mortgage.

'Thank you for letting me say goodbye.' Nicole attempts a smile. 'I'll leave you with her.' They all nod, no one knowing what to say, and she leaves with a heavy heart.

As she walks to her car she lets the tears fall and allows herself to fully embrace the pain and the guilt. Then she quashes the wave of relief threatening to flood her. With Bex gone, only one other person knows what happened, and she has as much to lose as Nicole. The truth cannot escape now.

Her phone buzzes with a message and she rolls her eyes, frustrated she has no time to process her last visit here. One of the twins will be demanding a lift somewhere no doubt. *Not now,* she thinks. Then she looks towards Joe in the car, waiting for her. The sudden image of her husband trying to offer her comfort she doesn't deserve makes her want to walk away from him forever.

Pulling the phone from her bag she stares at the screen and stops dead.

A text from an unknown number. Five words.

> I know what you did.

Then another. Only two.

> Own up.

THREE
EMILY – 2022

'Fuck's sake,' Emily mutters as someone rushes out of the shop to her right and bumps into her.

Wincing, she rubs her arm and throws them a glare she usually saves for when she's had enough of the teenagers she teaches. Nicole would apologise. Not Emily.

'Watch where you're going,' she snaps and walks away. Her bad mood fuelled by the encounter, she's hoping a glass of wine – or five with a couple of tequila chasers – with Nicole will help soothe her, and tonight it is only the two of them, no Bryony.

The end of term is looming and her temper is always frayed during the last couple of weeks where the children have had more than enough of her and of school. And this term – the first term of the year – is always the one she hates the most. The multicoloured leaves begin to fall off the trees leaving them bare and ugly, their branches stretching out like arthritic fingers. The bright blue sky of summer turns grey and dark before anyone is ready to hunker down. Remnants of long summer days still fizz in everyone's minds and no one is in the mood for Christmas, even though the shops are already stocking mince pies with sell-by dates in November.

The pavement is peppered with chewing gum, fag butts and the odd mask and she spits her gum out, knowing the huff from behind her is designed to provoke.

Ignoring the cries of 'Pick it up, dirty bitch,' she walks into the bar and sees Nicole already there, halfway through a large glass of white wine. Emily is late, again, but after many years Nicole is used to her tardiness, says she likes to have some time on her own away from the kids and Emily is doing her a favour by not arriving on time. But tonight, Emily is tardy because she debated about whether or not to even come.

Sucking her frustrations and fears deep inside her, she inhales and walks over to Nicole, playing with a smile on her lips.

'Hey babe,' she says, and Nicole looks up from her phone. Her eyes are puffier than usual and her nose a touch red at the end. She's been crying, Emily is sure. And then, when Nicole grabs her and pulls her in for one of her death hugs, Emily knows why.

Tears prick at her eyes. Emily never fucking cries. She hates her body for trying to make her. Nicole holds on a fraction too long and Emily pulls away and orders a double vodka and coke. Wine isn't going to be enough tonight. They don't speak for a while. Taking a tissue from her bag Nicole dabs at her eyes and sniffs. They knew this day was coming, and you'd think after twenty-five years they'd be prepared. But this raw emotion brings back every ounce of grief and guilt she's ever experienced. The loss of her parents, as a child. Her divorce, three years ago.

But most of all, that bloody day on the beach.

'Sorry.' Nicole blows her nose. 'I didn't expect to be this upset. It's been... so long, I thought I'd done all my crying.'

'Grief is a funny old thing, Nic. Better out than in.' The counsellor had told her this after her parents had died on the same day, when she was nine years old. She'd thought the counsellor had meant she needed to poo more often.

'Yeah, but I mean it's not like I've lost a child. Or a parent.' Nicole grimaces. 'Sorry.'

Emily waves her apology away and empties her glass. 'Don't be a twat. You've had your fair share of shit. It's fine. You're allowed to be upset.' *So are you*, a tiny voice in Emily's head says, but she doesn't respond.

Nicole glazes over and Emily clicks her fingers in front of her face. 'Hey! No mist nonsense please.' Emily hates Nicole when she does this. 'Not now, Nic. You don't need to escape me, okay?'

Nicole had told Emily about her coping mechanism when they were younger. How she'd started losing herself in an imaginary mist, probably around the time her uncle first went to prison and her parents, adamant she must not follow him, became even stricter. But her zoning out drives Emily fucking nuts.

'Sorry.'

'And stop saying sorry, seriously.' Emily is regretting coming. She looks at her drink and spins the ice around in the glass. 'Did you see her?' Emily asks, glaring at the floor.

Nicole nods her head and cries again. 'Yes, briefly.' A look passes across Nicole's face that Emily can't read. For a moment Emily thinks she's going to tell her something, and then changes her mind.

Ordering another drink, Emily processes everything. Nicole was good to have gone and seen Bex, but then she always does the right thing. Emily had lied when they'd called and asked her to go as well. She'd said she was caught up at a parents' evening at school.

The barman puts a couple of drinks for someone else next to them on the bar and without thinking Emily picks one of them up and downs the shot before placing the glass beside Nicole's.

Nicole doesn't say anything, but her disapproving glare speaks volumes. When the barman returns he looks puzzled.

'You okay?' Emily asks him.

He ruffles his hair. 'Swear I made two drinks and put them here,' he says.

'Only saw you put one down.' Emily watches Nicole's eyebrows rise.

He shakes his head in disbelief. 'Didn't sleep too well last night, feel like I'm losing my mind.'

Emily laughs and tells him she feels the same at times and when he is ready she could do with another double vodka and coke.

'Coming right up.'

He totters off and Emily winks at Nicole. She looks tired, thinks Emily. Her hair is a bit greasy as though she skipped washing it today. And her skin is paler than usual. But it's more than how she looks. Nicole is slumped on the bar stool instead of sitting up straight as she normally would.

'You still feel guilty, don't you?' Emily narrows her eyes. She knows the answer. Nicole feels enough guilt for the both of them.

'Of course I feel guilty. And now, even though I thought I'd feel better when this day came, my God, I feel so much worse.'

'You need to let everything go. I've been saying so for years.'

'But I can't. And I don't know how you've been able to.'

'We can't change the past so why worry about it. Bex chose to come with us. We didn't force her to do anything.'

'No, we didn't force her, but we did lie to her. And then, if we hadn't done what we did then maybe, just maybe…' Nicole stops as more tears well in her eyes; her hand goes to her mouth. She picks at the skin on her lips.

Emily looks at the door, wanting to escape. 'Nicole, get a fucking grip.'

'Is your heart totally made of stone?'

'No. I simply don't see the point of crying over an event from so long ago–'

'But there should be consequences,' Nicole interrupts. 'We did the wrong thing, made the wrong choices, and she's the only one who has suffered ever since.'

Jeez, Nicole and the bloody rules. Her uncle's actions ruined any chance she ever had of caring about other people less.

'There are consequences.' Emily throws her hands in the air. 'Your guilt is one of them.'

They sit in silence. Laughter drifts over from the table opposite. Four women nurse glasses full of Prosecco. Their cheeks flush, they clutch their stomachs and their shoulders shudder as they giggle. At no point in her life has Emily had a group of female friends she can laugh with like that. Not even with Nicole and Bex back at school. Their competitiveness over boys, as well as Emily falling for Bex's older brother, Grant, often got in the way of their friendship. And many of the women she'd called friends after she married Grant, sided with their own husbands when they separated. Their fake friendships were as dead as her marriage.

'I need to talk to you about something else.' Nicole's glare is intense. She has her phone in her hand, like she wants to show Emily something on it.

'I'm listening.'

Nicole continues to stare and Emily shifts in her seat, uncomfortable, feeling as if she is about to be interrogated. But then Nicole shakes her head.

'Never mind. Let's change the subject.' Nicole puts her phone down. 'How's work?'

'The usual. One of my class called me a stupid idiot today after I told him to stop playing on his phone.'

'Nice.'

'It's the go-to abuse at the end of term.' Emily signals to the barman she'd still like that drink, potentially the one to tip her over the edge and confirm she can no longer hold her booze like she used to. 'They've all had enough of me and I of them. But hey, three more days and counting.'

'The boys are knackered too; they come in from school and do nothing but sit in front of the TV or the computer. They might have to have a lot of screen time over the half term. I haven't got the energy to challenge them.'

'You're too soft.' Not for the first time Emily is grateful she doesn't teach at the same secondary school as Nicole's kids. She's often amazed at how Nicole's parenting style is the polar opposite of her parents'. All she had were rules; her children have none.

'I can't be arsed with the arguments.'

A waft of strong aftershave shrouds them as a group of men walk past to a table at the far end of the bar. Inhaling, Emily closes her eyes and tries to remember the last time she was close enough to a man to smell his aftershave. Neglected parts of her body tingle as the scent hits the back of her nose, before she shakes the feelings off, puts her desires back into a box, and tries once again to throw away the key.

'And Joe, how is he?' she asks.

'Always at work, but fine I think. He drove me there last night even though he still has no clue why I am so upset about everything.'

Emily clenches her teeth as Nicole brings up the one thing she doesn't want to talk about again. 'I'm thinking of signing up to Tinder. Wanna help me swipe right?' She grabs her phone and changes the subject.

Nicole's eyes narrow, but if she's irritated by Emily, she doesn't show it. Maybe now they can get some closure and finally move on.

Otherwise, now it's all over, Emily may have to move on from Nicole.

FOUR
MEL – 1997

I didn't want a friendship with them, honestly I didn't. But I did want to be included so I could tell them to sod off, just once. They weren't even the cool group, the populars, though they were not the geeks either. Just some kind of weird middle-ground group, and what pissed me off most about them was they were so happy with each other. Like they didn't need anyone else. I didn't know any other sixteen-year-olds who felt so comfortable and secure. Although, I had heard them arguing about Michael the other day, so maybe not everything was rosy.

'Beans please,' I snapped at the upper-sixth-form student handing out the lunch today.

'Cheese too?'

I hesitated, then nodded. Mum would be cross I'd caved and gone over my calorie intake for the day, but I didn't care. When she weighed me later I'd tell her I'd got my period and was bloated. I'd only had one bar of chocolate at break, so everything should be evened out. Those three didn't know how lucky they were being skinny and not ugly. I moved along to the dessert table and hovered beside the cinnamon cakes and custard, my least favourite of all the desserts they offered here for lunch, but better than nothing. Double physics this afternoon required sugar.

Walking out into the refectory and down the middle of the long tables jutting out from either side, I looked for somewhere to sit. The only spaces available were the seats at the end of the tables, where no one ever wanted to eat their lunch because then you had to take up everyone's dirty plates for washing when they'd finished eating. The students weren't meant to start sitting on a new table until those dreaded seats were filled, but everyone did. This act of defiance annoyed me because the whole process of lunchtime was then even longer and, aside from the eating, lunchtime was the worst part of the day for me.

The teacher on duty today wasn't paying attention and I could have walked on by and sat at a new table, but I didn't. There was an irritating part of me always forcing me to do as I was told. I looked down at my plate and at the cheese I was not meant to eat. I scraped most of the melted cheese off onto the side of my tray, gloopy and glistening with oil.

Without making eye contact with anyone I sat at the end of one of the long wooden tables next to some third-formers. They looked so young, so fresh-faced and full of hope. Not yet worn down by the small injustices that happened daily as you went through school.

I choked on a baked bean as a loud laugh came from the door behind me and I turned to see the three of them walking in, arms linked as though they could never bear to be apart and not touching. Bex was in the middle as usual. So much confidence bursting from her, but then everyone wanted to be friends with her because they fancied her hot older brother, Grant. Bex could pick and choose her friends, but she'd picked Emily and Nicole and the three of them didn't want anyone else. I went to primary school with Emily and Nicole and they'd never needed anyone else. I was surprised they let Bex in, but then, Emily *was* snogging her brother.

They nudged my chair as they walked past.

'Move in, fatty,' one of them muttered, Emily I think, and I hung my head so low my chin nearly touched the beans on my plate. They knew I couldn't move my chair in, and I was grateful they didn't nudge me again.

One day I would call them up on their shitty behaviour. Nicole and Emily were never like this at primary school. They were close, yes, but they weren't bullies. Bex had changed everything. Changed them. Secretly, I hoped Michael would get between them and break the toxic trio up. But really, I wanted him to choose me.

I stacked the third-formers' dirty plates and as I took them up to the dirty washing bench I glanced over at Nicole. She was looking right at me, smiling and looking apologetic. But then Bex reached out and grabbed her arm, pulling her so close no light passed through the point where their bodies met.

Gritting my teeth, I dropped the knife I clenched into the sink, and walked away.

FIVE
NICOLE – 2022

Nicole stares out of her car window, still unsettled by the nasty texts. She tries to recall seeing anyone else on the beach that day who might know what they did, but the weather had been awful and visibility poor, and twenty-five years on she's tried to erase most of the memories. Assuming the texts were about then, and not something else.

At first – and she felt bad for even doubting her friend – she did wonder if they could be from Emily. Mistrust and Emily go hand in hand, Nicole knows how devious her best friend can be, and yet not with her. Emily has always had Nicole's back, and so if the messages are from Emily, why now? Nicole doesn't know why she didn't simply ask her outright last night at the bar. Then she flicks the doubt away. No, not Emily. Not her style. She'd be direct, not mess about behind her back.

Nicole is stuck in traffic on her way to see her parents. The dutiful daughter visiting once a week, tidying whatever needs tidying and listening to whatever moan her mum needs to offload. It's often about her last visit to Uncle Tom. Or, very rarely, an explanation of why she couldn't visit that particular week.

The road to their house, the one Nicole grew up in, passes the beach where the accident happened. Often Nicole will drive the long way round and avoid the coastline altogether, but she's in a rush today and so chose to drive alongside the shoreline. A decision she now regrets.

The weather has taken a turn. Gone are the warm autumn days of September. Cold has flooded the small seaside town. Everyone wears winter coats and hats. Shops where customers bustle all summer are boarded up for the winter. Every year Nicole thinks the change happens overnight, with no warning. She is often still wearing her flip-flops when everyone else has switched to boots and thermal socks.

Her week sucks so far, and to top everything off she is having a nightmare period. Why your body doesn't stop menstruating the minute you decide children are no longer an option for you, Nicole doesn't know. She dreads this time of the month, rage and irritability more present with every one. Spending time with her parents when she feels like this isn't ideal. She wants to go home and curl up under a blanket with a hot-water bottle and sleep until the cramps and anger subside. But at home there won't be any rest. Dinner will need cooking. Clothes will need washing. Joe will need servicing.

A loud beep from behind makes her jump and she sticks her middle finger up at the driver in the car to her rear. The van in front has only moved a couple of inches at best; she's got nowhere to go.

'Bog off,' she shouts and then regrets her words when she sees the impatient driver get out of his car and walk over to hers. Her heart thumps in her chest. She grips the steering wheel and calms her breathing. She checks the doors are locked. *Crap, he looks really angry.* Why did she flick him the bird?

The man bangs on her window. 'Open up.'

Nicole is too scared to even crack the window a little bit in case her trembling fingers won't be able to stop a gaping hole from appearing beside her. She imagines his big hands reaching in and grabbing her neck. She can't swallow. 'I'm sorry,' she mouths to him through the glass. Her hands lifted beside her head in mock surrender. 'I'm having a bad day. I don't know what came over me.'

'Don't take your women's crap out on me, love.' He is pointing now. People walking by avert their gazes; no one looks as though they would be willing to challenge this man. She is safe in her car. But what if he follows her when the traffic moves again? Her stomach cramps get stronger, and she puts her hand below her belly button and rubs the ache away.

'I said I'm sorry.' She sounds braver than she feels. He looks like the wolf about to huff and puff his way into her car, his stale breath seeping through cracks she can't see.

At times like this she wishes she could be more like Emily. This man, this horrible aggressive man, did not need to beep his horn at her to get her to move less than a metre up the backside of the car in front of her. *He* is the one who is being unreasonable, and yet she feels as though she is the one in the wrong. Emily would sit here now with both middle fingers pressed against the window, Nicole knows it.

'I'm really sorry.' Nicole tries to be strong; she cannot continue to apologise. Her chest tightens as though she is having a contraction and her lungs are giving birth to her fear. 'But you beeped me for no reason. I can't move anywhere.' She gestures to the road in front of her, where there isn't even enough space to swing her parents' cat.

'I'm late for a meeting,' he shouts, not giving up.

'That's not my fault.' She bites her lip. *Do not say he should've left earlier and given himself more time*, she tells herself. *Do not say it.*

'You're a fucking joke.' He bangs the window with his fist

and for a second Nicole thinks the glass might shatter. She holds her breath. The air in the car is charged with energy. Feeling like she should stand up for herself, she contemplates getting out; unbuckles her seatbelt, inhales deeply. And then, before she can face him on the road outside, he throws his hands in the air and goes back to his car.

Trying not to cry Nicole blinks and looks upwards. Shame and loathing wash over her. She hates how she allows people like him to make her feel bad about herself. Ever since she was a child, after the very first time her mum had slapped her cheek for misbehaving, she hasn't been able to do anything wrong, even by accident, without guilt weighing her down. *You'll end up like Uncle Tom, in jail, alone.*

Do the right thing, is her mantra. *Be kind. Put others first. Don't stick your middle finger up at dickheads who might then want to shout at you about your poor behaviour.*

She sobs, wiping the tears from her cheeks, remembering the red blush of the slap, of the shame. And of the fear she'd do something wrong and be taken away from her home and locked in a cell with no windows and no light.

Looking to the left she sees an elderly couple making their way along the promenade. Bright lights, dimmed in the daylight and ready to burst into life as dusk falls, hang above them and sway in the breeze. They walk arm in arm, hers linked in his as though he is holding her up and pulling her along. She wonders if this couple have always told each other the truth, or whether, like her, they have hidden parts of their lives or themselves, from the person who is meant to love them unconditionally.

Nicole isn't sure why she never told Joe the truth about the accident. She is certain Emily hasn't ever mentioned that day to Grant either. And so, if those two things are facts, then Emily must be the one who sent her those threatening messages because she is the only one who knows what happened. But again, why now? Nicole cannot figure Emily's motivation out. She shakes her head. Not Emily. But then, if not Emily, who?

The old couple have stopped to stare out over the English Channel. Her head rests on his shoulders; his arm snakes around her back.

They must've been through so much together, Nicole thinks. And yet here they are, side by side, embracing by the sea, holding each other up.

She thinks of her parents. If they were to walk along the promenade they wouldn't be arm in arm. Her mum would march ahead, arms either folded across her chest, or swinging by her side as though she is in a hurry. And her dad would amble behind, trying to take everything in breath by breath, not wanting to change anything, least of all her mum.

Acceptance is a hard concept to grasp for some, but not for Nicole. No. She'd accepted her fate from the day she was first shown by her mum how she would only be loved if she behaved. And if she didn't behave, she'd end up alone.

A loud beep blares behind her and she jumps again. The cars in front have moved a little way ahead and she's angered the man behind even more by not following them within seconds and closing the miniscule gap.

This time she doesn't stick her middle finger up at him, but instead holds her hand up by way of apology.

She is disgusted with herself.

Idling once more she looks at the threatening messages on her phone.

Maybe she should send one back.

SIX
EMILY – 2022

The supermarket's lights shine through the darkness and Emily pulls up outside. She is only here for booze and maybe some comfort food on her way home from work. Another bloody evening looms ahead of her with nothing to do and nowhere to go. But at least she has nearly reached the end of term intact, and so have her students.

Yawning, she opens the car door and walks towards the shop before swearing under her breath and heading back to the car for forgotten bags. Every. Single. Time.

'Ha, me too,' a deep voice to her right says.

She smiles and rolls her eyes at the stranger, an unexpected warm feeling of reassurance she's not the only one spreads through her.

The car park is full and the shop will be packed with customers, tired at the tail-end of a busy week and in need of convenience food for dinner. A young couple walk in front of her holding hands. They take turns to stare at each other and smile. Instead of their obvious love giving Emily hope, their public display of affection makes her feel empty.

You push away anyone who loves you, Grant had said before

they were divorced. *Except Nicole,* he'd added and Emily has always wondered if he'd been jealous of their friendship, or if there was more to his words. She and Nicole were the ones who came out of the accident unscathed. The same could not be said of his sister.

It's a wonder they got married, her and Grant, she often thinks, but by the time he proposed there was a bond set too deep for her to even contemplate not saying yes. Then – after several years of not speaking to them once his parents had divorced – he'd decided to reconcile with them, the final nail embedded in the coffin of his and Emily's marriage. After that, Emily was no longer excused from visiting Bex.

Bex was there on their wedding day, in body, but not in mind. Emily remembers her eyes and the way they had stared right through her as though trying to tell Emily she didn't exist, that she was invisible. Unimportant.

The message Bex's eyes had portrayed then hurt more than if they'd revealed anger.

The bashing of rattling trollies as someone tries to shove a pound in a free one brings Emily back to the present.

'Bollocks.' The man standing by the trolleys looks at her as though she is responsible for his distress. 'I've lost my pound coin. It's stuck.'

'I reckon they make them faulty on purpose,' she says. 'Every penny counts, more like.' The corners of his lips turn upwards in the hint of a smile.

'Here.' She hands him a trolley token with a smiley emoji on the front. 'Have one of my tokens. They do the same thing as a pound coin, but don't anger you as much when they get stuck. I've got loads.'

His smile now reaches his eyes as he takes it, brushing the back of her hand as he does so. A tingle runs up her arm. His eyes are a piercing shade of blue and she swears she sees the flash of a suggestion or thought flutter over them as he looks at her.

'Thanks,' he says, holding up the token. 'You sure?'

'Positive. It's my duty to go around saving people from the thieving trollies. Now don't lose it!'

'Ha, I won't.' He inserts the round token into the trolley. 'Thank you. Have a good weekend.'

'You too,' Emily says, and for some reason salutes him. Her cheeks flush red. Without hesitating she grabs her own trolley, suppressing every instinct she has not to turn around and see if he's looking back at her.

The supermarket is heaving and she skips the fruit and veg aisle and heads straight for the pizzas, picking up one with a little bit of veg on so it's not all crap. There'd been donuts in the staff room earlier and she'd had three for lunch. With the threat of perimenopause looming she is determined to take full advantage of her metabolism before everything goes tits up or, in all probability, tits down.

Her favourite wine is on offer and she takes this as a sign to buy three bottles, vowing not to drink them all before Monday, even though she has nothing better to do.

The queues at the tills stretch far back into the aisles behind them. Hoards of hurried customers tap their fingers on the trolleys and frown into the distance. Some check their phones. Others open packets of grapes and feed them to their impatient children. Her heart quickens and her palms are sweaty. She wants out, and now. She wants to go home and put her pyjamas on, curl up under a blanket and shut out the world.

She walks over to the self-service tills where the queues are smaller and waits. A child shouts to his mum about how he hasn't seen his cousin for a long time and is going to go now whether she likes it or not. An old man, hearing aids in both ears, roars at his companion about how he'd been to Stan's funeral, which had been lovely. She stands and listens. Everyone's voices blend into one painful intrusion and her head hurts. The tills beep. Cutlery crashes from the café to her right. Plates smash together as they are cleared. Chairs rub against the wooden floor as people stand up and sit down. She hears laughter. Freezer doors slam shut after their frozen contents are picked out.

'Hey, lovely.' Bryony is waving and shouting at her from the queue to her right.

Emily pretends she is engrossed with her phone, even though it'll make no difference to Bryony.

'Emily,' Bryony shouts again. 'Yoo-hoo!'

Emily waves and smiles, but doesn't move out of her line. *Thank fuck for queues,* she thinks as Bryony is also stuck in hers, loading her shopping – quinoa and smoothies Emily swears she only buys for show – onto the conveyor belt. Emily sends up a silent prayer, hoping she can be through the self-service tills before Bryony and shoot off. She hasn't got the excuse of someone waiting to be fed at home and Bryony knows it. Then she feels guilty. Bryony is a nice person; Emily simply needs to be in the right mood for her.

'Sorry,' Emily mouths as a till becomes free. She scans the wine and places the bottles in a shopping bag.

Glancing over she sees Bryony is being served. Emily doesn't scan anything else, but simply packs the remaining items into her bags.

The member of staff supervising the tills is fraught and doesn't glance at her basket or bags when she confirms Emily is over twenty-five years of age without so much as clocking the wrinkles under her eyes. Emily holds her breath. Her skin tingles. Bryony is loading her trolley with the last of her fully scanned goods and is delving into her bag for her purse. No time left. Emily cannot get caught in conversation.

Using her phone to pay she waits for the beep and races out of the store, a pilfered pizza and a tub of double-salted caramel ice cream burning a hole in the heavy bag nestled amongst the bottles of wine.

With seconds to spare, she gets into her car and locks the doors before pulling away, her wheels making a screeching noise as she does. She grits her teeth. Bryony emerges from the supermarket, struggling to control her overloaded trolley, as Emily sails past the main entrance giving her the silent finger.

'Fuck you, Bryony,' she shouts in the car and then bursts out laughing. She hasn't stolen anything for years, but fucking hell the rush is still amazing. Her senses are sharpened, blood bursts from her hurried heart and fires up every muscle. *You need to go back and pay,* Nicole's imagined voice says. But Emily shouts, 'Fuck you too, Nicole,' and drives on.

For too long she has felt like she is sleeping through life with one eye open, waiting to be caught out. Kleptomania was a secret habit of hers after her parents passed away. But as an adult the rush is harder, higher. She feels as if she has taken all of the drugs, and not the ones half cut with brick dust. Pure, solid gold, class A drugs.

By the time she arrives home twenty minutes later the buzz has dulled, but she still feels no guilt. She steps over the post on the doormat, ignoring the envelopes containing unpaid bills, walks into the kitchen and pours herself a large glass of wine. The wine she paid for. Then she turns on the oven and unpacks the stolen pizza. *It's only pizza,* she tells herself. She spends enough money in that damn shop; this won't kill them.

Emily sits at the breakfast bar and opens up Facebook. Over the past few years she's wanted to delete her page, but curiosity often gets the better of her and she checks in once or twice a day to see if any of her exes have messaged, or if any of her own school friends – not that there were many beside Nicole and Bex – have joined her in the divorced club.

Louise is the one person she wishes would. She was always chief bitch at school. The one who named them 'The Goodies' and left them out of any illicit parties she held when her parents were out of town. Thank fuck Facebook hadn't been around back then as Emily knows she'd have spent most of her evenings trawling through her feed for evidence of Grant, who was always invited, snogging someone else. Or maybe she'd have wasted hours looking for Nicole and Bex in the background of a photo, in case they had lied to her about not being included when the invitations were handed out.

She smirks as she realises if Facebook had been around when she was at university there would no doubt have been many a drunken photo of her on there.

Sipping her wine she scrolls through the adverts for bras and mattresses and then, as her wine goes down the wrong way and she splutters, she stops on a post that takes the wind out of her. Bex's death has been announced in the way all deaths are announced nowadays. Her parents have updated her page, Bex's Army.

Emily doesn't know why they've called themselves an army. It's been many years since Bex was able to go to war in the physical sense. She reads on.

> We are heartbroken to announce Bex passed away peacefully in her sleep with her close friends and family beside her. She was courageous to the very end and her bravery will inspire us all to continue to live and love without her. Her funeral will be held next Friday, and then as we do every year on the anniversary of her accident, a memorial service will be held on the 28th October. Details to follow. Donations to St Luke's Hospice.

Emily doesn't want to, but she sobs anyway then gulps the rest of her wine before refilling her glass to the top and downing the drink in one. Twenty-five years ago was the last time she'd seen Bex at the beach, but she'd thought about her every day since even though she'd tried not to. That day hadn't changed her. Instead, the tragedy had exacerbated what had lurked inside of her for years. Accidents happen. First her parents. Then Bex.

She doesn't want to take the blame for any of them, but the truth is they'd all still be alive if she'd made different decisions on the days their lives had changed or ended, so she has no choice but to take the blame.

The oven beeps. She slices up the pizza and leaves nothing but crumbs on her plate.

SEVEN
NICOLE – 2022

'Mum, what do you fancy for dinner?' Nicole shouts through to the living room. She swears her parents save up their dishes for when she comes over knowing she'll sort the dishwasher they never use and tidy up for them without question.

Her older sister, Lily, never does, even though she lives five minutes away from them. In fact, she contributes to the mess even though she is over forty and married herself. She pops round for a home-cooked meal from Mum every Tuesday evening. Her freezer, unlike Nicole's, is stocked with cottage pies and fish pies their mum has made for her. Whereas when Nicole comes she's the chef, the cleaner, and very much the adult in the relationship, not the child.

'How about the lovely casserole you do?' Nicole's mum appears at the doorway. 'We haven't had that for a while.'

She looks well, Nicole thinks. Her hair shows signs of having been professionally cut and highlighted – her mum refuses to go grey. And her nails are red and shiny too. Her mum has never wanted to grow old disgracefully; appearance as important to her now as when Nicole was younger. A value Nicole has tried to shrug off, but struggles. Still she cannot leave the house without mascara on. Ever.

'Do you have the ingredients?' Nicole inhales deeply, praying her mother will say yes.

'The shopping delivery is coming in an hour, and yes I've ordered the ingredients. I've been craving casserole all week.'

'Great. And I'll be here to help you unpack and put everything away too.' Nicole is positive her mum doesn't hear the sarcastic tone to her voice, but she can't be sure.

'Wonderful. I didn't know if your father would be home from golf in time to help and you do know how my hands struggle to carry the bags what with my arthritis.'

'I do, Mum, yes. How are your hands?'

Her mum rubs at the base of her left palm. 'Sore, but not too bad.'

'Shall I make a cuppa while we wait for the shopping then?'

Nicole's mum looks at the clock. Nicole knows she's deciding if it's an acceptable time to have a gin or not. 'Yes, a cup of tea would be lovely.'

Nicole can't remember the last time someone made her a cup of tea. Her parents aren't bad people – they don't steal or lie, and they never hit her after the first, painful slap – but they do put themselves before anyone else. Nicole wishes she could put herself first more often, but people-pleasing was so ingrained in her, she wouldn't know where to start in order to change. Plus, she doesn't think her family would know what to do or how to cope if she did.

'Get those nice biscuits out the cupboard too,' her mum shouts from the hallway.

Nicole stands next to the kettle as the water boils and waits for the mist to come and give her five minutes' peace, but the gap beneath the doorway remains clear.

She takes the tea through. In the lounge Nicole's mum is sat on the larger of the two sofas reading a newspaper. 'Did you see this article on Brexit?'

'No, Mum.'

'Scaremongering again they are.'

'Probably.'

Her mum doesn't look up from the paper, but tuts and Nicole tries very hard not to roll her eyes.

'Bex died,' Nicole blurts out and for a fraction of a second her mum doesn't move. Then she closes the newspaper and puts it down on the coffee table in front of them. 'How sad,' she says. 'Did you go and see her?'

'Of course, but I doubt she knew I was there. Her parents said she'd mostly been slipping in and out of consciousness for a few days beforehand.'

'Did Emily go with you?'

'What do you think? As far as Emily is concerned Bex died on the beach. She's never visited her. Her refusal to do so is one of the reasons her and Grant finally split up.'

'She always did ignore anything she doesn't want to deal with.'

Nicole bites down frustration. Her mum and Emily had never got on.

'She's been through a lot, Mum.'

'She had a wonderful upbringing, even after her parents died. Living in a big house with her aunt.'

'Emily lost her parents when she was nine. No amount of money or love can make up for that.'

'Well, it's better than when I was a child with that brother of mine.'

Here we go again, thinks Nicole. 'She was very close to her aunt as well, and she also died. Emily has had to deal with so much, Mum. So many losses.'

Her mum shakes her head and waves her hand. 'Of course, I

do remember you know, she was here all the time, but it's not the same. My brother, growing up was hard for me.'

'I forgot the biscuits,' Nicole says and, before her mum can tell her she's drunk her tea and has nothing left to dunk them in anyway, she gets up and marches into the kitchen.

Grabbing the worktop she steadies herself. Her mum can be so judgemental at times, and play the victim. Growing up in an end-of-terrace house with damp in the corners of the ceilings and sharing a room with three siblings, one of whom became a criminal far too young, is not the same as losing both of your parents as a child, Nicole thinks. She saw what Emily went through. The process of coming to terms with everything was horrific.

Grabbing the biscuits, Waitrose Finest no less, Nicole heads back into the lounge with her composure intact.

'Here you go.' She hands the packet to her mum before taking a biscuit herself.

Photos of her and her sister's children are on display in various frames around the room. Lily and Robert on their wedding day too.

'Where's the photo of Joe and me on our wedding day?'

'Your dad managed to smash the frame while dusting. Haven't had the time to buy a new one.'

No, but you've had the time to do your nails and hair, Nicole thinks and then catches herself being as judgemental as her mum.

'I'm going to go to Bex's funeral, but wondered if you wanted to come to her memorial with me? It's on the 28th.'

'Oh, I can't, love. That's when I have badminton. But do pass on my condolences to her parents, and Grant.'

Nicole sighs. 'Of course.' Acknowledging a funeral and a memorial so close together is a lot. She tries to understand how this all is from Bex's parents' point of view. But she can't. Do they feel guilty too? She wonders, remembering someone once telling her how every death injects remorse into all involved.

Nicole's mum picks up the newspaper again, indicating the conversation to be over. Nicole doesn't understand why her mum won't come to the memorial. Bex had been a regular fixture in their house for years when they were teenagers.

But then she concluded there was no point in trying to understand how other people's minds worked, when she didn't even understand her own. 'Might nip up to my old bedroom before the shopping comes. I want to look for something.'

Her mum nods, but does not look up.

Nicole takes the stairs two at a time and crosses the landing to her old bedroom. She recalls many a night, when as a teenager, she'd been tempted to sneak out – knowing Emily wanted to gatecrash the latest house party they weren't invited to – but couldn't quite bring herself to leave on so many occasions. Her parents would never have known if she had. Her dad sleeps as though he is dead, and her mum pops at least three pills so she does the same. And yet, as a teenager, Nicole couldn't ever fully rebel as often as she'd wanted to.

Her parents have never redecorated her bedroom; the wallpaper is the same as when she lived here, as is the bedding. Blue and yellow swirls mix with green leaves. Nicole used to find the colours soothing as she'd lie on her bed and follow the patterns when falling asleep, but now the walls look as though a toddler has been allowed to go wild with some poster paints.

She walks over to the far corner below the window and pulls the bookcase away from the wall. Reaching in, her hand touches the cold metal of the object she is looking for, amongst dust and spider webs, still there, hidden from sight for twenty-five years. Nicole is grateful her mum is a terrible cleaner and would never think to dust behind here.

Wincing as she twists her arm to pull the hidden hip flask

out, she turns the cold metal in her hands, unscrews the top and has a sniff. Only a dank metallic scent resides inside.

Two initials are stamped on the front, NH, belonging to Emily's dad. Emily doesn't know Nicole has the hip flask or that she took it from her bag that day. She hadn't wanted Emily – never one to think things through – to leave the flask anywhere that might reveal the truth about what happened to Bex. Even though Emily would understand the significance of someone else finding it on the beach after the accident, Nicole couldn't risk leaving the incriminating evidence in her hands. The flask holds little significance now and can't be tied to the events of that day. But still she won't throw the damn thing away.

Pulling her phone from her back pocket, she opens up the recent threatening messages. Whoever they are from, she must not let them intimidate her. For once she has to stand up for herself.

She reads through them once more, and then she types back.

> You know nothing. Leave me alone.

Putting her phone back in her pocket, she slides the hip flask behind the bookcase once more. No one else knows it's here. No one else knows anything.

And she is determined for things to remain that way.

EIGHT
BEX – 1997

'We shouldn't be here.' Bex studied her friends, but there was no sign of agreement. Not even from Nicole, who kept glancing over her shoulder towards the back of the beach. Emily smirked.

October 28th saw the first chill of autumn. But by the middle of the afternoon the air had warmed and rain dripped down the back of Bex's coat onto her neck. Her short fringe stuck to her forehead. She wished she'd brought an umbrella. The dark sky loomed in the distance as though night-time approached.

'Pass me the lighter.' Emily held her hand out towards Nicole. She lit her cigarette and exhaled a long, slow river of smoke. 'You sure you don't want one?' Emily asked for the second time, holding out the packet of cigarettes.

Bex shook her head, biting down the frustration.

'Fair enough.' Emily shrugged, but Bex knew Emily didn't understand why she'd refused. Emily didn't understand anyone who didn't want the same things as her. Smoking, in Emily's eyes, was the ultimate rebellion and today they were rebelling.

Funny how the world hated people who followed the rules from an early age, Bex thought, as though conforming was an infectious disease. And strange how people viewed teenagers who broke the rules as attention-seekers. Today, Bex knew how those attention-seekers felt. She thought about Michael, and wondered if he'd come today like she'd asked him to. She needed him here for what she had planned.

The sea salt hit the back of her throat as she looked out at the waves in the distance. Raging in, one after the other, their roar drowned out the call of the herring gulls hovering above. White foam, carried along the top of the waves, washed up the beach and rested there as the water retreated. In and out, one after the other, no break, no gap. Rolling up the beach. Rolling back out to sea. She ached to dive in. To feel the cold water tighten her skin and take her breath away. She buried her bare feet in the sand, pushing deeper as the rough grains dug under her toenails and brushed against the blister on her heel.

'Do you think anyone will wonder where we are?' Nicole frowned and looked at her watch. 'I mean, I told my parents I was going to the library to study, but they might check and find I'm not there.' Her legs shook and Bex wasn't sure if the movement was down to nerves or the chill in the air.

'I don't care.' Emily stubbed her cigarette out in the sand and pulled her hood down as the rain eased. 'That's why we're doing this, right? My aunt is at work until late anyway today.'

'Right.' Nicole nodded, but looked unsure.

No, Bex wanted to shout. That wasn't why she was here. But they wouldn't think to question her motives. These days Emily and Nicole believed Bex to be the sheep, the one who followed, not the farmer she once was. An act she'd perfected over the last few months, giving Emily in particular the control over her she craved.

But, not anymore. Today, here on the beach, everything was about to change.

They were the ones who wanted to break the rules.

And Bex was going to decide the consequences.

NINE
EMILY – 2022

'Are you sure you're okay, Em?' Anna asks. 'You look a bit rough?'

Emily has worked with Anna at this school for a long time. They aren't close enough for Emily to consider calling her a friend, but she is a colleague Emily trusts. Throughout Emily's divorce Anna would often tell her she looked as though her body had been through an earthquake – the force crumbling her outer layer of defence – and broken. Anna is an English teacher. She loves a simile or a metaphor, thinks Emily.

'I'm fine,' Emily replies and Anna winces. 'Why, do I smell?' She sniffs under her arms, but is met with the scent of the deodorant she'd sprayed on five minutes earlier.

'No, not at all. It's just some of the kids in your class said you... well, you got a bit irritable with them earlier and said "fuck" under your breath quite a few times.'

Emily sucks air in through her teeth and shakes her head. 'Brandon was being a dick.' She notices Anna grimace at her speaking about a student that way. 'You know what he's like, he was in one of his moods and he went too far. Touched a nerve, that's all.'

'Okay, if you say so.' Anna holds her hands up. Emily reassures herself Anna's not the head of year or even anyone who would need to act on this, simply a colleague who can lend an ear. 'Can I do anything?' Anna's eyebrows are raised.

'Take my class the next time I've got Brandon? Last period I think.' Emily laughs knowing Anna is not allowed to do this, nor can she because she doesn't have a bloody clue about anything to do with maths.

'Wish I could, Em, but I've got English with the year sevens then. Oh the joys.'

'Might nip out for a quick fag. You wanna come?' Not sure why she asked, she's hoping Anna says no, craving a few minutes by herself.

'I'll come with you, but I'm not going to stand anywhere near you. You know I don't smoke.'

'Yeah I know, but it's never too late to start.' Emily ignores the wave of irritation rushing through her. She's out of sorts, uncomfortable in her own body even. Bex's death has brought back the emotions she felt after the passing of her parents and her aunt. She hates how grief does that. Lies hidden, below the surface, then attaches itself to any loss regardless of how significant and explodes back into full force. When her aunt died she didn't think she would ever be able to function again. The grief had been overwhelming.

They walk in silence out through the side doors of the staff room and onto the little patch of grass outside, invisible to all students. An old chair – left out in the rain so many times a shiny blanket of green slime adorns the plastic – rests against the building. The caretaker was meant to remove the chair ages ago, but hasn't and Emily isn't sure why. Maybe he feels it's outside his remit, and will not do as he's asked this one time after all the other times he's been put upon and has gone above and beyond to make the school safe and presentable for everyone.

'So how are the kids?' Emily exhales a long, slow plume of smoke, not caring what Anna's answer is, but feeling like she needs to put the focus of this conversation on Anna, and not her.

'All good.' Anna waves her hand in front of her face even though the smoke from Emily's mouth is being blown in the opposite direction. 'Martin's settled in at uni, although I'm still adjusting to him going, and Esme is in her final year now. The moment I get rid of both of them, one will be bloody coming home soon. Children can't afford to buy or rent anywhere these days.'

Emily smiles and then for a second gets lost in thought. She's not too old to have children now, but she's never wanted them. Anna's youngest child, Martin, is friends with one of Nicole's twins – they went to Scouts together and hit it off – unlike Nicole and Anna, who have never warmed to each other. Anna thinks Nicole is a goody-two-shoes, and a bit virtuous with it. She's told Emily before about how Nicole makes her feel inferior, especially if she ever hovered on the double yellows by the Scout hut when picking up her son. Nicole would park miles away and walk, head held high, as though proving a point. As if she was better than anyone else for doing the right thing. Emily understands the irritation Anna feels, but also understands why Nicole behaves the way she does.

'Right, best get back.' Emily stubs her fag out with her foot. She inhales deeply, the stale smell of smoke already coating her tongue. She needs gum and some body spray before going into class.

'You sure you're okay to teach?' Anna asks. 'Do you need to take the afternoon off?'

'Honestly, I'm fine. Didn't sleep well last night. We all have off days, right?' *Please don't pity me*, she thinks.

'Right.' Anna shrugs, but Emily knows she isn't convinced.

She probably thinks Emily is hiding a secret. Wouldn't be the first time. 'I'll see you later.'

Back in the staff room Anna waves a hand as she leaves, and Emily notices she's left her bag on one of the long and uncomfortable chairs no one ever sits on, unless a staff meeting is so well attended they have no choice. They are covered with scratchy material that makes your legs itch.

Emily looks around the room and contemplates taking Anna's bag to her classroom. But then a bubble of danger pops in her stomach and her heart picks up the pace. She needs chewing gum; maybe Anna has some in her bag. At least, that'll be the excuse she gives if she's caught.

Walking over, she grabs the handle and moves the bag onto the table, right next to her own. Then she makes herself a coffee in a dirty cup and pours in two sugars.

She stands by the bags. A bead of sweat drips down the base of her spine. She closes her eyes and shakes her head. Stealing from a large supermarket is one thing; from a colleague is entirely different. Emily isn't even sure what Anna could have in her bag she would want to take. But her hands fizz as though they are out of her control and she knows she's going to look; no amount of mental back and forth is going to stop her. Placing a hand in front of her mouth she breathes into her palm, checking the smell of her breath, looking for signs of smoke, starting the façade.

The bell trills for third period and she has minutes before she is due in front of her GCSE maths top set, a class of students who could descend into chaos if she is even a second late. Footsteps shuffle outside the staff-room door and she stops to sip her coffee, the hot liquid stinging her mouth. Then silence.

Without a pause for breath she unzips Anna's bag and looks inside. Tampons, a wallet, some painkillers fill the space within, and a faint smell of Anna's body spray. Nothing special. Nothing Emily wants. The fizz fizzles out. But, as she is about to close the bag, she catches sight of an item she didn't expect to see, right there, at the bottom. She looks closer. Tucked into a corner of the inner fabric is a green lighter.

Lying bitch, Emily thinks. *She does smoke after all.* Emily pulls the lighter out and into her back pocket. She throws Anna's bag back onto the uncomfortable chair, picks up her own and heads to class. A smile plays on the corner of her lips and satisfaction washes over her.

Laughing, she pats the lighter in her pocket. Stealing is so easy, she thinks, and yet so effective at making her feel good. Better than a shot of vodka or a drag of a cigarette.

When Emily had introduced Bex to her little stealing secret all those years ago Bex had described the sensation perfectly – simple little thefts packing an adrenaline-fuelled punch.

The trouble is, as Emily knows all too well, soon she'll need to start stealing more and more, with added risk, to get the same hit.

Without getting caught.

TEN
EMILY – 1997

Emily came in here every day after school and always nicked chocolate or sweets. She'd been stopped leaving before, after the owner had caught her stuffing a Twix up her sleeve, but she'd screamed he was harassing her, that he had touched her inappropriately even though he'd only put a finger on her shoulder to make her turn around. She knew the looks he'd got from other shoppers had made him fear he'd get a reputation and worry his business would suffer. Now, every time she came in, she smirked at him, knowing damn well there wasn't a bloody thing he could do to stop her stealing.

She'd tried to get Nicole and Bex in on the act. Nicole didn't want to be involved ever, and would stand outside, her arms folded, a scowl on her face. She'd give the occasional huff as she peered through the glass of the door before looking away again. But Bex was tempted. Thought Michael might think she was cool for nicking stuff no doubt.

'Emily,' Bex called over as she stood reading a magazine she wasn't going to pay for. 'Twix or Mars?'

Emily bit her lip and looked at the ceiling in thought before replying, 'Both.' Bex stuffed a Twix up her sleeve, and then took two Mars bars to the till. They didn't steal everything. Emily smirked.

'You gonna make me pay for these or what?' Bex's voice was smooth, confident as she spoke to the shop owner.

'That'll be 58p please.' The owner held out his hand and she handed him a jumble of coins that spilled out onto the counter. Then she grabbed the chocolate bars and left before he could even count the money and see if she needed change, although Emily suspected Bex hadn't even given him enough anyway. Emily put the magazine on the shelf and turned to leave.

'She's got issues, that one,' a voice said from behind the magazine shelves. 'You need to be careful being friends with her.' Then Mrs Farrow stood beside her, leaning on her walking stick. Emily swore this woman only came into the shop for gossip.

'Don't we all?' Emily replied, and walked closer to Mrs Farrow, who had a basket in her free hand with one apple, one banana and a crossword puzzle book inside it.

'True.' Mrs Farrow nodded as though she was an expert. 'But on my way here yesterday I had to walk past her house, and oh the racket coming from inside. Made me blush to hear it.'

'What do you mean?' Emily knew she was prying, but she couldn't help herself.

'Screaming about this and that. If you ask me, I think her dad's been having an affair and her mum doesn't want him back, but he's refusing to leave.'

'Are you sure?'

'I know what I heard.' Mrs Farrow's voice is a whisper. 'She screamed that this wasn't the first time and that she's had enough.'

'She could be screaming about anything. You're a nosy old bat.'

'I don't care what you think of me. But I'm telling you he looks shifty, like the type to cheat, you know? Grease in his hair and a stupid fancy car.'

Emily thought then that Mrs Farrow might've been watching too much TV and the type of programmes she liked had propelled her mind into overdrive. She needed a better hobby than spying on people.

'None of your business really, is it, Mrs Farrow?' Emily leant in.

'It is my business if they are going to scream so loud I can hear them when I am walking past. What if he'd got violent, he could've stormed out of the house and attacked me.' She lifted up her walking stick and Emily was certain Mrs Farrow would be more than comfortable using the wooden pole as a weapon if provoked.

'Only those today?' The shop owner pointed at Mrs Farrow's basket in an attempt to shut her up and get Emily to leave.

'Yes.' She turned to face him, her back now towards Emily. 'Got my son coming to stay and much as I hate him ignoring me, he does love a crossword puzzle.'

The owner put Mrs Farrow's shopping in a bag for her and watched, eyes narrow, as Emily slowly made her way out of the shop, her pockets empty.

Outside, Bex, who was sat on the wall, threw a Mars Bar at her. 'What took you so long?' Nicole was beside her, scowling.

'Tried to steal the old bat's purse, didn't I?'

'And?'

'She didn't have one, just a load of coins in her pocket.'

Bex jumped off the wall and the three of them walked towards home, Emily shoving the chocolate in her mouth, and wondering what secrets Bex was hiding about her home life. Her parents had always appeared so cool, allowing Bex to do anything she pleased. But maybe that was the lie.

For the first time, Emily wondered which was worse – no parents, or ones who didn't care at all.

ELEVEN
NICOLE – 2022

Dressed head to toe in black, a simple burst of colour as requested in the form of a bright-pink scarf, the reflection in the car mirror tries hard to convince Nicole she looks the part she has to play today, of the guilt-free, grieving best friend.

She contemplated not going, anxious her remorse would pour out of her, leaving only the painful truth behind for all to see. A result the person behind the threatening texts would revel in. But Nicole wants to set fire to the memories. She wants the smoke to filter up her nostrils and leave an acrid stench in the small hairs until everything is burned away.

Entering the church – even though she is two hours early and no one else will be here yet – makes Nicole's guts lurch. Outside is miserable; she needs to seek shelter for a minute or two until the rain eases off.

She's been to many funerals before but this one is different. She has to prepare herself. Her tongue sticks to the roof of her mouth as though she's eaten rancid food and is trying to lick away the taste.

Since Bex died everyone keeps telling her, as though she should be reassured when she is not, that Bex is at peace now. Everyone thinks what happened was a tragic accident, and this collective belief makes Nicole grateful. Other people have formed a narrative of Bex's demise, of how Nicole must feel. She isn't going to be the one to change their stories.

She walks up the aisle, reminded for a brief moment of doing the same on her wedding day, and looks at the altar. Tall, stained-glass windows loom over her. Flowers, a mix of white and yellow, stand proud in vases at either side. A grey-haired man is playing the organ. Nicole listens and smiles. She doesn't recognise the tune, but is soothed by the melody even though she often thinks organ music sounds like tone-deaf singers struggling to hit the right note.

She picks up an order of service from the pile on a table at the end of the aisle, but she can't look at the photo of Bex on the front without a lump forming in her throat. Bex is grinning from the middle of a wave, her arms thrown up high above her head; an interesting choice of photo given what killed her. The picture reminds Nicole of simpler times, when all they had to worry about was getting their homework in on the right day or recording the charts without the DJ speaking over the music.

'Hello?'

Nicole turns as a hand rests on her shoulder.

The vicar smiles at her. 'You're here early.' He clasps a bible to his chest and looks puzzled.

'I know,' Nicole replies. 'I'm not a huge fan of funerals. I wanted to get all the emotion out before everyone else is here. Is that okay?'

The vicar smiles again, his head tilted to one side. 'Of course it's okay. We're getting ready for the service. You're lucky we don't have one beforehand today like usual.'

'Thank you.' She takes a step back. The vicar is standing too close to her and she can't catch her breath. 'I'm heading to Bex's house in a second to wait for,' her mouth is dry and she licks her lips, 'the hearse.'

Nicole wonders if the vicar knows she doesn't want to look at the coffin, touch the wood, be anywhere near Bex's body. The thought makes vomit rise to the back of her throat. She rubs the base of her neck.

'You do whatever you need to do.' The vicar puts one hand on her shoulder again. She can smell his aftershave, musky and slightly stale. Nicole takes another step back. 'Today will be tough, but the service will be a wonderful celebration of her life.'

'Of course.' Nicole walks out of the church, stops and turns at the door. 'I'll see you later. Thank you.'

The rain has stopped, but puddles line the pathway back to her car. She turns the keys in the ignition and switches the radio on. Within seconds she realises what song they are playing and she punches the radio off. She can't listen to the song. Why is that tune on the radio now? Today? She hasn't heard these lyrics for years. Is Bex watching from beyond the grave?

'Barbie Girl'. How they'd loved and loathed that song in equal measure. Nicole imagines Bex laughing and pretending she's singing the lyrics, 'undress me everywhere' to Michael.

Nicole wants to cry.

She turns the radio back on. The song has ended and the intense emotion of remembering Bex and October 1997 dissipates. Nicole will need to learn to deal with these little reminders hitting her when she least expects them. That's when she notices the absence of the mist again, frustrated the silvery cloud isn't seeping in between the cracks of the car doors and through the air-conditioning vents, enveloping her in a trance as usual. She hasn't got the headspace to wonder why she can't access the release she craves.

The journey to Bex's passes in a blur. Checking her phone Nicole sees she has three missed calls from Joe, probably wondering where she is. She hadn't told him she was planning on going to the church first. He might be at home waiting to drive her to Bex's. She sends him a quick text to let him know she is already here and gets out of the car. The front door is open. A cold draught from the entrance to the house surges through the hallway, and seeps uninvited into all of the rooms downstairs.

'Hello?' Nicole calls out from the hallway.

'In here.' They are in the lounge. Grant is in a chair in the far corner and Bex's mum and dad are on the sofa, holding hands, which is unusual given they divorced twenty years ago and couldn't stand the sight of each other afterwards. They'd had argument after argument over Bex's care. The odds of staying together after her accident too much for them to beat, especially for a couple who'd had problems to begin with.

Bex's mum, Sylvia, dabs her nose with a tissue and looks out of the small window beside them.

'Nicole.' Sylvia embraces her. 'Thank you for coming. Is Emily with you?'

'No. I think she's meeting us at the church,' Nicole says, realising she's not even spoken to Emily today.

'Right, okay. I need to go and sort a few things,' Sylvia says. 'The hearse will be here soon.'

Grant remains mute. Bit odd, Nicole thinks, but then funerals are never easy and maybe he's trying to hold everything together for his parents. He'd reconciled with them separately at first, whilst he and Emily were still married. Today – and the day of Bex's death – are the only two times Nicole has seen them all in a room together since Emily and Grant's wedding for which they'd magically put a pin in their estrangement. Emily had never told her why Grant had fallen out with them back then, but Nicole suspected the reason was because they didn't like Emily. She knew they'd never been her biggest champions. Maybe they'd asked Grant to choose between them and her, and when he stayed loyal to Emily they'd all stopped talking to each other.

Nicole had seen a statistic once about the amount of families who are destroyed by life-changing accidents, and so she isn't surprised Bex's family struggled. But her guilt is compounded by the fact that two marriages are broken because of the choices she made that day.

Happy family photos are dotted around the room and in the far corner a large board filled with photos of Bex, both before and after her accident, stands in the space where they'd once huddled together and watched scary movies as teenagers. Nicole looks down at her hands, ashamed. Her stomach grumbles. She hasn't eaten today and a burning sensation drives its way into her throat.

'The hearse is here,' Grant says, and walks into the hallway, followed silently by Bex's dad. Nicole's acting skills haven't always been up to scratch, but today she leaves the guilt she feels here in this room, and sucks every other emotion in.

In contrast to earlier, the church car park is full. Nicole's head throbs and she rubs her temples. They'd ridden here in silence. She suspects Grant is trying to be stoic and not cry. And she still hasn't heard from Emily.

The funeral director opens the door for Nicole to get out. She watches Bex's coffin being unloaded from the hearse, and the lump in her throat is making her wonder if something is stuck in there. Grant's shoulders slump and his face screws up in pain. Nicole reaches out and rubs his back, but he pulls away.

Inside the church, people have already gathered and are huddled close together with their coats still done up. The mourners wear weary looks. They smile at Nicole as she walks down the aisle and takes her seat near the front, moving the reserved sign onto the floor. She looks around for Emily, but cannot see her among the throng of people; maybe she is using the toilet. Nicole sends her a quick, *Where the hell are you?* text and then switches her phone to silent. The organ player bashes the keys and plays the tune Nicole had heard earlier. And then, Bex lies there in her wooden casket.

The service passes in a blur. Hymns are sung. Then come the readings, one from Grant, another from a godmother who Nicole knows Bex disliked, and a eulogy. As everyone leaves, Nicole watches Grant and his mum and dad shake hands and kiss the cheeks of people she knows and those she doesn't. They thank them all for coming as they exit the church. Nicole embraces Sylvia. She rubs her back and tries to offer some comfort, whilst swallowing down the contents of her stomach. Sylvia's eyes are red and her arm is firmly locked in her ex-husband's, who has also not stopped crying.

'I'm going to find Emily,' she tells Sylvia. 'Before we head to the wake.'

Nicole reminds herself Emily lost her parents when she was a child, and then her aunt; maybe grief is why she isn't here. This funeral would obviously bring up some unpleasant memories for her. But still, it's odd. They started this together; they need to gain closure with each other too.

Fresh flowers brighten up several of the graves near the entrance of the church. Nicole stands near one and scans the crowd for Emily's wavy hair. In the distance a woman stands alone, as though hiding, behind a tall gravestone. Her hands wring together in front of her body. For a minute, Nicole thinks she knows the woman, her outline, the way her shoulders gently hunch, but she blinks and the woman is gone.

Nicole looks down at the flowers on the nearby graves and bends over to touch the petals. The petals hold fast to the stems and stand tall. They smell fresh. Nicole looks around again for Emily and shivers. But she can see no sign of her friend and before long Sylvia comes to take her to the car, and the wake.

'It was very quick at the end,' Nicole hears Sylvia repeating over and over again. And the reactions of the listeners are the same every time. Their heads dip to the side. They scrunch up their faces in sympathy. This funeral is becoming tiresome and Nicole is getting increasingly angry with Emily for not being here with her.

'Oh, how awful for you,' says a woman stood with Sylvia who Nicole doesn't know, her hand on her chest in mock horror. 'I can't imagine how terrible watching her die must've been. I don't know how I would react or what I would do.'

This behaviour is something Nicole is seeing a lot of today, both at the funeral earlier and at the wake. People are trying to put themselves in the position of the grieving parents, as though they have some innate morbid desire to experience how those who were close to Bex are feeling. Are they preparing themselves in case the same fate befalls them one day?

Nicole doubts they are actually trying to empathise. People always have a morbid fascination and want to know the minute details of how the death happened, or where and when. Maybe these people want to add the answers to those questions to the list of 'things not to do so I don't die'. They don't realise some deaths can be controlled, whilst others are beyond all control.

'Well,' Sylvia says to another couple of funeral attendees, 'I was lucky Grant,' she pauses, 'and Richard were with me when she died. I'm grateful I could be there with her, unlike–'

Suddenly she looks as though a balloon full of emotion has burst inside of her. 'Excuse me,' she says. 'I need to go and find someone.'

Nicole clenches her teeth at the subtle nod to someone else who isn't here today. She thinks back to the woman at the graveyard, and shakes her head, the thread of familiarity tugging at her once more. No. The woman wasn't her.

Nicole retreats into the kitchen and finds Grant sat at the table. Having the wake at their family home, even though they had not lived there as a family in many years, had seemed like a great idea, but people are hanging around and not leaving after a respectful amount of time and Nicole imagines he's had enough of staying strong now. Maybe if she clears away the sandwiches and nibbles then people will take the hint. She puts her hand over her mouth to stifle a yawn.

'Grant, are you okay?' Nicole asks at the doorway, not wanting to intrude.

His eyes are puffy, his shoulders high around his ears, having inched up throughout the day.

'What do you think?' he snaps and she thinks he has a fair point. 'But at least you showed up.'

'I'm annoyed at Emily too, you know.' And she really is. Nicole sits down and faces Grant. He doesn't say anything else. They hold hands across the table. His skin is smooth. His hands haven't been pummelled by life in the same way hers have. They are not worn down. No burns from cooking. No sun spots from spending days outside devoid of sunscreen. His fingers are slim and delicate, his ring finger bare. As far as Nicole knows he's not been with anyone since Emily and he divorced a few years ago. But then, how would she know?

As they sit here, tied by their grief and their hands, the back door bursts open and shatters their quiet moment. The calm sensation in Nicole's chest is snatched from her by the sound of the wood slamming against the dresser behind the door.

Emily stands in the doorway, the bright autumn sunshine outlining her silhouette as though she's risen from the dead.

'Fuck you both,' she says, and storms back out.

TWELVE
EMILY – 2022

Screw them. A rush of blood floods her head. An inner demon raised and taking control of her, she heads back to her car, spitting her chewing gum out on the path. Seeing Nicole and Grant hand in hand had made her want to punch them both. Showing up today, even if she'd missed the actual funeral, had taken every ounce of her strength. Hours spent pacing around her home, far too many cigarettes smoked, only to walk in on them holding hands across the table. *They can go fuck themselves.*

'Em,' Nicole calls from behind, but Emily doesn't turn around.

She'd chosen to come in through the back door because she wanted to slip in, say a private goodbye and slip out again unnoticed. Emily doesn't do sympathy, giving or receiving.

When they were younger, they hadn't needed to sneak in or out of Bex's house. Before they'd divorced, Bex's parents hadn't cared whether they were there or not, or if they were sober or not. There were no disapproving looks for wearing skirts too short. No harsh words berating them for applying excessive make-up. In fact, Sylvia would grab her handbag, pull out her deep-purple lipstick – the colour of a fresh bruise – and make them apply a thick coat before they left. Not that they were ever going anywhere except each other's houses or back gardens anyway.

Once, Bex held a party at her house when her parents were away, invited the whole year, but no one had come, which meant the five bottles of Lambrusco they'd bought had been drunk solely by the three of them. Nicole had thrown up for two days straight afterwards. Emily had a headache for a week. Bex had been unscathed.

'Em, will you slow down? It's not what you think.'

Emily swung round. 'Gee, where have I heard that before?' Her heart aches. Grant has always denied having an affair, but she can't quite bring herself to accept the raw emotions tied to him filing for divorce for no concrete reason. As though she alone is to blame for him leaving. Not worthy of love. Maybe having to choose between reconciling with his parents, and staying married to the woman who refused to acknowledge his sister was still alive, hadn't been a hard decision for him after all.

Nicole stands in front of her with her hands on her knees, panting. They haven't even walked far, Emily's car is literally down the road. But Emily's breath is coming in shallow waves too, as though she's been in a fight instead of bracing for one.

'It's not, Em, I promise.' Nicole takes a deep breath in, her voice high and strained. 'He's understandably upset. His sister just died.'

'She died years ago, Nicole. Don't tell me he's been holding onto his grief all this time, it's bullshit. He used to be glad we never visited her; he felt the same as me.'

Nicole straightens herself up, but her chest is still heaving. She shakes her head, puts her hand on her heart, her fingers splayed, clutching at her clothes. She glares at Emily.

'What?' Emily says. A bubble of anger catches fire inside

her throat. 'Why are you behaving as if I am the one who is being unreasonable?'

'Because you are being unreasonable.' Nicole pauses. 'In fact, you're being a bitch.' Nicole gasps at her own words. Her eyes are wide.

Now, Emily stands tall. Nicole never answers her back. She is a people-pleaser. Someone who sucks up their frustrations and discomfort and lets everyone else get away with being rude or unreasonable.

And Emily has played on this weakness for years.

'Excuse me?'

'I am so fed up of dealing with your crap, Em. You act like you are the only person who has ever suffered. Like you're the only one who deserves sympathy. Grant is clearly dealing with some challenging stuff today, no matter how he felt when Bex was alive or when you were married. He's not himself at all.'

'But...' Emily starts, but she has no words. The fireball in her belly will turn any she does have to pure venom if she speaks.

'You waltz around as though life owes you. I know what has happened to you is cruel, your parents dying when you were nine is horrific, your aunt too, but my God most of the rest of it,' she pauses and inhales deeply, 'this,' she points behind her towards Bex's house, 'this is all you. Bex's accident was *your* fault.'

You're wrong, thinks Emily, her body crumbling. *I killed my parents. Not Bex.*

'You were there on the beach too, you know.' Emily is seething. She speaks through gritted teeth. 'You've got as much to lose as me if anyone ever finds out.'

'Right, yes, you're right I was, but what you did wasn't my idea. I'm not the one who hurt our friend, put her in danger and then hid the fact from the whole world. I'm not sure you've ever felt guilty.'

One of the funeral guests walks past them, dressed in black having ignored the request to wear bright colours, head bowed in a nod to let them know they've heard the argument, but don't want to intervene or get involved. Emily doesn't recognise them anyway, and even if she did she's far beyond caring. As though a dimming light has finally flickered out inside her, she's lost all of her fight.

'Screw you, Nicole.' Her voice is as calm as the sea before a storm. 'Screw you and your "do good" attitude. Go and tell them we were there too, that Bex wasn't alone, go on.'

'That's what you want, isn't it?' Nicole frowns at her. She looks winded. 'You want me to tell everyone the truth. That's why you sent those messages to me.'

'What messages?'

Emily stares at her friend. She waits for a comeback, daring Nicole to challenge her further.

But Nicole rubs her forehead as though trying to press the frown away and smooth the deep groove settling in between her eyebrows. Emily knows what's coming next. Nicole will become vacant, her stupid mist allowing herself to detach from a difficult moment instead of facing reality. Nicole will run back to Grant, burst into tears and his arms will pull her close and rub her back and then they'll bond further by slagging Emily off and saying how selfish she's become. Hell no, has always been. Her self-absorption is one of the reasons why he left her. Isn't it?

They stand in silence for a while, neither knowing what to say or why they are waiting for the other to speak, instead of leaving. Emily looks down to the pavement and at the scattering of brown and yellow leaves in the gutter, blocking the drain and mingling with mud and crisp packets. No tenner there, hidden beneath the leaves; nothing by her feet worth stealing.

Then the realisation hits that the thrill from taking Anna's lighter has dampened to a dull fizz.

'Okay, Nicole. You win. I'm going.' And she walks away, her steps shaky as though she is teetering in high heels on a cobbled pavement. Then she stops and turns. 'Trying to be a saint won't fix this, Nic. Behaving in such a way won't ever make the guilt of what happened go away.'

'But being good helps me,' Nicole says, her eyes wet, her voice cracking. 'You know that. I need to do the right thing. Always.'

'Or you'll end up like Uncle Tom? That's bullshit and you know it. Most of the rules you claim to follow are your own made up set anyway. No one cares about whether you follow them or not. No Diet Coke after 3pm, only one packet of crisps a day, never drink more than two thirds of a bottle of wine in one sitting, always say please, park only in marked bays even in an emergency, even if it's only for two seconds. These actions don't make you a saint, Nic, but they do make you think you're better than everyone else.'

'I'm only doing what's right, Em. I care about other people, about the impact my actions might have on them. Look what happened the last time I didn't.'

'I care too,' Emily shouts, her fingers tapping at her chest. 'You sound so fucking preachy. Trouble is you've nothing else in your life that's important. You have no purpose; but following rules gives you one.' *This conversation needs to end,* Emily thinks. Nicole is never going to see things her way and her rule-following actually does have more to do with her estranged uncle in prison than anything else. But she's not going to bring him up again now. Bad shit happens, they might as well get what they can out of life in the meantime.

'And don't call me later to apologise because you think it's the right thing to do,' Emily calls over her shoulder.

Nicole throws up her arms and walks away.

Emily gets into her car and chucks her bag onto the empty

passenger seat, knowing she's potentially ended the only good relationship she's ever had, one spanning decades. Staring at her lap she waits to be overwhelmed by emotion, but instead she's numb. Without hesitating or looking back she starts the engine and pulls out of Bex's parents' road. But she doesn't head home.

Instead, she heads to where this all began.

THIRTEEN
NICOLE – 1997

'There you all are, together again,' Mr Jones said as he walked by. But he didn't make them go to class.

Yes, Nicole thought, *we are always together, always whispering.* And now they'd got a new menace in their eyes, like a fresh injection of hormones had infused them with an element of nerve. Since she'd joined their twosome, Bex Williams was always in the middle, Nicole and Emily on either side of her as though they were holding her up and balancing her out like counter-levers.

Nicole knew Mr Jones had always found the dynamics of their threesome fascinating, watching them and saying he'd never encountered anything quite like them in all his years as a teacher. As he walked into his office she thought back to when they'd first started at school here. Her and Emily were firm friends when they'd arrived at secondary school; they were so close she didn't think anyone would be able to penetrate their outer wall. Mel had tried, and failed. But Bex had somehow managed to smash the bricks and then rebuild the wall around them, with her safely inside the fort.

Nicole gets why the three of them confuse him. Their

reports from primary school had said Nicole and Emily were model students, even after Emily's parents had died suddenly. She appeared to have bypassed the angry, rebellious part of the grieving process. But Bex wasn't the same. Her report wasn't as glowing even though on paper she had no reason to be disruptive. At home were two parents, still together, and a brother, a prefect, was heading to university and leading by example. They had money too.

Nicole often thought – if she admitted to believing in such things – a touch of something beyond human understanding had brushed Bex and lived inside her. A part of her dormant, like a field mouse in winter, waking in spring and turning into a different animal, one who liked to cause trouble. Bex behaved as though another force swelled in her body, overtaking her mind and making her act out of character, before retreating again moments before a serious incident occurred. The opposite of Nicole, and yet those qualities attracted her to Bex.

Nicole turned and saw Mr Jones watching them through the glass in his office door. They were standing in the corridor when they should be in class. He ought to have told them to 'run along', but he didn't and she wasn't sure why.

Being late to class didn't have an impact on anyone but themselves. Tardiness was a grey area and never really punished. Girls often needed the toilet for personal reasons at awkward times, and Emily and Bex abused this, so them coming into class late was rarely questioned. To be honest, she thought, sometimes the teachers were mostly grateful the children turned up to class at all.

Nicole looked at her watch and tapped her foot. She didn't like being late, but couldn't admit she was uncomfortable bunking off. Bex laughed now, always the loudest, before Nicole leant in and used her hands to indicate they should maybe be a bit quieter. She moved backwards, and looked left and right as though checking they weren't going to be caught. This was the effect Bex had, making Nicole do things not within her nature.

But she was running out of patience. She hoped Mr Jones would help her out, make them go to class after all. But he'd sat down, closed his office door, his hands on the armrest of his chair.

'I'm going,' Nicole said and stormed off, knowing Bex would be shrugging and rolling her eyes at Emily. What would Emily do now, she wondered? Torn between her oldest, loyal friend, and the one who had offered her something a bit fresh and new. Nicole turned at the end of the corridor, watched as Emily hovered beside Bex, who unwrapped a stick of gum and threw the paper on the floor in front of her.

This was one step too far for Mr Jones and Nicole smirked as he opened his office door.

'Pick that up, Rebecca,' he ordered, pointing to the paper. 'Put it with your gum into the bin and then get to class.'

'Yes, sir,' she replied, just about managing to keep her eyes from rolling backwards again. She picked up the paper, spat out her gum and folded the wrapper up before putting the rubbish back in her bag.

Emily's cheeks flushed pink and she looked at the floor before they scurried towards Nicole.

One day, Nicole thought, *those two are going to get in some serious trouble, and if I'm unlucky, then they might take me down with them.*

FOURTEEN
NICOLE – 2022

'Doesn't look like any tables are free.' Bryony cranes her neck to peer further into the café as though she's missed a hidden corner they could nestle in, away from the cold air conditioning making Nicole's fringe flutter.

Nicole's limbs feel uncoordinated, her skin itchy. She is churning inside even though her body is still.

Bryony stands next to her, muttering under her breath. Nicole is unsure if she's meant to be paying attention or not.

'What do you want to do?' Bryony asks.

Leave, thinks Nicole, who isn't sure why she agreed to come in the first place. She wants to do nothing but hide under her duvet. In her mind, she skips into the future and pictures them stood frustrated in the centre of the café, their trays full of sandwiches and cappuccinos, scouring the room for signs of someone about to leave. Praying for silence amidst the noise as someone pauses their conversation to pick up their bag, or put on their coat.

'The queue is a bit long,' Nicole says. 'I'm not sure we'll get a seat. Maybe we should go.'

Bryony huffs then leans in and whispers, 'We could always

save a table?' She raises her eyebrows and shrugs, turning her back on a large sign politely, but firmly, requesting all customers wait until they have purchased their food and drinks before sitting down. Her bright-pink cheeks flaunt themselves on top of her dark foundation and bronzer.

Nicole rubs her own cheeks and pinches them to encourage some colour. She hadn't bothered to put any make-up on before she came out, like she usually would, and regrets this decision.

She shuffles on her feet, looks at Bryony then towards the seating area and back again. A fire ignites in her stomach, the heat flushing her cool chest. One of the women in the queue ahead of them, wearing a bright-orange scarf, is also umming and ahhing about whether to remain in line or ignore the large sign and nab a table before she has purchased anything.

Nicole's stomach rumbles, her tongue is dry. She's eaten no breakfast and drank nothing other than water this morning. Whether she wants to be with Bryony or not is irrelevant, she is starving. *I'll show you, Emily,* she thinks. *I can be reckless.*

'Sod it.' Nicole takes a step forward. 'Get me a cheese toastie, a packet of salt and vinegar crisps and a cappuccino. I'll be over there.' She points to a free table in the distance.

'You sure?' Bryony looks relieved Nicole has volunteered herself as the risk taker.

'Hell yes,' Nicole says. *Forget the past,* she thinks. *Forget everything.*

The woman with the bright-orange scarf faces them with the same determined look Nicole knows is in her own eyes. She's planning to nab a table before ordering too, and Nicole is having none of it.

The clatter of plates and cutlery recedes as she hears the pulsing of her heart in her ears. She rounds the cake table and marches blinkered past the cashier towards the only free table in the café. The other woman is a blur of orange out of the corner of Nicole's eye. A definite threat, and yet also a source of comfort to Nicole. She isn't alone in her misbehaviour. Striding wider than is comfortable she reaches the chair first and throws her bag onto the plastic armrest, turning her back to the other woman.

She feels no guilt. Instead she buzzes. The other woman stands for a moment before another table becomes free. *Nothing bad has happened,* Nicole tells herself. *I haven't hurt anyone. We've all got a table.* Nicole smiles. The shift that has taken place inside her is invisible – she was darkness, she is light.

After a few minutes Bryony joins her and the light inside Nicole burns a little brighter. She is feeling brave and is not going to sit here and listen to Bryony's inane drivel. She'll be honest. Tell Bryony how she feels. But maybe not the whole truth –she won't admit she's only here because she's missing Emily and has no other friends.

'I got you two sugars,' Bryony says, as though she knows how Nicole takes her coffee. The reality is although their children go to the same school and Bryony likes to think she's one of Nicole's best friends, she isn't. Nicole knows she is partly to blame for this: she should've cut Bryony off a long time ago and stopped using the mist as a tool to zone out every time they speak. But then loyalty kicks in, and she can't quite let her go. They've known each other for too long. Maybe Bryony is a closer friend than Nicole would like to admit.

'Actually I don't take sugar anymore.'

Bryony looks taken aback. 'Sorry–' she starts.

Nicole waves her hand in dismissal. 'It's fine, honestly. We haven't drunk a lot of coffee together recently.' Again she has a sharp edge to her words. Another dig.

'How are the boys?' Bryony asks, and Nicole is disappointed Bryony hasn't retaliated.

'They're good,' she replies and looks down at her

cappuccino. In truth, she doesn't know. They come in from school and deposit themselves on the sofa or in their bedrooms, barely say a word during dinner and then disappear again. They've stopped doing all their clubs too.

Nicole has tried to enforce family mealtimes in an attempt to foster conversation, debate, to do the right thing and be a model family, but the boys hate it. They grunt when asked a question. Sulk when made to clear the table. Roll their eyes when she asks them to *please* make an effort. Old habits are sneaking back in. She is happier eating alone anyway. Joe is always home too late from work for them to eat together. 'About to choose their GCSEs,' she offers. 'Does James know what he wants to do?'

James is Bryony's eldest and at one stage had been close to Nicole's sons at primary school, but since going to secondary school everything changed and they rarely spend any time together.

'Oh you know James.' Bryony throws her hands into the air. 'He doesn't even know what he wants for dinner let alone which GCSEs to take.' She laughs and Nicole tries to join in, but hasn't got the energy.

'And Emily,' Bryony asks. 'Have you seen her recently? She's gone a bit off-grid.'

Bryony and Emily are not good friends and never have been, so this comment is odd to Nicole. 'What do you mean?'

'She hasn't come to yoga for a few weeks, that's all.'

'You go to the same yoga class?'

Bryony licks her spoon. 'Yes, down at the sports hall, been going for a while now, which is why it's so unusual for her not to be there. I was going to text, but thought better of it. She doesn't normally reply anyway.'

'I didn't know Emily did yoga.' Nicole feels wounded for

some reason, even though Emily is an adult and can do whatever she wants without Nicole joining her.

'She's good too, very flexible.'

'Right.'

'So, you've not seen her then?'

'No, not for a few weeks either.'

'That's not like you two.' Bryony looks smug.

'Oh it happens, when you've been friends for so long you can go without seeing each other for a while and then pick up where you left off. We're not dependent on each other, you know. We don't have to talk every day.'

'Of course.' Bryony uses her hands to bat away the very suggestion Nicole is needy. 'I wondered how she was after your friend died, that's all.'

Nicole's heartbeat picks up a pace. Her and Emily had vowed a long time ago never to talk to anyone about Bex, at least not to anyone who they hadn't known back then. What else had Emily told Bryony? There was a bitter taste on her tongue and she willed her cheese toastie to hurry up. Sipping her coffee only heightened the sensation.

'They weren't close,' Nicole lies, 'and so I think she's okay. Her death was expected as well. Bex had been ill for a while.' Nicole shrugs as though throwing off any remnants of guilt. But the guilt had layered over the years and was seeping into her skin. 'Did Emily tell you about what happened to her?' Nicole held her breath. *Please, please say no.*

'Oh no, she only said what happened was a tragic accident and that's as far as we got. Never any time to talk after yoga; she's always rushing off.'

To an empty house and the comfort of having no one to share the space with, Nicole thinks. Sometimes she wishes she could do the same. Not be at anyone's beck and call, even though sometimes she suspects if she disappeared no one would even notice until the washing piled up and they got bored of eating pizza. Joe might notice before that, maybe.

'Yes, what happened was a tragic accident.' Nicole doesn't want to talk about that day, although for a split second she considers purging her soul and confessing all to Bryony. She'll deny having ever said anything if Bryony gossips, or she will tell everyone Bryony is delusional. And then she stops her train of thought, not convinced Emily will back her up anymore. Emily might use the opportunity to put all of the blame on Nicole. Pulling her cardigan tight around her, she shivers.

No. Best to not say anything to anyone for now. But she is so sick of living the way she does.

'I can't imagine what her parents must've gone through.' Bryony's voice cuts through her thoughts.

As Nicole goes to reply, toying with the idea of mentioning the other parent affected by that day, she is knocked from behind. She turns to see the woman with the orange scarf from the queue earlier. She has shoved past her and allowed the studded corner of her large handbag to bash into Nicole's back.

'Sorry, love.' The woman smirks.

You bitch, Nicole thinks, turning away from the woman before she can see how much she's hurt her. Her toastie arrives and she burns her fingers on the hot, melted cheese as she takes the plate from the waitress's hand. Tears well in her eyes and she blinks them away. Her back throbs.

Breaking the rules or not, she is always the loser.

FIFTEEN
EMILY – 2022

This, Emily thinks, *is the house where I changed, where everything changed.*

She is standing on the doorstep and wondering if this is such a good idea after all. She first drove here after arguing with Nicole at Bex's funeral and then changed her mind and went home without even getting out of the car. Almost every day since, she's been back

'Mrs Smith, are you there?' She peeks through the letterbox, but all she can see is a pile of post on the mat in the hallway. A faint smell of dampness, as though no one has inhabited the building for a while, wafts through the gap. Not like when she lived here with her parents and the house would smell of roast chicken, or cottage pie. Or a Victoria sponge cake her mum had decided to make one afternoon.

Maybe she should go round the back. Mrs Smith is probably having an afternoon nap in her bedroom at the rear of the house. A large plant pot has been placed next to the side gate, no sign of any flowers growing inside, and for a second Emily considers using the pot to propel herself over the metal bars. But the lock is loose, thanks to years of rust building up, and is easy to open.

The gate squeaks. She hopes the sound will alert Mrs Smith to the intrusion, making her come and see who is banging on her doors and windows.

The back of the house is dominated by decking and the bi-folding doors everyone is installing these days. She doesn't understand the obsession with these types of doors. For starters, smoke from the barbeque coals always infests the inside of the house, weaving through the large space the doors leave when fully open.

The bi-folding doors in front of Emily are shut, however, and the blinds are pulled across, blocking out the tiny bit of late-afternoon sun managing to peek through the storm clouds brewing above.

'Mrs Smith, are you there?' Emily shouts and knocks on the glass doors, nearly slipping on a greasy film coating the wooden decking beneath her. Her body flushes hot and she wonders if she is coming down with a bug, then recognises the emotion as anxiety.

I need to come in, she thinks. *I need to lie on the bed in what used to be my bedroom and close my eyes, indulge myself and imagine my parents are downstairs, huddled on the sofa and watching the television. I need to feel safe. To forget how alone I am now.* She shakes the thought away.

No answer. Mrs Smith is either in a deep sleep, or unconscious.

Bollocks.

Emily looks over to some upturned garden chairs on the grass. She flips one over and flops down in it, then pulls a packet of cigarettes from her bag and lights one with Anna's lighter.

Being angry with Nicole and Grant had been a marvellous distraction from her guilt. Bex finally dying should've absolved her of all of it, her suffering finally over, but instead Emily has started feeling guilty for all of the things Bex should've been able to do – get married, have children. All the things robbed from her. Trying to figure out whether Nicole's guilt would prove too much for her is another burning issue. Of late, Emily has thrust all of these anxieties to the dark depths of her mind – the place covered in cobwebs where unpleasant thoughts go to die and where memories fade and turn to dust – but they are all starting to stick bony fingers up from the depths of the soil and wave.

The back of the house is worn and the windows and bi-fold doors stand out against the aged brickwork. New and old not quite meshing together, each only further highlighting the contrast between the two. The dusty chipped bricks make the windows appear whiter and fresher than perhaps they are.

Emily shudders as a chill runs through her. She blows a long plume of smoke from her mouth.

Then a movement catches her eye; a flicker from one of the blinds behind the doors.

Mrs Smith bloody well is in.

'I saw you,' Emily shouts and runs over to the doors. 'I know you're in there. I want to come in for a bit, like I used to. I won't stay long, I promise. You know I'm never any trouble.' She bangs on the glass and then stands back and waits. And then hears a click, and the door opens, but only a fraction.

'We agreed the last time would be the last time.' Mrs Smith's voice is gravelly. She is dressed in a robe and looks, and smells, like she hasn't washed in weeks.

A stench of alcohol wafts through the air towards Emily. She wants to retch. 'I know, but please can I come in?' Emily throws the rest of her cigarette to the decking and stubs out the end. 'This really will be the last time. My friend just died and I need my bedroom.'

I need the shadows of my parents, she doesn't add. *And I need to check the fireplace.*

But then, looking beyond Mrs Smith and into the mess of the kitchen, Emily almost wants her to say no. If Mrs Smith stinks this much then Emily doesn't want to know what the rest of the house is like. She can't stand the thought of her bedroom being soiled.

'No,' Mrs Smith says. 'This is for your own good.'

'No, it isn't.' Emily wants to cry. 'Please.'

Mrs Smith tries to close the door, but Emily puts her foot in the gap and blocks her.

'Please. I really, really need this.' She's crying now, but makes no effort to wipe away the tears, wanting Mrs Smith to see how desperate she is, to understand how much this means.

The door opens a fraction, but this time Mrs Smith moves her body in between the door and the wall and blocks the gap, then she takes a packet of cigarettes out of her dressing-gown pocket and lights one, inhaling deeply then blowing the smoke in Emily's face.

'Want one?' Mrs Smith asks, puffing on the cigarette again.

'Thanks.' Emily takes one and inhales as Mrs Smith holds her lighter to the end of the white stick. Emily can feel her parents; she can hear them from the lounge calling her in. She turns to look at the garden. Tries to conjure up memories of when she skipped on the grass as a child, mud caked between her toes where she refused to wear shoes. Snippets of lost laughter dance around her and she wipes the wetness from her cheeks.

They stand there and smoke without talking. This is as close as Emily is going to get to her past today and the realisation crushes her.

'Right,' Mrs Smith says, breaking the silence. She throws her stub onto the floor to fizzle out. 'Now bugger off.'

This time Emily is too slow and the door bangs shut,

catching her big toe. She hops and rubs her foot, biting her lip to shut out the stabbing pain.

Emily goes back through the gate and to her car. The Rembrandts' 'I'll Be There for You' blares from the radio as the engine starts, and she smiles through the tears as though she has been sent a sign. Emily and Nicole had danced around Bex's bedroom playing the tune over and over again when the song had first come out. They'd used their hairbrushes for microphones and pretended to mix records like DJs. Emily had told them she'd been tempted to have the track for her first dance at her wedding to Grant, but he'd vetoed the idea. They were good times.

Emily turns the radio up, drives away, belting out the chorus at the top of her voice.

She is desperate to be lost in the safety of the past, but she knows she has no choice but to deal with the present.

SIXTEEN
NICOLE – 2022

'Fine,' Nicole snaps down the phone, 'I'll bring his bag in now.'

Having vowed to put herself before anyone else, Nicole is already failing.

Kieran, the most forgetful of her twins, always leaves his PE kit at home. She's tried everything to help him be more organised – a whiteboard of important weekly events hangs by the front door and is ignored as he walks past every day – but at least once a month she has to drive his bag of PE clothes to the school after a panicked text or phone call from him.

Nicole knows she should let him take the punishment for forgetting his kit; but she also knows where detention leads. Kieran and his brother, Luke, must stay on the straight and narrow, not follow the route of her uncle. Her mum claims detention was where his delinquency started and so Nicole has no choice but to take the PE kit to school, even though doing so inconveniences her.

After several frustrated minutes, she locates the kit shoved under his bed with its contents still muddy, sweaty and unwashed from his last lesson. She also finds an empty cigarette packet crumpled there. There'd been a hint of stale smoke in Kieran's hair when she'd forced him into a rare bear hug last week. She'd assumed the smell had come from him standing too close to the culprit and had dismissed any suggestion the culprit was in fact Kieran.

Some parents on the school WhatsApp group fail to see their children's flaws and Nicole has vowed never to be one of those parents who excuses rudeness or believes every word coming out of their child's mouth without question.

Her boys are often rude to her and they don't appreciate her. Whilst she knows this behaviour is not okay, she tolerates their indifference as long as they don't behave badly in public or at school. When outside of the four walls of their home they need to keep up appearances, as does she. The pressure to do so is overwhelming at times.

Flicking off her slippers and slipping on her trainers, she grabs her car keys and heads to the school, with what feels like the weight of the world on her shoulders.

Surrounded by double yellow lines and zigzags, parking at their secondary school is never easy. Of course, Nicole never dreams of parking – even for a few minutes to drop something off – on any of the forbidden yellow-lined areas, but plenty of parents do. Their actions infuriate her and sometimes she finds her thoughts darkening, imagining the worst, wanting them to be caught out somehow. Not that she'd want a child knocked over to prove her point, of course not.

Sure enough, as she drives past the staff parking entrance, a large, black car is on the yellow zigzags out the front of the school.

The driver is probably a middle-aged, privileged white male, she assumes, fully accepting she is being hideously judgemental but not caring. Parking where they have tells everyone they have no regard for children's safety, and they don't even care who knows this. For a second, Nicole imagines a world where she doesn't worry what everyone thinks about her – just like the driver of the black car. Then she grips the steering wheel tighter knowing such a world doesn't exist.

She passes the no-parking zone and finds a space a few minutes' walk away from the school, up the road as usual. She opens the car door and steps out into a puddle as the first drop of rain from a fresh shower lands square on her forehead. She wipes the water away, shakes her foot, and exhales slowly out through pursed lips, scrunching her eyes closed. She doesn't need to be anywhere else right now, but still she resents this.

The walk to the school gates burns off some of her frustration, but not all. Her ears ring, a symptom that's been bothering her for the last few days. Intrusive thoughts tell her that her blood pressure is too high or a brain tumour is affecting her hearing. This is a new kind of anxiety she's not experienced before.

Refusing to listen to the thoughts, she shakes her head and instead tries to focus on other noises. The whooshes of cars racing down the road. The high-pitched sound of their spinning wheels splashing through patchy puddles on the tarmac as the rain falls heavier; the distant roar of an aeroplane engine. Her racing heartbeat thuds in her chest beneath her wet jumper.

In the school office, she smiles at the receptionist. 'Hi, Kieran in tutor group 10S, I've got his PE kit.'

The receptionist doesn't even bother to glance up at her, continuing to type on her keyboard instead.

'He forgot it again.' Nicole attempts a feeble laugh.

'Tutor?' the receptionist asks, finally looking at Nicole.

'10S,' she repeats.

'Is he expecting you to bring his stuff in?'

'Yes, I'll text anyway as usual and let him know it's here.'

'He shouldn't have his phone on in lessons.'

'Of course. He knows that.' Nicole feels scolded as though she is the one on her phone when it's not allowed. 'Could you let him know it's here then?'

'He'll have to come down when he needs it. I have no idea what lesson he'll be in now.' And then she snatches the bag from Nicole and focuses her attention back on her keyboard and computer screen. Nicole can see a timetable, in fact several timetables, on the noticeboard behind the receptionist and is pretty sure the woman could locate her son in an emergency. A forgotten PE kit clearly not important enough.

'Thank you.' Nicole tries not to sound sarcastic, but fails. She turns to leave and instead of closing the door behind her as she usually would, she leaves it open, the wind blowing shards of rain into the reception area and onto the blue carpet.

Smirking, she walks down the ramp and through the car park, not caring about her hair, frizzing more and more with each drop of rainwater.

The black car is still on the zigzags, no one in the driver's seat, no one to argue they are simply dropping an item off and won't be long. No one she can glare at to let them know she fully disapproves of their actions.

As she walks back to her car, with every plod of her feet, she grows taller, as though developing some kind of rule-following fatigue. That's what any good doctor would diagnose her with now.

Your poor woman, they'd say. *No wonder you snapped, you've been so virtuous, so well-behaved, and you have never been thanked or rewarded, only judged.*

Without pausing to think, Nicole turns the engine of her car on and does a U-turn so she is facing towards the black car parked on her side of the road. A fresh fire ignites in her belly and expands with each inhale. The flames spread down through her pelvis, her thighs, and into her feet. Her right toes burn and she presses down on the accelerator. Faster. Faster still. Checking in her rear-view mirror she confirms there will be no witnesses. Gritting her teeth and holding her breath she swerves towards the black car, passing close enough to knock its wing mirror clean off with a loud bang.

The sound jolts though her and she lets out a piercing whoop, then she moves back into the road and speeds away. The black car's alarm rings in her ears as she turns right and heads down a steep hill and into the road running parallel below. Her sweaty hands slip on the steering wheel and shake as she changes gear. She glances left. Her wing mirror is folded in as though cowering from the collision. What has she done? She bites her bottom lip, her eyes wide.

God, that felt good, she thinks. She tingles all over as though she's had the best sex of her life.

'Fuck you,' she shouts in the rear-view mirror even though she can no longer see the car. The owner will no doubt be able to afford a new wing mirror. Heck, they're probably the kind of person who will claim on insurance anyway or wriggle out of payment somehow. Lie about where they were parked so there'll be no doubt they weren't to blame. Arsehole.

Pulling over, Nicole gets out and pulls back her wing mirror, wiping off a small smudge of black paint. A tiny scratch where the mirrors collided is the only evidence. She'll tell Joe she found the scratches there after parking in the car park in town. Some idiot obviously knocked her wing mirror while she was there, she'll say, and Joe will shake his head and sigh. The scratches won't get fixed, Joe is rubbish at stuff like that, but she won't mind. She'll look at them, touch them, and remember the first time she showed someone the effect of their selfish actions.

And she has a feeling this time wouldn't be the last.

SEVENTEEN
BEX – 1997

We'd got back from yet another holiday at the bottom end of Cornwall yesterday. The part of the county no one went to unless they had family to visit there. And I was so pleased to be home, snuggled under my duvet, headphones on and music blaring, drowning out any sounds from inside the house, fantasising about the next time I was going to see Michael.

On holiday I'd decided, one day whilst we were walking along the beach we always walk along, looking at the huge waves as we do every single time we're there, I couldn't continue to live the way I had been anymore. And now we were back, I was going to put my plan into action. Michael would finally notice me – everyone would.

Mum, Dad, they'd fought the whole time we were away. I wish they'd just get divorced already. Mum had apparently found an object giving her solid proof of Dad's affair, although I wasn't sure what the object was. A condom packet maybe, or a dirty thong? Either way, small enough to fit into Dad's jacket pocket, and obvious enough for her to scream at him with conviction.

Then she'd smoked all week, and drank every day from the moment she woke up to the moment she passed out. Nothing except alcohol passed her lips as far as I could see. She was a vile drunk too. Shouting obscenities one minute and weeping about how she was going to kill herself the next. The glass by her bed was filled with neat vodka, not water, I swear it. The mug of tea was bourbon. And the empty wine bottles piled up in the garbage.

Mum didn't hide her drinking from anyone anymore. She wanted the world to know of her hurt and distress, to invite them to share her pain through watching her pickle her insides. Drinking gave her the attention she'd always craved elsewhere. Shame the attention wasn't the kind she needed.

'It's over,' my dad had shouted at her before muttering, 'dumb bitch' under his breath. But so far he showed no signs of actually leaving.

Mum had cried a lot too, last week. I could hear the wails followed by quiet sobs from my bedroom, which was next to theirs. Dad, meanwhile, snored on the sofa.

Then, when we walked along the beach for the millionth time, had been the only day of the entire holiday when neither of them had shouted or cried. The whole thing had been disconcerting.

Then, one night last week, Wednesday I think, as I was on my bed hugging my knees, I heard mum's muffled cries again and felt like crying too and a realisation hit me; I'd never known my parents happy. They had money, whatever they wanted they could buy, but they didn't put down a deposit on anything other than making each other miserable. And I was sick of the hate and mistrust. They should've got divorced really, and a long time ago too. I didn't understand why they were more concerned with how being a divorcee would look to the outside world than their own happiness, or mine and Grant's. And

Grant was in denial. He refused to even talk to me about their behaviour. He was infuriating.

I decided then and there, last Wednesday, huddled with wet cheeks under my duvet in the holiday house, I needed to do something drastic. They needed to notice me. Realise what they were doing to their only daughter. Maybe they'd fall in love again too. Grant didn't need to know. He already got enough attention what with him being the favourite, and anyway, he was leaving home soon for university. First one in the family to go. The Golden Boy.

I'd looked around the room, listened to the crashing of the waves outside and the ensuing deep roar as the sound echoed against the cliffs, and began to formulate a plan. A plan that might work, but I knew I would need a little help to put my ideas into action.

As I'd plotted I'd thought about asking someone else to help me, but didn't know who to enlist. Not Nicole with her insistence on behaving. Plus I didn't want to give Michael any more reason to like her over me. Maybe Emily, but then she thought everyone with parents should be grateful they've got them, even if they suck, so she would be of no use. Shame they didn't get how I felt.

No, they'd never understand why I had to go ahead with my plan.

I had to do this alone.

EIGHTEEN
EMILY – 2022

'Miss?'

Emily looks up from the pile of papers she's marking to see Chloe, one of her brightest students, in the doorway to her classroom.

'Hey, Chloe, you okay?'

'Can I come in, miss?'

Emily puts down her pen. Her heart quickens. She's not in the mood to be Chloe's confidante today, for many reasons, but doesn't have the energy to say no. Chloe should go and find her academic mentor, but Emily has a strong suspicion as to why Chloe has chosen to come and see her instead. She hopes she's wrong. Kicking her bag further under the desk, she waits as Chloe closes the door behind her and sits on a chair opposite the desk.

'This is a bit awkward, miss.' She bites her lip and Emily's mind races.

Oh God, thinks Emily. *No, she can't want to talk about that. There's no way she'd know. I've been so careful.* 'I'm listening.' Emily shifts in her chair and prays to a god she doesn't believe in.

'The other day, while I was doing PE, I lost my watch.' Chloe pulls up her sleeve to show Emily her wrist. A faint white strip wraps around the centre even though summer is long gone.

A knot tightens in Emily's stomach. 'You know, Chloe, this actually isn't the best time. I've got all of these papers to mark. Have you been to lost property? That's always the best place to look for lost belongings.'

Emily picks up her pen and opens one of the papers in front of her. She looks down, away from Chloe's gaze. She needs her to leave the classroom. Now.

'The thing is, it's not in lost property, miss. I know where my watch is.'

Emily freezes and the words on the paper in front of her blur. All she can hear is the blood rushing in her ears. *No. No. No. No.* She puts her pen down in a controlled manner instead of slamming the biro on the desk like she wants to. She is the adult. The teacher. This meeting will not go any way other than the way she directs it.

'If you know where your watch is then why are we sitting here and having this conversation?' Chloe, although bright, has been in trouble before. The senior leadership team will believe Emily over her. Emily is convinced.

'I think you know why, miss.' Chloe narrows her eyes.

Emily clenches her teeth. Why does she keep saying *miss* as though she's interrogating Emily?

'I haven't got a clue, Chloe. But before you go any further I'd advise you to be very careful. You are talking to a teacher, not a mate.' Emily's voice quivers and she hopes Chloe hasn't noticed. Her shoes knock against her handbag under the desk.

'Yes, I know. But I'm talking to you and not a mate because you've got what I've lost. You've got my watch. But you know that already, don't you, miss?'

'I need you to leave now, Chloe. Close the door on your way

out.' Emily's hands tremble and she places them on her lap under the desk to hide the tremors.

'But, miss–'

'*But, miss* nothing. You've accused me of being a thief, Chloe, and that's not okay without any proof.' *Please don't let her have proof,* Emily begs the universe, squeezing her eyes shut.

'I saw you. In the classroom when we'd all gone out for PE.'

Emily glares at Chloe, words she will regret dance on her tongue and she bites down hard and swallows them.

'Your watch will turn up when you least expect it, I am sure.' Emily ignores Chloe, tilts her head to one side, picks up her pen and smiles. 'Now if you don't mind, I have work to do.'

'But–'

'But nothing. You need to watch your mouth.'

'I can easily go and tell the headteacher what you've done, right now, you know.' Chloe's hunched posture doesn't match the threat of her words.

'Yes, you could.' Emily places her pen down on the table. 'But then I could say how troubled you are. How many times have you been to isolation this week? I'd say you were making everything up. Who do you think they'd believe?'

For what feels like minutes, Emily holds her breath as Chloe, knowing she's defeated for now, jumps up from the chair and marches out. She pauses at the door, but Emily's gaze remains on her pile of unmarked papers, the words on them blurred and swimming across the page. After a moment, Chloe leaves and closes the door behind her.

Tears well in Emily's eyes and she bites her bottom lip to stop herself from crying. Her bag screams at her from under the table. She pushes her chair back and pulls the handles from underneath her feet. Glancing at the door to check Chloe has gone, she opens her bag. And there, on top of her purse, is Chloe's watch.

Emily had taken the offending item while Chloe had been in a PE lesson yesterday, like she'd said. She couldn't help herself. After Mrs Smith hadn't let her into her childhood home to get the comfort she craved she'd gone looking for solace elsewhere, exactly like she'd been doing since the day her parents died.

Stuffing Chloe's watch to the bottom of her bag, nestling alongside the stolen lighter, Emily closes her eyes and can't help but be transported back to the day when her world had been damaged beyond repair.

'Are we nearly there yet?' she'd asked, knowing full well what the answer would be. No. They were nowhere close.

The sky had turned from blue, to bruised purple, to black as they'd whizzed down the narrow, bumpy lanes to their holiday caravan and her bum cheeks were beginning to ache. Plus, she needed a wee. Her legs wouldn't keep still either. There were bubbles or ants or something weird in them and she had to keep switching position, which made her think she was going to wet herself every time she did.

'No, sweetie,' her mum said, 'but we're over halfway. Why don't you read your book?'

'Finished it.'

'Already? Hang on.'

Emily's mum had rustled in her bag and then as if by magic handed a new book to her over the back of the seat. Always prepared her mum was. Emily swore her bag was like the one Mary Poppins had, full of anything they'd need at any given time.

'Thanks, Mum. But I need a wee.'

'We can't stop, love. Can you hold on?'

No toilet in the bag for an emergency like this one then, Emily thought. 'I don't think so. I'm desperate.' She scrunched up her face and wiggled her legs to prove her point and clutched in between her legs with her hands. For once, her mum had let her have a large lemonade when they'd stopped for dinner not long ago, a decision they were all regretting now. Her mum hadn't complained when Emily burped and then laughed while drinking the fizzy sweet liquid. Dad had rolled his eyes and smothered a grin. Everyone had been in the holiday spirit.

Emily glanced over at her dad and saw him shrug his shoulders at her mum as if to say, *If she needs to go then she needs to go,* and her Mum twisted round to face Emily. 'Okay then, we'll stop. But you'll have to go in a bush. No one's around, so you'll be all right.'

Emily nodded and put her hand between her legs again to hold her wee in. The sudden urge to go was huge. 'Now, Mum, I need to go now.'

'Pull over, darling.' Her mum placed her hand on her dad's arm, but Emily could see there was nowhere he could stop. They were driving along a single-track lane, cushioned on each side by overgrown hedges, with no passing places at all.

'There.' Her mum pointed to a gate as they rounded a corner. 'We can wait here and she can hop over the gate. Here–' She handed Emily a torch from her bag. 'Be quick.'

Emily's mouth was dry. She didn't want to go over the gate and into the field on her own. What if there were some cows in there, or a bull? What if they sensed her fear and trampled on her while she was weeing? But she was so desperate she knew if she didn't go in the field then she would wet herself in the car and although she knew she wouldn't get told off for doing that, she'd still feel ashamed. She was nearly ten years old. Nine-year-olds didn't wet their pants. Nine-year-olds didn't need their mums to come and watch them wee either.

'Okay, I'll be quick.' She opened the car door. 'Can you leave your door open too?'

There was no moonlight outside, and there weren't any

visible stars either. The torch clicked on and she could see a mess of mud at the base of the gate. Thankfully there was no smell of muck and so she convinced herself the field had no cows grazing there and she was safe to use the space as a toilet without being trampled on. The metal of the gate was cold to the touch and there was dried mud along each rung.

Her heart raced. Though an only child, she hated being alone. But she knew she had to be brave. Her own company had unnerved her from the day she was born, as her parents had often reminded her. They said right from the minute she took her first breath she'd found a way to be with someone else all the time. Emily imagined being with her parents forever – not ever leaving home for university or marriage. The thought made her smile and feel safe.

The countryside was silent and dark that night, and then it wasn't.

Emily didn't understand what was happening at first. She thought the sudden noise was from their car radio and that her mum had turned up the volume so Emily could hear the music and know she wasn't alone, reassure her they weren't far away. But Emily was puzzled as the music wasn't the type of music they liked to listen to. More drums. More beats. More crashing and banging. There were whoops too and as she pulled down her trousers she knew they weren't from the mouths of her parents, but from other people nearby. Strangers.

Her heart raced and she missed the ground and weed all down her leg and the new noises were scaring her and so she didn't quite manage to pull her trousers up properly and then she fell, face first, into a mound of mud. The music, the whooping, the revving of a car all got louder and louder and she knew, she knew she needed to get back to her parents as quick as she could so they could drive far, far away from the monsters who were getting closer. She knew they were bad. She knew they'd hurt them. And she didn't want to be alone in a dark field when they came.

But, as she looked up, as she peered through the grey, metal slats of the gate in front of her – the barrier standing between her and the safety of her parents – there was a flash of light and then the loudest bang she had ever heard. Louder than any firework, even the ones bursting into a million tiny bright lights lighting up the sky.

At first she thought the bang had made her heart stop. Then she thought the bright lights had blinded her.

The silence returned, apart from a dull thud in her ears. She felt the soft ground beside her for the torch she'd dropped when she'd tripped over her trousers. And as she stood up her foot felt the cold metal lodged in the mud. She pulled the torch out and shook it until a faint light glowed. Then she took a deep breath and pointed the beam of light at the gate. And with a gasp she saw what had made the sound of the world ending.

Two dark-blue cars, kissing and crumpled.

'Mum!' she screamed. 'Mum. Dad.' Her breath caught in her throat. *Maybe I'm dreaming,* she thought, she hoped, and scrunched her eyes closed. Was she dreaming? This was all too horrible to be real. 'Please, please let this be a dream,' she muttered under her breath, her lips quivering.

Running towards the cars she yelled again and again for her mum and dad, but as tears fell down her cheeks she knew they weren't going to answer. If they were alive then they'd have gotten out of the car and she'd be wrapped in their arms. They'd be telling her everything was okay. But she needed to see for herself; to know she wasn't dreaming.

And then, as she stumbled through the mud and over the gate to the car, the sickening realisation the accident was her fault hit her as hard as the drunken driver had smashed into her parents' car.

If only she'd held on. If only she'd been stronger then they wouldn't have stopped. All she believed was that, right there and then, her parents were dead because of her.

And she deserved to be alone forever as punishment.

Emily looks down and sees her tears have dropped onto the student's work on her desk. She tries to wipe them off, but the paper frays beneath her trembling fingers and small shards of white bundle together at the edge of the work.

That was the worst night of her life. She remembers her aunt, eyes red and puffy, coming to collect her from the local police station. She remembers pocketing one of the policemen's handkerchiefs as she was escorted out. The material had smelled of his aftershave and she'd held the fabric right under her nose, tight in her fist, for the whole night pretending the smell belonged to her father, that she was buried in his chest, his arms tight around her. That was the first time she'd taken an object which didn't belong to her.

She'd managed to stop stealing stuff for a while in her early teens, until the accident on the beach, and then the kleptomania had started up again and had nearly got her into a lot of trouble at university before she swore she'd stopped forever.

She isn't sure why she's started taking people's things again. In fact, she doesn't even want to think about why. Even Nicole doesn't know about this little habit of hers, and Emily definitely can't talk to her about her problem now they've fallen out.

She kicks her bag back under the desk, sniffs and wipes the tears from her face before inhaling deeply and shaking the grief and guilt away.

Maybe people need to learn to be more careful with their stuff, she thinks.

NINETEEN
NICOLE – 2022

Nicole imagines it's hard not to feel angry when you live in a tiny bungalow in your parents-in-law's garden, your husband works away more than he is home, and your dogs are constantly trying to trip you up by getting under your feet, which is why she excuses Bryony's scowl as she opens the door to her.

Yes, Nicole thinks, you can dance in your kitchen like no one is watching – the building faces away from the main house. But Bryony is constantly moaning her stupid in-laws knock on the door at all times of the day and so Nicole concludes Bryony can't dance with abandon whenever she feels like it. Nicole never dances anyway.

'Hey,' Bryony says, 'sorry, thought you were the in-laws again.'

Nicole snaps out of her thoughts and smiles. 'Nope, only me.'

'Thank feck for that, they've just left. Popped down to ask if I wanted some milk from the shops when they know damn well I had a food delivery yesterday because they helped me unpack it.'

The old Nicole would be like Bryony, she thinks, so bloody polite and people-pleasing. Bryony might moan about her in-laws, but to their faces she sucks in all of her negative feelings and plays the part of the dutiful and grateful daughter-in-law. But then, Nicole is playing the part of the dutiful friend too, not wanting to spend any more time in Bryony's company, but also not quite brave enough to say no. She misses Emily.

'Bless, they must love being with you.'

'No. They don't.' She rolls her eyes. 'What they're doing is checking up on me to see I haven't damaged their precious building in any way. Honestly, their stupid grinning faces make me want to punch them. They make me feel so guilty for not inviting them in every time they come knocking.'

Bryony locks the dogs in one of the bedrooms and then beckons Nicole inside and carries on as they walk through to the kitchen. 'I mean yes, they are getting on a bit, well, a lot, and might cark it soon, and so I know I ought to make more of an effort, if not for them then for Mark, who as you know, thinks the sun shines out of their arses and doesn't understand why I find them so infuriating. But then he doesn't have to spend as much time with them as I do. He gets to escape to work.'

'Breathe.' Nicole sits down at the breakfast bar. Bryony's little home is quaint. A large open-plan kitchen-diner-lounge, with a log-burning fire warming one end and a swarm of beanbags covering the wooden floor at the other; and a television dominating the space. No sofa, which never fails to amuse Nicole. She doesn't think her knees would be able to cope with repeatedly getting up from the beanbags if they were all she had to sit on.

'So how's tricks?' Bryony asks, even though they saw each other recently. Nicole is starting to enjoy her company again more.

Bryony fills the kettle and gets two large mugs out of the

cupboard. They've been friends for a while now. Nicole likes having a friend who didn't know her at school; but over the years Bryony has become more and more competitive with regards to their children, and Nicole doesn't have the strength to compete anymore.

Being asked how she is makes Nicole think of Bex and Emily and the pain of everything and, without her being able to stop it, her mind closes. She watches with glee as the mist rolls in from the hallway towards her.

'Hey, Nicole, are you there?' Bryony claps her hands in front of Nicole's vacant face. 'What's going on with you today?'

'Doesn't matter.' Nicole picks her cup up from the worktop before placing it back down again and wrapping her hands around the china.

'Yes, it does.' Bryony rests her hand on Nicole's arm. 'Come on, I know something's up.'

'You know, we spoke about what happened at coffee. She died, my friend,' Nicole says, not knowing if Bryony will fully understand. She doesn't even contemplate mentioning the threatening texts. There haven't been any more and Nicole is hoping the whole thing is some crazy wrong number incident.

'Oh, of course. I'm so sorry.'

Yes, they've talked about Bex and what happened at school before, but on Nicole's terms and she's only ever given the most basic of information to Bryony.

'Not your fault,' Nicole says, before staring up at the ceiling to avoid eye contact because she is convinced if Bryony looks straight into her eyes then she'll know. She'll know Bex's death is Nicole's fault.

'I feel so guilty.' Nicole wipes a lone tear from her cheek. She's never cried in front of Bryony before. She does not want to be vulnerable in front of someone who might use the information as next week's gossip. In fact, she rarely cries in front of anyone.

'Why?' Bryony looks confused. 'From what you've told me, she had an accident. These things happen. Don't feel guilty. Sad, yes, but guilty? Hell no.'

For a minute Nicole looks at the floor and they sit in silence.

'Stuff happened back then.' Nicole shrugs. 'We don't talk about it, heck as you know, Emily refuses, but what everyone thinks happened that day isn't what actually happened.'

Bryony sits forward; ears pricked like a dog hearing a mate barking in the distance. 'What do you mean?'

'We were with her, Emily and me. On the beach.'

Bryony doesn't say anything.

'No one knows. We lied. But the truth is, we were all there, the three of us. It was in the holidays and we were meant to be revising together for our mocks. I don't know why I agreed to the lie. I also don't know why no one sussed. Emily told everyone she had a sickness bug and had been in bed all day. No one had checked. My mum and dad had been visiting Uncle Tom and assumed I was studying at the library. Lying was all too easy.

'Bex's parents thought she'd gone to the beach alone. They didn't care where she was most of the time anyway. And Emily, she was adamant we had to run, to say we weren't there at all. I've felt like shit about what we did for years. I didn't even want to go to the beach, but Em and Bex were so persuasive and I was scared if I didn't go, then well... then Em would finally drop me as her best mate and I'd be cast out of the group and have no one. She always preferred Bex. Bex was more fun than me.'

A moment's silence hangs between them.

'You told me Emily only liked Bex because she fancied Grant.'

'No, it was more than that, I think. They connected and were friends because they chose each other. Em and I are only friends because we grew up together and know no different. Our friendship isn't a choice.'

'You're talking rubbish, Nicole. You and Emily chose to stay friends. That says a lot.'

'Yeah and then after that day on the beach we were forced to stay friends, bound together by all of the other lies we told.'

'What other lies? What do you mean?'

Nicole stands up; she's done with being questioned. The half-truths she's told Bryony are unravelling the lies she needs to keep buried. 'Yeah. You're right, not my fault, I know.' Nicole bats her hands at Bryony and takes her empty mug into the kitchen space. 'Ignore my stupid waffling. Reckon my hormones are playing up. I feel guilty for everything these days.'

'You're too nice, that's the trouble. Don't ruin your life simply because Bex lost hers.'

'You sound like a clichéd self-help book.' Nicole grins over her shoulder as she stacks her empty cup in the dishwasher. 'It doesn't suit you.'

'Bog off then.' Bryony sticks her tongue out.

'Sorry,' Nicole says. 'I am trying to be a bit more forthright, you know? Stand up for myself.' She thinks of her wing mirror.

'Good. I'm impressed. What's brought that on?'

Nicole shrugs. 'I'm not sure, a combination of things really. I know I let people walk all over me and maybe Bex's death has, you know, made me realise I'm not living life as I should. God, now I sound like a self-help book.'

'You are a total people-pleaser, at least you have been since I met you anyway.'

'I know.' Nicole sits down on one of the beanbags not caring if she can't get back up. 'Being good was the only thing my mum gave me praise for as a child, and so the behaviour stuck I guess, especially at school. Mum's brother, my uncle, he went to prison as a teenager and has been in and out ever since. Following the rules was drummed into me from an early age. And then that day with Bex when everything went horribly wrong made me never want to be naughty ever again. Stupid really.'

Bryony doesn't need to know about the first time Nicole's mum gave her no choice but to be the child who behaves, Nicole thinks. How scared she was at the thought of her mum's hand making contact with her cheek again. Or worse. The constant threat of being sent away to prison.

'Not at all. Makes perfect sense to me.' Bryony nods. 'But you're right. It's no way to live. Everyone messes up at some point. Bex was unlucky.'

'But that's what bothers me. I hate people who go around without a care in the world doing as they please with no regard for anyone but themselves, and who never ever see the effects their actions have on others. They get no comeuppance.'

'Like Emily, you mean.'

Nicole's shoulders slump. Is this what her new attitude is all about, resenting Emily? Hating the fact she doesn't appear to think about anyone else? That she only has herself to worry about, whereas Nicole puts other people's feelings before her own before she does anything, even people she doesn't know? She's pathetic. 'I guess.'

'Nicole, when someone dies we get messed up, I should know. You're grieving and grief always comes with guilt in some guise.'

'I've been feeling guilty for nearly twenty-five years though.' *Carrying the blame for me and Emily,* Nicole thinks. And she's had enough. Yesterday, when she took the wing mirror off the car she'd felt alive for the first time in years. Of course, she's still waiting for the guilt to show up, but nothing has yet and the absence of remorse is firing her on to dish out more karma.

Maybe Emily needs some too. Bex's accident was mostly her fault in Nicole's eyes, and Emily has never ever accepted that.

Instead, she has spent her whole life dismissing the truth and living as though no one matters but her. After all, Nicole has acknowledged she can't keep living the way she has been, doing everything *right* at her own expense. Sat here in Bryony's lounge she's angry she's let that one day define her in a way Emily hasn't.

But then she remembers the look on Emily's face on the beach: at first horror and then nothing. Her expression had been blank. No frown or fear or twitch. Nothing. As though she hadn't cared, which is what her behaviour since also implies.

Nicole has had enough. *No more,* she thinks. *We need to own up. We need to face the consequences that come with being honest.*

'Sorry, Bryony.' With fresh energy Nicole hauls herself out of the giant beanbag. 'I've got to go. I need to do something.'

TWENTY
EMILY – 2022

The text beeps in the middle of the staff meeting and Emily rushes to find her phone in her bag. 'Argh, sorry.' She hoists the bag onto her lap. 'I can't find my phone.'

'Switch it off when you do, please,' the headteacher says – as if Emily is an awkward adolescent, clueless about workplace etiquette – before carrying on as if she is not important.

Emily hasn't been listening anyway; she doesn't give two hoots about student well-being when she is struggling so much with her own, even though this makes her a heartless bitch and crap at her job. Well-being hadn't even been a thing when she was at school and is a load of bollocks right now as far as she is concerned.

As she delves deeper her hand brushes against the cool metal of Chloe's watch. She's tried to find a time to return the watch, has even snuck into the girls' changing room to look for Chloe's bag when she had PE. But there'd been another student in there running late and then Emily couldn't remember which bag was Chloe's and didn't want to be caught snooping around and so she'd left with the watch still in her back pocket.

Everyone knows she doesn't get along with the PE teacher,

and so she couldn't even say she was looking for her to excuse her presence in the changing rooms.

Then she considered putting the damn watch in the lost property box, but thought that might be too obvious given it's where she suggested Chloe look.

So here the watch is, hiding in the bottom of her bag, being slowly suffocated by old receipts and tampons.

When she finally locates her phone she twists it round inside the bag and taps on the screen to have a quick check to see who is messaging her at work. Very few people message her these days. She's intrigued, but hopes the message isn't from Nicole, who she's still pissed off with.

Grant sent her a text the other day too, to say he hopes she's okay and to reassure her again about how Nicole was only comforting him at the funeral, nothing more. She hasn't replied and has deleted the message.

The phone number the text is from isn't one she has saved, and at first she thinks the message must be from a scammer, but then, as she reads on, her breathing picks up a pace.

> I know what you did. And if you don't own up, then I will tell everyone the truth.

Her hands tremble.

'Emily, are you with us?' Everyone in the staff room is staring at her. Her headteacher is tapping his right foot and glaring, arms folded tight across his body and his lips formed into a circle of distaste.

'Yes, sorry. Nothing important, I've switched my phone off now.'

'Good, so, as I was saying–'

Her headteacher's words fade into the background and Emily plants her feet on the floor to ground herself. She closes her eyes and then she gasps out loud as she realises who the text is from.

Chloe.

Of course. Chloe, who has probably watched too many cop dramas, has decided she can take the law into her own hands and threaten Emily to get her watch back.

Silly little bitch, Emily thinks, but recognises she does need to get the watch out of her bag pronto. Although, how did Chloe get her number?

'Sorry,' Emily interrupts the headteacher, who again does not look pleased. 'I need to nip to the loo, haven't been able to all day. And well, time of the month. You know what it's like.' Emily smirks. Her headteacher has forgotten how teachers train their bladders to only empty at regulated times of the day. Plus, she hasn't got her period, but no one will question the suggestion. A couple of her male colleagues even grimace.

'Be quick.'

Without hesitating Emily grabs her bag and dashes out the door. She cringes as the metal slams behind her, but ignores the noise and rushes to the girls' changing room again. No after-school clubs are running today and she is confident the room will be empty of everything except a stale stench of sweat. Glancing left and right along the corridor as though she is being hunted, she opens the door to the changing room and heads down the steps inside. A lone scarf hangs off one of the pegs and a pair of muddy trainers hides under the bench opposite. Nothing worth taking here.

Pulling Chloe's watch out of her bag she looks around for a hiding place where Chloe wouldn't have already checked. Then decides the location doesn't matter. Thankfully this room has no cameras in, for obvious reasons, and therefore there will be no proof she is the one returning the lost item. Holding her breath as she yanks out one of the muddy, smelly trainers, she deposits the watch in the space behind, before replacing the shoe. Then she brushes her hands down her dress, deletes the warning text from her phone, and heads back to the staff room.

The rest of the staff meeting passes in a blur – although she has downloaded the breathing exercises app recommended for staff well-being. Now Emily is in her car on the way home.

After a few minutes she passes the turning to her childhood house and bites her lip to stop the tears falling again, annoyed with herself for being emotional all the time. Maybe she is due on after all.

Regardless of where she is in her cycle, she needs her old bedroom, and not simply because being in there – where the wallpaper remains unchanged along with the curtains – gives her comfort. She hid an item there a long time ago and needs it back. At the time, leaving it there was the right thing to do. She vowed to leave everything behind when she moved out, the memories, the objects, all of it.

The text message is playing on her mind too. She's positive the threat was from Chloe, but she is still puzzled as to how Chloe got her number, and this unnerves her. Kids are pretty savvy these days, she knows, and Emily would bet it's easy to find someone's number.

Her thoughts turn to Nicole. The break-up of female friendship isn't often talked about, but as Emily is finding out, causes no less pain than the break-up of a marriage. Emily keeps finding herself looking on her phone at old photos of her and Nicole together as though she's grieving. Or she'll read through their last messages to each other. She wants to reach out, to tell Nicole about the text message from Chloe, but every time she opens up her phone to do so, she stops and she turns the screen off again without typing a single word.

At home she pours herself a large glass of wine and rests on the sofa. Looking around the room she sighs. On the coffee table in front of her is a pile of unopened bills. Probably final demands too. She places them there after picking them up from her doormat because she feels this small act shows she intends to pay them at some point. And yet, she never does, at least not on time, and then they charge her late payment fees and the problem gets worse and worse. She gulps her wine and refills the glass. And then her phone beeps again.

She doesn't want to look, but is compelled to. She'll reply this time. Tell the person sending her these stupid messages to fuck right off.

But it's not from the mystery number.

It's a message from Bex's parents inviting her to a small memorial on the beach on Saturday where they will scatter her ashes. A final goodbye. Twenty-five years since her accident. They've done this on the same day every year since. The gathering started out as something else, for someone else, but over time the day and its meaning became about no one but Bex.

Nicole goes every year to the gatherings on the beach, and tells Emily about it; about how Bex is in a wheelchair, her eyes glaring at Nicole. At least today Bex won't be there to make her feel even more like the piece of crap she is.

But Grant and Nicole will be.

Emily takes a deep breath in and blows the air out of her lungs slowly as though through a straw. She doesn't want to go, but suspicions will be raised if she doesn't this year, especially after not being fully present at the funeral. As far as Bex's parents are aware they were all best friends and Emily was distraught when Bex's accident happened.

Emily hopes Mel's mum won't be there either; according to Nicole she had stopped going, but Emily suspects she might this year.

Bex wasn't the only person whose life changed that day.

TWENTY-ONE
NICOLE – 2022

Sometimes, at the gathering they hold every year here on the beach, the weather is calm and Nicole struggles to recall the ferocity of the storm that blew in when Bex decided to go for her fateful swim. Nicole remembers sharp rain showers, hoods pulled up and tugged down over and over again as the drizzle came and went, before the wind arrived and whipped around them, extinguishing their cigarettes, then sweeping away anything that dared enter the sea.

Today the wind has returned as they all gather on the beach to remember that day and everyone involved, and Bex now she's died. Nicole has prepared herself to see Emily today and she has also prepared herself to finally speak the truth to Bex's parents, to hell with the consequences.

She's not opening up to absolve herself of guilt, she tells herself, she's confessing because she and Emily, after all these years, finally need to pay for the part they played. Plus, if someone else knows and is going to out her and Emily, then she needs to be the one to do so first.

'Hi, Mr and Mrs Williams. How are you?' She walks over to

them and gives them a loose and uncomfortable embrace, air-kissing the salty sea breeze instead of salty skin.

'Hi Nicole, we're doing okay thanks.' Sylvia speaks quietly, slowly. Her voice is measured and Nicole recognises the great deal of restraint and control she's employing to hold everything together today. The reply is rehearsed, as though if Bex's mum gives a different answer in a different tone, she'll fall apart. Bex's dad remains silent as usual.

'Would you mind if we had a chat at some point today?' Nicole asks, wringing her hands.

'Of course. Come and find me before you go home. After we've scattered the last of Bex's ashes maybe?'

Nicole nods and sucks her bottom lip before walking away and leaving them free for their next embrace, a line of mourners growing behind her.

The reality of Bex's ashes being scattered here hasn't occurred to her, until now. A knot tightens in her stomach. She isn't sure Bex would want to be scattered here. Why would you want to be remembered in the very place where a few wrong decisions and choices damaged your life forever? Nicole wants to be buried somewhere far away from any painful memories. Somewhere where her family and friends can feel at peace when they visit her grave, not in a place that will torment them.

This beach is already tainted for Nicole, and from now on she'll imagine trampling on grains of Bex washed up by the sea every time she walks across the sand. With each footstep she'll push a part of Bex deeper underground. Beneath a shell. Under a rock. Pressed against a fragment of sea glass.

More and more people gather, many faces Nicole recognises and some she doesn't. Maybe doctors or carers of Bex's, she thinks. Or maybe people who are feeling guilty they'd never attended this event before, even though it's been happening for years. But then, this wasn't always about Bex. Lots of lives were changed. Nicole half expects to see Michael emerge from the sand-dunes.

A gust of wind takes Nicole's scarf from around her neck and as she turns to catch the end before the whole thing races across the sand, she spies Emily in the distance. Her coat is wrapped around her body, held firmly in place by her folded arms.

She doesn't look good, thinks Nicole. *Troubled.* But then when has Emily ever not been troubled? Picking up her scarf Nicole averts her gaze and stands next to a small group of people she doesn't know.

'Hey.' A hand touches her shoulder and she yelps, the people beside her turning, alarmed.

'Grant, you scared me.' Nicole is already on edge today, fired up for her confession; the simplest of touches causing her heart to clench.

'Sorry.' He attempts a grin. 'You okay?' He glances over towards Emily, his expression fraught.

Nicole rolls her eyes. 'She's perfectly welcome to come and talk to us, but I know she won't. We know how stubborn she can be.'

'She's impenetrable when she's like this. Was a big part of what infuriated me when we were together. Now it's tacked on to all the other crap about her that drives me mad in spite of this weird sense of loyalty I have towards her as my ex-wife.' He looks down as though he's said too much.

Nicole isn't sure what he's hinting at. 'I know. Me too. She closes off, which is why I'm not even bothering to go over. Absolutely no point in talking to her until she's ready.'

'Do you think she'll ever be ready this time? Since Bex's death she's different. Her current behaviour is more than stubbornness. She needs to sort herself out on a deeper level, an emotional one.'

'I know what you mean, but we can't help her unless she wants us to, and she clearly doesn't want us to.' Nicole shrugs.

They glance over to catch Emily glaring at them. They are far enough away to not hear the huff they can see emanate from her lips, but close enough to catch the roll of her eyes.

'I've tried calling and texting and she ignores them all,' Grant says.

Nicole looks down at the sand and carves a line with her shoe. She hasn't reached out like Grant has and suddenly feels ashamed.

'Do you know who these people are?' Grant tips his head at the strangers.

'No, I don't think so,' Nicole says. 'I did wonder if that was Mel's mum, but she looks so different. Older than I'd expect. But then, I've not seen her for years. She hasn't ever come to this before.'

Mel's mum had stopped coming to these days a long time ago and Nicole never knew why. Maybe they remembered privately instead. *Somewhere away from here where the tragedy happened,* she thinks.

'I think it is her. She's got a mole on her cheek, remember?'

'Vaguely,' Nicole replies. The truth is, she can't remember a lot about Mel and the realisation mortifies her.

A waft of salty seaweed smell is blown over them by a sudden gust of wind and Sylvia Williams steps forward. 'I won't keep you long,' she says. Her hands shake. 'Thank you all for coming to remember Bex.' She glances at Mel's mum and then at the ground. 'Today marks twenty-five years since our lives were changed by the tragic accident here, when, for reasons we still don't understand...' she pauses and puts her hand to her mouth, '...for reasons we still don't understand, Bex decided to go for a swim. Alone.'

Nicole glances over to Emily, who looks up at the dark sky.

Maybe today isn't the time to own up, Nicole thinks. She needs to talk to Bex's parents privately, not in front of everyone here on the beach when they are already distressed. But the weather is cold and windy and she doubts people will stay long. An opportunity to talk might appear and she might feel being honest is right after all.

'Today,' Sylvia continues, 'we also, as always, want to give thanks to everyone who bravely tried to save Bex.' Frowning, she turns to Mel's mum, who has separated herself from the group in front of Nicole and is slowly edging forward. She appears to want to speak, but Bex's mum carries on talking about Bex. The irony that her mum is now making sure Bex is the centre of attention is not lost on Nicole. But she feels for Mel's mum too.

A murderous frown covers Mel's mum's face as she retreats. These events can do funny things to people, Nicole thinks. Once again, she pushes from her mind the thought of being without one of her children, or Joe. It's too painful to even contemplate.

A dog walker in the distance bends down to scoop up their dog's mess. Nicole hasn't even ever lost a pet. The only people she's ever had to grieve for are her grandparents, who died when she was too young to even remember them; and Bex. Unlike Emily, who has lost more than her fair share of family and friends.

'We're going to scatter the last of her ashes now.' Grant leans in and speaks softly to Nicole, his arm around her shoulder. 'I'll catch you later?'

'Okay.'

All of a sudden, Nicole feels exposed. As though she is the cliff in the distance being battered by the relentless waves. The tide is retreating, leaving patches of water looking as though someone has spilled a drink on the sand. Her eyes sting, the wind filling them with salt. She blinks the tears away as she watches Bex's family each take a handful of her ashes and throw them into the sea. She looks up, the sky two different shades of blue, separated by a stark line of grey clouds.

She's transported back, stood near the rocks responsible for taking Bex's life away. Their dark and ragged edges had barricaded her from the shore and safety. Had broken her bones, her brain.

Nicole can't breathe. She pulls her scarf away from her throat. Rubs the base of her neck and tries to calm herself, but nothing works. The silver mist can't save her here. She's never been able to lose herself in its comfort on the beach.

In the distance, Grant envelops his mum in his arms, his dad placing a hand on his shuddering shoulders. Nicole has to go. She cannot own up. What was she thinking? She cannot cause them any more pain. They're suffering enough. Maybe this is her consequence, she thinks. To never quite live a full life. To never fully be free of guilt and blame. To hate herself always.

Confessing will absolve her of some guilt, but she deserves to suffer; both her and Emily do.

Somewhere above her a herring gull calls out and Nicole imagines the bird is Bex, laughing.

Serves you both right.

TWENTY-TWO
ANGELA – 1997

'Hello sweetheart, how was school?'

Mel's eyes were wide, her grin reached across her whole face.

This is a change from usual, Angela thought. She had recognised years ago the sadness in her daughter's expression. Angela had always worried about her 'ever so slightly always depressed' daughter, as a doctor had once described Mel. From her first day at playgroup she'd struggled to make friends. She was always too old for her years, as though the fun and carefree element of being a child had never fully formed.

Angela believes she made Mel wrong in the womb. She thinks she neglected to give her the vital element needed to ensure she was always happy and fitted in.

'School was great, Mum.' Mel threw her bag down at the base of the stairs. 'Can I have a friend round?'

Wow, Angela thought. Mel had never asked to have a friend round before.

'Of course.' She hid her surprise. 'Anyone I know?'

'Don't think so, but you'll like her. She'll come by in about half an hour. Okay if she stays for tea?'

There's not a lot in the fridge, Angela remembered, and then worried. If Mel was going to have a friend round then they'd need to be fed well so they wanted to come and visit again. Angela didn't want to be known as a poor cook or host. 'Yes, I'll nip to the shop and get food for dinner.'

'Not pizza or fish fingers.'

'How about a spaghetti Bolognese?' She could cook that easy enough. Get one of those sauces.

'Yes, but not with grated cheddar. Can you get some nicer cheese? What's the Italian stuff they do at Pizza Hut?'

'I know the cheese you mean.' *Looks like yellow dust,* she thought, but didn't say.

'Great. Thanks, Mum. Just going to get changed!'

Angela watched her daughter skip up the stairs as though she weighed half what she did. Her weight was another reason for Mel's lack of friends, no doubt. Angela remembered her own school days. She was the fat girl who never fitted in. Ang-jelly-belly they'd called her. She'd hated school.

The shop hadn't had all of the ingredients Angela had needed for the Bolognese – she'd wanted to put mushrooms in – but she'd picked up some garlic bread, which she hoped would elevate the meal somewhat.

Back home she could hear Mel laughing with her friend upstairs, pop music playing in the background a tad too loud for her liking. She worried about the neighbours complaining – the walls were so thin. Even though the sound of her daughter's laughter was unfamiliar to Angela, the giggles sounded a little fake, exaggerated, as though Mel was trying too hard.

An ugly thought popped into Angela's head. What if this new friend was taking advantage of Mel? No, she shook the thought away and stirred the dinner. Just because she couldn't find any common ground with her daughter, other than their weight issue, didn't mean everyone felt the same. Mel would be different with people her own age, Angela was sure, and now she was older she would be more understood and accepted by her peers. This new friend would like Mel for who she was and not because she could be manipulated as she was so desperate for companionship.

'History will not repeat itself,' Angela said out loud, and called up to the girls to say their dinner was ready.

Walking in behind Mel was a girl who was her exact opposite. Long legs, long hair, and a smattering of freckles across her defined cheekbones. Angela's breath was taken away a little bit by this girl's presence, as though a wave of energy had blown in with her. She'd injected Mel with confidence too. Her daughter stood taller, smiled wider and spoke louder.

And now, Angela's instincts were on high alert.

This girl, this new friend who had transformed her daughter within a matter of hours, couldn't possibly want to be friends with her for genuine reasons.

No, this girl wanted something from Mel, Angela was convinced.

But there was no way in hell she would let this new friend take whatever she desired. She'd protect Mel at all costs.

Keep your enemies close, she thought. *And keep your daughter's enemies even closer.*

TWENTY-THREE
EMILY – 2022

'Emily please,' her headteacher says, his hands wide, pleading the same way hers had been the day she'd begged Grant to stay. 'You are the only teacher with free periods now. If you don't go and invigilate this exam then the students can't take it.'

'But it's only a mock; can't they reschedule?'

'No. Look, I know I asked, but my question was rhetorical really. The agency didn't have anyone else they could send. You have to go.'

'Fine.' Emily grabs her pile of workbooks and makes her way to the hall. She turns back at the classroom door. 'But I am doing my marking in there or you're giving me this PPA time in lieu.'

The head's eyebrows rise before he gives a resigned sigh. For a mock, marking work whilst invigilating clearly isn't a deal-breaker for him. Emily won't be the only teacher in the hall, but normally doing anything but standing bored out of your fucking mind and staring at the children is strictly forbidden.

The sports hall has already been set up – row after row of tiny desks waiting for the students to find their place and fidget on their chairs. Each desk is numbered and the exam papers are on top, already in place. At least she's got out of setting the room up. The last time she had, one of the agency invigilators had stunk of cigarettes and coughed in her face as they'd worked together to check the students' place cards had matched the seating plan.

Emily had then smelt of smoke herself for the rest of the day, a dull taste of tar setting up home at the back of her throat, making her crave, and then smoke, cigarette after cigarette.

She nods at the other invigilators and forces a smile. She recognises a couple, but others she doesn't. One nervous short woman hovers by the main table at the front awaiting further instruction. Emily isn't going to give her any.

She dumps her pile of marking on the nearest free desk and stands arms folded at the front of the hall. She'll stand here as the students pile in and the exam starts. Then she'll sit and mark. And not think about the memorial at the weekend. Or Nicole and Grant looking cosy, huddled together against the wind like penguins sheltering in a sodding snowstorm.

The doors at the back of the hall burst open and students file in, in silence. Exam conditions start the second you enter the hall and if you're caught talking then you're disqualified. Harsh, but necessary.

All of a sudden Emily's breath catches in her throat as Chloe walks in and clocks her. She has her hair up today, pulled back into a tight bun, stretching the skin on her face. She reminds Emily of someone, but she can't put her finger on whom. Chloe comes out of the cupboard where the students leave their bags so they can't cheat, and sits down at her desk.

Then she puts her hand up and looks at Emily, eyebrows raised.

None of the other invigilators are near or appear to have seen, and so Emily grits her teeth and walks over.

'Forgot to take my watch off, miss,' Chloe says, a look of

mischief on her face, her lip twitching as though she wants to laugh. 'Could you look after it for me, please?'

Watches aren't allowed in any exam and Emily is pretty sure Chloe knows this and is messing with her on purpose.

'You found your watch then?' Emily stands firm.

'Yep. Right where you left it.'

'Lost property?' *Two can play at this game,* Emily thinks.

For a second Chloe looks beaten, before she regains her composure and hands Emily the watch. 'Don't forget to give my watch back at the end of the exam now, will you, miss?'

Without replying Emily walks back to her spot at the front of the hall. Her palms are sweaty and she is light-headed. Teenagers getting the better of her happens more often than she'd like, and is a part of the job she hates. *No more stealing at work,* she thinks. *Too risky.* But her fingers twitch as they stroke Chloe's watch in her pocket.

The fabric of the strap fraying. Emily catches a thread between her fingers and pulls. All the while Chloe watches her, a smirk playing on her lips.

The deputy walks in and begins the exam. This is the worst part of the process for Emily – those first few minutes knowing she can do nothing but stand and stare for the next hour and a half. She feels suffocated, as though all of the air in the room has been sucked out. Chloe can't stare at her for the entire length of the exam, surely?

Ignoring her, Emily goes to another student and begins the task of fulfilling the inevitable and endless requests for tissues. She isn't sure why exams make noses begin to run. Chloe doesn't join in with the mass tissue requests and Emily is relieved. She walks over to her marking, but hesitates and doesn't sit.

Chloe.

If Emily does her marking when she is meant to be

invigilating then Chloe will have more to hold over her and Emily cannot let her have such power.

Chloe has no proof about the watch, but this time she will have proof of Emily bending the rules, and if anything goes wrong with her mock exam then Emily will be to blame because she won't have fully paid attention. *Fucksake,* she thinks.

So she stands. She glances around the room. A handful of students yawn, and a surprising number appear to be asleep, heads down and resting on top of their folded arms on their desks. Others are scribbling away, checking and rechecking their work. She watches as Chloe writes a few words, pauses, then looks at Emily, before writing again. She repeats these actions over and over. Then Emily stops watching.

She adds up the blotches of leftover Blu Tack on the display board on the wall in front of her instead. Sixty-one.

Stretches her calves one after the other.

Counts the rows and columns of desks and tries to calculate how many students are in the hall right now. One hundred and ninety-eight.

Leans against a wall before recoiling as she spots several blobs of chewing gum all over the concrete.

Watches the green light flash on the fire alarm, counting the seconds in between the flashes. Three. She could press it, she thinks, smash the glass and make them all have to leave, but then realises that will only prolong the agony as the exam will simply resume once a real fire isn't discovered.

Or she could start one. No.

She catches Chloe's eye again.

There've been no more texts since she returned the watch and so Emily hopes it's all over. The question of where Chloe got her number from still nags at her, but she doesn't have the energy or the inclination to confront her. Chloe will never admit to sending the text anyway, just like Emily will never admit to taking and returning the watch.

Emily looks at the clock: still an hour to go. Papers are shuffled and noses are wiped and pens are dropped and chairs are moved and the students sneeze and cough and sigh and Emily is going out of her tiny mind with boredom.

She's transported back to when she took her GCSEs. Goodness knows how she hadn't failed them all. That had been a time in her life when she'd not cared about anything, Bex not being the best of influences, and Emily ripe for corruption.

Nicole had always tried to follow the right path, but they'd broken her too eventually. Sneaking out after dark – without Nicole at first because she was too scared to escape her house – smoking and drinking cider in the local park where no one ever ventured. They'd thought they were invincible, but had nearly been caught once. That night was the one time Nicole had come, she'd perfected the positioning of her pillows so her parents thought she was sleeping, and Emily remembers feeling strangely proud of her friend for rebelling as she did. Emily hadn't thought Nicole could do so. But then Bex had changed and the fun had ended anyway.

Emily looks around the room at row after row of teenagers taking an exam they don't want to because they have neither a clue what they want to do with their lives nor the motivation and energy to decide. They aren't capable of looking far into the future, just as she hadn't been. Live for the moment and screw everyone else had been her MO.

Maybe that attitude should be fully resurrected.

She looks at Chloe one last time, and this time she's the one to smirk. *Fuck you,* she thinks, and sits down to do her marking.

'You won't win,' Emily mutters, 'because I've nothing left to lose.'

TWENTY-FOUR
NICOLE – 2022

Joe is splayed on the sofa, one hand tucked in the top of his trousers as he does when he's eaten too much, the other holding his phone. He looks tired. Working late has taken all of his energy out of him. Nicole has little sympathy. When he's closed off he takes her for granted and she hates it.

She hides her hands behind her back, hoping he hasn't spotted the flecks of mud that have dropped to the floor. She should've washed the muck from her hands before coming to speak to him. If he asks her why they are caked in dirt she doesn't have a lie ready to tell.

'Have you fed the boys?'

He doesn't even look up. 'No.'

'Joe, it's seven o'clock.'

'It's what? I've been working. Didn't realise the time.'

'Right, I'll order some pizzas then, shall I? Do you want one?'

'Not really.'

'Well, there's no food in the fridge. I've not had time to go to the shops.'

'What *have* you been doing today?' he asks and she tenses.

Nicole knows he doesn't mean to sound accusatory, and even though she's hiding something, his questioning angers her. 'None of your business.' She turns to leave. 'Get your own dinner, I'm having a pizza.'

She storms upstairs, slamming the bedroom door behind her, orders the pizza and then goes into their en suite and locks the door. A shower; she needs a shower, needs to wash the day, what she's done, off her.

Under the hot water she closes her eyes and inhales deeply, looking up so the water splashes against her face and neck. She can't believe what happened today.

If she'd answered Joe honestly when he'd asked her what she'd been up to he'd have been shocked. Dishing out karma is becoming an obsession, but isn't making her feel as good as at first, when she'd knocked the wing mirror off the car. But still she can't stop. Rage burns like a hot coal inside her stomach and an internal scream rings in her ears.

She wipes the brown dirt off her hands and digs mud out from beneath her fingernails. And then she laughs a little as she remembers the look on the woman's face when she came back to discover her car, parked on the yellow zigzag lines beside a busy primary school entrance, with its windscreen covered in soil from a nearby garden. Nicole is pretty sure no one saw her throw the soil, having watched the owners of the garden drive away in their car a few minutes previously – but she can't be sure.

She hadn't stuck around to find out either, but reckons she's done the residents of the road a favour. They are all sick to death of the inconsiderate and dangerous parking. There'd been constant emails from the school when the boys had attended, asking the parents to park considerately and to not block drives or park on the yellow lines, but there is always someone who thinks the requests don't apply to them. Maybe a bit of mud and inconvenience might make them think twice the next time they want to park illegally because they can't be arsed to walk more than five feet to pick up their children. Uncle Tom would be proud.

A loud banging on the en-suite door interrupts her thoughts, but she ignores it.

'Nicole,' Joe shouts through the crack at the side of the door where he'd sawn off a little too much when trying to fit it. 'I'm going down the pub with Grant, okay?'

'Whatever,' she shouts back. *Good,* she thinks, glad not to have to grit her teeth and sit next to him on the sofa while he scrolls on his phone all night, ignoring both her and the TV show they're meant to be watching together. She gets out of the shower and wraps a towel around her in time to hear the doorbell.

'Can someone get that?' she shouts, but both boys will have their headphones on and won't hear her or the doorbell ring. She growls and runs down the stairs, her wet hair dripping down the back of her neck.

Grabbing the pizzas with one hand for fear of dropping her towel and revealing all to the poor delivery boy, she kicks the front door shut and goes to shout to the boys again, but she swears they have a sixth sense where food is involved because they've already appeared at the bottom of the stairs.

'Thanks, Mum,' they each say. Then grab a pizza box and head back to their rooms.

Nicole stands alone in the hallway. Goose pimples pop on her damp skin – a puddle forming below her on the floor. One hand grips the towel around her and the other grasps the smallest of the three pizza boxes. *Life wasn't meant to work out like this,* she thinks. She had aspirations of being an artist, or a fashion designer. All taken away from her the day she'd watched her friend being thrown about by the stormy sea.

'Make sure you bring the empty boxes down,' she calls up the stairs, knowing she'll be the one to retrieve them from under their beds tomorrow morning sometime. Putting her pyjamas on she flops onto her bed and opens up the pizza box.

They've got the order wrong. Of course they have. She ordered a Veggie Supreme and here, hiding under red and green peppers, is some ham. She picks the slices off and bites down. Then her phone beeps with a text message.

> I still know what you did. And if you don't own up, then I will tell everyone the truth.

Nicole spits out her pizza and coughs as her sharp intake of breath causes some of the cheese to go down the wrong way. Who the hell is this new message from? And what the hell is it about this time? Did someone see her take the wing mirror off the car, or throw the mud, after all?

She stands and paces around the bedroom. No, not them. How would they have got her number for starters? Without thinking she goes to WhatsApp Emily and then stops herself. Then she goes to message Bryony, but realises if she talks to anyone else about this then she'll have to admit what she's been up to lately and she cannot face judgement for any of her actions.

> Who is this? Leave me alone. They deserved it.

She presses send and then throws her phone onto the bed. She can't face eating any more of the pizza and so closes the box and places it on the floor. Then a thought strikes her; maybe these messages are from Emily after all. Emily has always resorted to tactics like this when she's angry. At school once, when Emily had been in a mood with Mel, she'd taken to writing her nasty anonymous letters and putting them in her bag, or coat pocket, when she'd been in the toilet. Nicole had tried to stop her, but Emily hadn't listened. Bex had laughed.

Nicole rolls her eyes at the memory and for a second is certain this new text message is Emily's doing as some kind of punishment for her being close to Grant at the funeral and memorial service at the beach. *Pathetic,* she thinks.

What exactly Emily is accusing her of eludes her, but with Emily, logic and reason are often absent. But if her accusation is about what happened to Bex then Emily has just as much to lose. Maybe these messages aren't from her after all. Nicole rubs her forehead. She is going round in circles.

She's tempted to drive over to Emily's and have everything out with her, but hasn't got the energy after today's antics. Instead, she grabs a glass of wine and settles down in front of the television, opening up the Facebook app on her phone.

At the top of her feed is a new post from Mel's mum on the Bex's Army page, which makes Nicole sit bolt upright on the sofa and spit out her mouthful of wine. Nicole grabs her glasses and reads.

> This is Mel's mum, Angela. I've kept quiet until now, but I cannot keep quiet any longer. My poor, gorgeous daughter needs to be heard and seeing as she won't post this, I have to. Mel's not a bad person. And I am not a bad mum. Children don't always tell their parents the truth. And vice versa. Mel and I should've been more honest with each other, communicated better. We didn't and I'm sorry. I'm so sorry, Mel.

Nicole chews her lip, confused as to what has triggered this outpouring of hidden guilt. And why Mel's mum has chosen to do so publicly on Facebook. Possibly, Nicole thinks, because she wasn't allowed to speak at the memorial. More than anything, she wishes she was on speaking terms with Emily as they would be on the phone, dissecting this update and reassuring each other this was in no way connected to them, because why would the update be?

Maybe she should go and see Emily after all. Talk in person and not over WhatsApp or the phone. She can explain again Emily was wrong about her and Grant, if that's even what Emily's problem is in the first place. Nicole can't deal with stuff like this alone, she's never been able to problem-solve by herself in a crisis. She always needs reassurance. And after the new threatening text and the Facebook update, she needs reassurance from Emily.

The roads are empty. Nicole has always liked driving alone at night, no music on the radio, no whinging children in the back or husband groping her leg over the gear stick in an attempt to be affectionate – not that he's done so in a while. Comforted by the darkness surrounding her car she sighs and lowers her shoulders. The calm is only broken by splashes of reds and yellows as cars pass and fade into the distance. She decides to take a detour and go the long way round. Take time to work out how to approach Emily, what she wants to say, as well as sulk a bit first.

She hasn't let Joe know she is nipping out, but she had at least told the boys before she left – they didn't care. She always knew parenting teenagers would be a challenge. Her own parents told her repeatedly about how teens have to pull away from you before they bound back, but she never expected to be this lonely. She thought she'd be the kind of mother her kids would want to talk with, open up to and confide in. That her house would be a house full of other people's teenagers, ones who are more comfortable in her home than their own. But no one ever comes. Instead, hers are the children who choose to spend time elsewhere.

She parks the car in a lay-by and closes her eyes. Then sighs, groaning as she expels the air from her lungs. The long drive has helped calm her, but the flicker of nerves about seeing Emily hasn't gone.

Emily's place isn't far from where she stopped in the lay-by and she is soon there. She can rarely find parking outside and Nicole drives along the narrow road searching for a gap in the cars parked bumper to bumper along each side. She doesn't even know if Emily is in. She does usually go out at the end of the week in the evenings. To where, Nicole doesn't ask if she's not the one meeting her. Being child-free means Emily can still indulge a hangover.

Nicole parks in a small space in the end near the junction, knowing the bumper of her car is hovering over the double yellow lines curving around the bend. She won't be long. It's dark. For once, she doesn't care.

She rushes down the road as pellets of rain pound her clothes – her coat hangs in the hallway at home. The puddles on the pavement glisten in the light of the streetlamps. Dots of rain pepper them and make them shimmer. Nicole is distracted for a moment by a memory of moonlight on the sea.

Then she hears a voice she recognises and the slam of a front door and as she looks up she watches Joe, her husband who is meant to be down the pub with Grant, leaving Emily's house. He pulls his hood over his head and turns in the opposite direction to where Nicole is standing. Her brain tells her feet to stay put.

Joe doesn't lie. His honesty is one of the things she loves about him. She trusts him. Always has and – until this moment – he has never, ever given her any reason not to. If he messes up, he owns his mistakes and she's forever grateful this quality has been instilled in their children. Or at least, that's what she thought.

Now, stood here, she is questioning everything, but in spite of that, she still very badly wants to trust Joe. She wants to believe he was at Emily's house for any reason other than the obvious.

A wave of nausea flows over her and she swallows hard. A car passes and the sound of the wheels splashing through a puddle snaps her out of her trance. The whoosh is like an injection of reality. The facts might be there, might've always been there, and she's been too trusting to notice or pick up on them. Emily and Joe are close, but in a brotherly and sisterly way, aren't they? At least, that's how Nicole has viewed their relationship.

Emily likes her men rugged, damaged, and Nicole has always assumed Joe too clean and sensible to be attractive to her. But people change. Tastes change. Relationships change. She tries to recall the last time Joe and her had been intimate and she can't. Not this month, or last. Maybe not even the one before that. Not since Bex died.

Looking up at the room she knows is Emily's bedroom, she watches the light flick on and then Emily fumbling and pulling the curtains closed. *Quickie on the sofa then,* Nicole thinks. *Or pressed up against the kitchen worktop.* She imagines Emily bent over, her husband grasping her hips from behind. She wants to vomit.

'No,' she says out loud. 'You have no proof. None at all.'

'You okay, love?'

Nicole jumps and turns to see a short old lady behind her holding a fluffy dog on a lead. The dog cocks its leg and urinates over a bunch of weeds sticking out of the bottom of the wall.

'Yes, fine, sorry,' Nicole says. 'On the phone. AirPods.'

Nicole points to her ears hoping her hair is covering the fact that she hasn't got any AirPods in right now. But she's seen enough people walking along the street appearing to talk to themselves to know it's a thing.

'Oh good,' the old lady says. 'Lewis here and I thought you might be having one of those mental breakdowns.'

'No, no. I'm fine. Just chatting to a friend.' The dog sniffs around Nicole's shoes and goes to cock its leg again. She steps to the side. 'I'm on my way to meet her, actually.'

'Oh, okay then, love. Glad you're all right. My friend Wendy went a bit mad once, used to talk to herself all the time, turns out she was talking to the voices in her head.'

Blimey, thinks Nicole. 'Oh gosh, I'm so sorry. I do need to go though.'

'Took her to some home they did. I never visited. She wouldn't have wanted me to. Wouldn't want to be seen that way.'

Nicole often used this as an excuse for having rarely visited Bex. She'd tell herself Bex wouldn't want her there, or for anyone to see her in that state. 'Of course, and that's okay,' Nicole answers.

'Dead now, of course. I'm the only one of my group left. My daughter visits, but she lives in Manchester so is a long way away. She does her best though.'

'How lovely of her, you're very lucky.' Nicole looks back at Emily's. All of the lights inside are off now. Emily must be sleeping off her post-coital glow.

'Anyway, best let you get on,' the old lady says. 'Bye then, love.'

Nicole watches as the lady shuffles down the road, stopping every two steps for her dog to leave its mark, and as she watches she sees her future mapped out in front of her. No husband. No best friend. Her kids will live far away and rarely visit. Her brain will close in on itself. She'll invent voices to talk to and keep her company. Get a dog. Talk to strangers on the street, or the check-out assistants in shops.

'Argh,' she groans, knocks her forehead with the heel of her hand and goes back to her car. In the front seat she texts Joe to say she's gone out to buy milk, and ask what time he'll be home from the pub.

He replies he's already back and is hopping in the shower, not even commenting on the fact she isn't there.

Liar.

TWENTY-FIVE
EMILY – 2022

Emily hangs up after leaving a voicemail to say she's not coming into work today. She licks her dry lips and reaches for the glass of water by her bedside table she doesn't remember putting there.

Going out and getting pissed on a Thursday night wasn't her best idea, but was all she could think of to calm her racing brain. She needed numbness, to be unconscious and block everything out, except the alcohol hadn't worked. And then, something awful had happened.

She pulls the pillows over her head.

Normally, she can cope with work and a hangover: several painkillers and a rehydration sachet do the trick. But not with Chloe eyeballing her every two seconds.

Emily can do without that, especially today. She glances over at the photo on the dresser of her with her mum and dad, taken a week before the accident. Today would've been her mum's birthday and it's a day she hates every year. Even now, a long, long time since her mum died, her birthday reopens the wound created and all of the grief and guilt sewn up inside pours out as though her jugular has been slit.

Pulling her pillow tighter over her face she screams into the soft lump. Then recoils as her breath reeks of alcohol and fags. When will she learn?

She stares up at the ceiling and toys with the idea of drinking again and continuing to do so throughout the day. Then she toys with the idea of calling Nicole. Last night showed her how quickly things can become muddied when emotions are involved. But she decides not to. She'll leave that to Joe. She's too mortified to speak to Nicole herself.

Events of late have tipped her over the edge of the fine line she works hard to balance on. She knows her bad choices are catching up with her and she cannot hold any more guilt inside.

That's when she remembers: Mrs Smith often goes to visit her children and grandchildren for the weekend. Having glimpsed inside the house the other day Emily understands a bit more as to why Mrs Smith's children don't come and stay with her – but she still wants what she hid there a long time ago and left there for safekeeping. A treasure she took and never gave back. As well as comfort.

Dragging herself out of bed, she doesn't bother to shower. She throws on some leggings and a baggy jumper, ties her hair up into a messy ponytail and then decides to make the effort to at least clean her teeth. The taste of last night's mistakes make her want to throw up all over again. Oh the shame.

Emily waits in the car sipping coffee from a thermos as though she is on a stake-out.

Mrs Smith's house looks empty. The curtains are open even this early in the morning as though no one has been around to shut out the darkness the night before. If Mrs Smith catches her here after last time then Emily may never be able to get into her childhood home or bedroom ever again.

Which might be a good thing, she thinks, recognising that holding onto this part of her past isn't healthy, but isn't nostalgia an activity all adults indulge in, whether orphaned or not? Or maybe only those who feel like they've lived two lives, she thinks – one full life with their parents, and one empty one without them.

There's no sign of life inside the house. Not even the tiniest twitch of a curtain. Looking up and down the road to check no one is around, Emily gets out of her car and heads up the pathway. She knows where Mrs Smith keeps the spare key because it's the same hiding place her parents used.

The pebble with the hole in the bottom had been a present from her dad to her mum after she'd locked them out of the house for the third time in a week. She was forever losing her keys or forgetting to put them inside her handbag.

A few chips show wear and tear on the bottom now, but the pebble is still right next to the plant pot overflowing with weeds by the front door. Emily picks the rock up and feels the familiar shape in her hand, before tipping it upside down and letting the key fall into her palm.

Without meaning to she holds her breath as she opens the front door as though waiting for the onslaught of smells from unwashed dishes or smoked cigarettes, but the air smells stale before the breeze coming in from the front door washes the mustiness away. No post on the floor either. In fact, the hallway is clear of shoes and coats and the usual objects she'd expect to find there. Mrs Smith must've been having an off-day the other day because this is how Emily usually finds the house when she is allowed inside. And it's how she likes it, with no clear indicators she ever lived here, but also no signs someone else now does.

She wonders then if Mrs Smith has done this on purpose, as though sensing Emily is going to come again at some point having not been allowed in the last time.

'Hello,' Emily calls out, knowing no one will reply, but still nervous there might be an unwelcome response. 'Mrs Smith, are you here?' She stands in the hallway for a moment waiting for a rustle from upstairs, or the creak of a door or floorboard. Looking towards the kitchen she has a vivid memory of her mother stood over the stove, calling her for dinner. She can imagine the cooking smells now, wafts of potatoes covered in cream and hints of tarragon chicken. Her mum had been an amazing cook. All of the goodness Emily was fed as a child makes up for the crap she eats now. The house feels alive, as though the walls and the floors have retained the memories of her life here and are releasing them as she walks through it. *Scratch and sniff wallpaper,* she thinks and smiles.

The stairs creak in all of the places they used to. The third step from the bottom, the one second from the top, where she used to sit when she was scared to go to bed whilst her parents were still downstairs. She'd huddle there with her teddy and listen to them as they chatted about their days with the television on in the background.

Often she'd fall asleep as they spoke, curled into the bannisters, and one of her parents would lift her up and carry her back to bed. They never told her off for getting out of bed after they'd said goodnight and sometimes, on very special occasions, they'd even let her stay downstairs and fall asleep with her head on one of their laps. She breathes in hard and tries to smell the scent of her mum's perfume, but all she can smell is dampness.

At the door to her old bedroom she pauses. The handle has been changed but the rest is the same, even the small pen mark near the bottom where she'd tried to draw the next-door neighbour's cat before being caught by her dad after only drawing the tail.

She pushes the door open and inhales the sight of her childhood bedroom. The single bed pushed into the corner, different bedding on there now, but the shape and position of the bed alone is enough to transport her back. Normally, she'd lie down on top and close her eyes and listen to the creaks and groans of the house and pretend she's nine again. But today she doesn't have time.

She goes over to the fireplace in the wall. As a child she was never quite sure what the vent was put there for and was always scared spiders were lurking behind the metal, ready to pounce while she was asleep and scurry into her mouth or up her nose. She'd even worn pants to bed in case they tried to go *up there* too. She shudders.

Hoping Mrs Smith hasn't discovered how loose the grate is, she gives the cool metal a tug and is relieved when the top square comes away from the wall a little the first time. Then she reaches in and feels around. Dust falls onto the carpet and she coughs. She can't feel anything. No one else knows this has been her secret hiding place for years and for a minute she thinks what she put here has disintegrated in the damp space. And then she feels the edge of part of what she is looking for – the slippery film of a photo – and pinches it in between her fingers, pulling the picture down with another clump of dust and debris.

Her heart thuds in her throat as though moving the photo from its hiding place has dislodged her internal organs and put everything out of position. She swallows the lump down and wipes the dust off the photo with her sleeve. Three faces appear as she cleans, as though they have been buried deep underground and are freed. Little by little their freckles and smiles become visible as the dirt is transferred to Emily's sleeve and the years in between when the photo was taken and now are erased.

Three girls giggling on a beach, storm clouds building behind them. Darkness coming and they had no idea of what the clouds or the future held. But here they are, smiling back at Emily from the photo on the day they thought they were being so rebellious.

'You stupid bitches,' Emily spits at the photograph. She remembers the moment the photo was taken by an outstretched wobbly arm – the camera almost too big to hold in one hand – in the days before mobile phones were widely used and selfies were a big thing. They didn't know if the photo would even work back then, no way to look and check, the moment hidden inside the camera until developed. Part of the fun back then was picking up a pack of photos and finding out if they'd chopped their heads off in every one. But they hadn't. They'd captured everything. The day of the accident. The proof they were all there. Not simply Bex going for a lone swim after an argument with her parents like the newspapers had reported.

Only Emily and Nicole know they were there that day too. Even Emily doesn't know why she had the photo developed, or why she didn't tear it into a million tiny pieces after she had. Maybe she knew she'd need the picture one day. Recognised even back then at such a young age that the past would catch up with them and they'd have to come clean.

She's needed to come and check the photo is still here ever since she received the fucking weird text, in spite of thinking the warning message was from Chloe about her watch. A part of her wonders if someone other than her and Nicole knows. Bloody stupid though, she recognises this, but paranoia has taken over.

Taking a deep breath she reaches her hand up once more and pulls out the final thing she came for, a journal. The handwriting inside isn't hers. This was the first thing she stole since the bars of chocolate from the corner shop. Her hands shake. She replaces the grate over the vent at the top of the fireplace and brushes away the dust as best she can.

Still undecided whether she is going to give the journal to the rightful recipients, or burn it, Emily stuffs the book into her bag along with the photo. She remembers being in Bex's bedroom after the accident. She'd sneaked in when Bex's parents and Grant had thought she was in the bathroom. She'd found the journal and taken it, knowing she needed to keep the secrets within hidden forever.

All too aware of how one bad decision can have devastating effects for years to come, and resisting the urge to lie on her bed and close her eyes, Emily puts the photo and journal in her bag, leaves the house as she finds it, and dashes back to her car before pulling away quickly in case any of the neighbours begin to wonder who she is and what she's been doing inside someone else's home for so long. Just like Bex's parents would want to know why she's kept their daughter's journal hidden in a wall vent for the last twenty-five years.

TWENTY-SIX
NICOLE – 2022

Nicole sighs as she packs the rucksack. She and Joe haven't spoken since the other night when she saw him coming out of Emily's place. She's googled 'signs your husband is having an affair' several times over the course of the last few days, but Joe hasn't fitted any of the stereotypes. He's not been exercising more or buying her extra gifts or flowers. In fact, he's exactly the same as he always has been. And she isn't brave enough to ask.

'Have you packed me some crisps?' Kieran shouts from the hallway.

'Yes, I've got two massive bags.'

'I don't want to share,' he huffs and storms back upstairs and she clenches her teeth. This morning she was tempted to not pack anything and then smirk as she tucked into her own picnic lunch, whilst her husband and children suddenly realised they had nothing to eat and had taken her for granted yet again. But she couldn't bring herself to be so selfish. Instead, she's dutifully made four sandwiches and packed them all in the rucksack she, no doubt, will be the one to carry.

'Who thought going for a picnic at this time of year was a

good idea anyway?' she asks Joe. 'The weather is bloody freezing.'

'The sun's out, it'll warm up.' Joe smiles. 'Your mum and dad probably won't want to walk far anyway so we won't be out for long.'

'I know, but I'm not sure why they want to do lunch somewhere other than the pub like usual for Dad's birthday. It's odd.'

'Not really. They fancy a change, that's all. We're allowed to break traditions, you know.' His eyebrows are raised.

Like the tradition of staying faithful in a marriage, she thinks, but doesn't say. She watches him put on his walking shoes and coat and thinks that even if he has changed maybe she simply hasn't noticed. She doesn't always pick up on the subtle shifts taking place over time. Joe is in front of her, day in and day out. She looks at him and wonders what she's missed. How many other times has he lied to her?

'Do you want your gloves?' he asks her.

'I've lost them.'

'No, they're in the utility room, in the cupboard next to the washing machine. Saw them there the other day, I'm sure.' He shuffles off and appears a minute later with her gloves in his hand.

'Thanks,' she says and they smile at each other. One of those rare moments when the hecticness of their lives pauses around them and they zoom in on nothing but each other.

'Come on, boys,' he shouts up the stairs and the moment passes. They trundle down, phones in their hands and massive headphones on their ears.

'You'll be taking those off on the walk,' Joe says to them and they roll their eyes. 'Now put your shoes on.'

Nicole pushes past them and heads towards the car. The weight of what feels like a bear rests heavy on her chest and a cloud of doom rumbles above her head. She's not in the mood for this. Not for any part of today. Nicole wants to ignore the world and curl up under her duvet. Everything anyone says or does pricks at her skin and makes her want to scream. But as usual, she keeps her mouth closed and massages the frown line between her eyebrows with her ring finger.

Read the instructions.
Play the game.
Be a good little girl.

The car clicks as Joe unlocks the doors and she climbs in, ignoring the judders of her children's knees in the back of her seat making her jerk forward.

'Do we have enough petrol?' she asks, knowing damn well she'd have checked before leaving, unlike Joe who gets some kind of sick pleasure out of running on fumes.

He turns the engine on and waits for the fuel gauge to do its thing. 'Yep.' He looks pleased with himself. She wants to punch his smug face. 'Should be enough.'

'Maybe we should stop and get some, just in case?'

'Nah, we'll be fine.'

In Nicole's car she keeps a blanket, a torch, a bottle of water and a packet of cashew nuts in the glove compartment. Everything you might need in case of breakdown. The nuts are probably out of date by now, she thinks, but that's not the point. In Joe's car they'd freeze to death after trying to survive on crumbs from the empty crisp packets littered over the floor.

'Okay, but don't say I didn't suggest getting some when you're walking to the nearest petrol station after you've left us stranded by the side of the road.'

He laughs, but she doesn't. In the back the boys have their heads down, eyes on their screens, the countryside whizzing past them without a second glance. Nicole often thinks their mental health must be very bad, as well as their vitamin D levels, as they never go for walks or runs. She's tried everything to get them interested in a hobby, but nothing has stuck. Even Joe has stopped playing football with his mates on Monday nights. Laziness is breeding laziness in all three of them – although maybe Joe is getting his exercise elsewhere.

'Have you spoken to Emily recently?' Joe asks without looking at Nicole. His eyes are firmly fixed on the road ahead. His face is relaxed, no sign of betrayal in his features; she checks carefully.

'No. Why do you ask?'

'Just wondered that's all. It's been a while. I thought you'd have made up by now.'

'You don't even know what we fell out about.'

'Yes I do. She thought you and Grant were too close at the funeral, right?'

'How do you know that? I didn't tell you.'

'Yes, you did.'

'I didn't. I'd remember.'

'Where else would I have heard that from?'

'You tell me?'

The car lurches forward, Joe unwittingly pressing harder on the accelerator than perhaps he means to. 'Nicole, you told me the other day she was being daft and you had no time for her drama queen behaviour. And then you told me why, remember? I advised you to give her some space.'

Nicole squeezes her eyes shut and thinks. Maybe she did tell him, but she can't remember doing so.

'Maybe Emily told you,' she says. There. She's questioned him even though she wasn't going to.

Joe remains quiet for a beat too long. 'Don't be daft, Nic.'

'I'm not being daft.' Her voice is raised.

'Where's this come from? Don't take your frustrations with

Emily out on me. I haven't accused you of being too close to Grant.'

'No. You haven't even given a shit,' she says. 'I've barely seen you since the funeral. You never ask me how I am. I can't even remember the last time you made me a cup of tea.' She almost rolls her eyes at herself then, she sounds pathetic.

He sighs a fraction too loud and Nicole feels as though she is about to explode like a volcano that's been dormant for millions of years.

'Mum, have you got a tissue?' Kieran asks from the back seat. Without speaking she reaches into her bag and pulls out a fresh packet of tissues placed in there before they left, alongside a blister pack of paracetamol, some plasters and some Savlon.

Then she's hit by the fact that because she's been the one planning for every eventuality in order to look after her family, she's actually fucked them and made them incapable of doing anything for themselves. She's the one assessing the risks and making sure everyone stays in line, but she never actually points out these risks to her children in order to educate them and ensure they have all the tools they need to not make the same mistakes she did as a teenager.

Her head pounds and no amount of rubbing removes the frown line nestled between her eyebrows. She breathes out slowly as though through a straw, but her ears are ringing and she bites the insides of her cheeks. Joe chooses this moment to reach out and place his hand on her thigh, rubbing a tad too high for her liking and the thought of having to give in to his demands too, tips her over the edge.

'Stop the car.'

'What?'

'Stop the car. I need to get out.' The space around her swims, her vision blurry. Her mouth is dry and she licks her lips and swallows hard. 'Stop the car!' she shouts.

Without speaking, and without the twins even looking up from their devices, Joe indicates and pulls into a lay-by. She flings the door open and falls out of the car, gasping at the air as though she's been underwater for too long and has only this second resurfaced.

Blinking away the flashing lights in her peripheral vision, she hears Joe's door slam and his footsteps as he walks around the back of the car to where she is pacing, rubbing her temples.

'Nicole, what's going on?'

She can't speak. Can't tell him what she's been up to recently and why. He wouldn't understand. Dependable Joe, who blindly assumes his wife lives as he does. Has Emily told him what they did? The thought pops into her head and scares her. Does he already know the truth about Bex and the beach?

She bends forward and rests her hands on her knees, dipping her head to her chest. He rubs her back. 'Nicole,' his voice is calm, 'we're going to be late.'

Standing, she shrugs off his hand. A dark emotion inside her, hanging by a thread, snaps. *Enough,* she thinks. *I've had enough of all of you.*

Everything she's believed in is stupid. She's stupid. How could she have been so certain everyone was safer with her 'instructions for living' in place? As though never being spontaneous or having fun was a penance she had to pay to ensure everyone's safety.

Prison or dead, that's the game they used to play when the boys were younger. Whenever they did something she thought was risky, she'd shout 'prison or dead'. The boys would laugh, point out that they were neither dead nor in prison, but she'd felt like she was keeping them safe. Giving them the tools and judgement to keep themselves out of trouble when she wasn't around to do so. But that's rubbish.

She can see the truth now.

She travels back in time. Emily was there too and what she did was far worse than Nicole's involvement. Her thoughts have been going round and round in circles for a while now, alternating between wanting to forgive Emily, and wanting to expose her. She hasn't checked Facebook again. She hasn't received another text, and yet still she is on edge as though she is being watched all the time. For one paranoid minute she'd even thought Bex had sent the text from beyond the grave.

She takes a deep breath and looks at Joe, even less in the mood for lunch with her parents than she had been. God help them all if they say anything to trigger her as she suspects her mouth isn't going to behave for much longer.

One push and she'll spit venom.

No, she thinks. *I can't go.* 'I'm not coming,' she says, matter-of-factly. 'Tell them I've got a migraine, whatever, tell them anything, I don't care.'

And she walks away.

TWENTY-SEVEN
EMILY – 2022

'Chloe, I have to get to class.' Emily uses the pile of books in her arms as a barrier to push past Chloe and out into the corridor.

Emily doesn't wait for a response. Nor does she look behind her to see if Chloe even cares. She might be stood outside the staff-room door waiting for another teacher. *Not everything revolves around you,* Emily thinks, and smiles as she remembers her mum saying this to her often as a child.

'Enough about me,' she'd say in jest, pretending to be Emily. 'Let me hear more about you. What do you think of me?'

She misses her mum the most.

The rest of the day passes without any drama or without Chloe reappearing, and Emily is relieved it's the last Friday of term and she can bugger off home early without feeling any guilt. Her diary for the next ten days is empty. Half of her is glad. And half of her feels lonely as fuck. Ever since they left school, her and Nicole have spent most of the October half term together, either shopping or going to a spa, or simply hanging out and watching movies whilst eating all the junk food. But they'd never go to the beach. October is the time of year where they keep busy and avoid anything to do with the sea and the sand.

Enough is enough, she thinks as she walks to her car. She pulls her phone out of her bag and texts Nicole, asking her to come over. She cannot do half term without her. Nicole and Grant weren't a thing, Emily knows that now after speaking to Joe about everything – she shudders again with shame at the memory – and now recognises how once more, she is pushing those closest to her away and isolating herself because she is overwhelmed with life. And death.

As she presses send, her breath shakes. There. She's reached out. Her old therapist would've been proud. She dumps the marking she knows she won't touch over the holidays into the boot of her car and heads home.

When she gets there Nicole is on her doorstep. Smoking. Nicole never smokes.

'Hey,' Emily says, taking her keys from her handbag. 'What the fuck are you doing?'

'Smoking. Want one?' Nicole holds out a packet of cigarettes and Emily can see at least three have been smoked already.

'Inside. Now.'

Nicole rolls her eyes like a sullen teenager and stubs out the cigarette and shoves the packet in her coat pocket. Then she folds her arms and marches up to the front door. Emily lets them in. She can feel the anger and frustration emanating from Nicole's body and wonders what the hell has gone on. Nicole is never angry. Ever. Even when Joe takes the piss or the twins are being spoilt twats – which is most of the time.

Nicole slumps on the sofa and Emily fetches two glasses, and a bottle of wine from the fridge. This isn't how she planned on starting her holiday even if wine had been on the agenda.

'Right, what is going on?'

Nicole glares at her. 'You. Tell. Me.'

Emily can't think what she could've done to piss Nicole off. They haven't seen each other. Or spoken. *Oh wait. Joe.* 'I have no idea what you're talking about,' she lies. 'But why do I get the impression you're angry with me?'

'Because I am, but if you own up then maybe, just maybe, I might not be quite so angry.'

'Nicole, you're making no sense.' *Joe's told her,* Emily thinks. She's mortified. But she still doesn't understand why Nicole is so angry with her. Maybe it's because Emily hasn't reached out to her before now.

Nicole's knees are jiggling and she picks at the skin around her thumbnail, an old habit meaning she's anxious. 'I saw Joe, leaving here the other night.' She moves to sit on the edge of the sofa. 'He told me he was down the pub. Is that why you were so quick to judge me and Grant at the funeral? Three fingers always pointing back at you and all that.'

'No, it really isn't what you think.' Emily stands and scratches the top of her head, her face scrunched up. 'Honestly.'

'Then why don't you tell me what happened?' Nicole sucks her thumb where the skin bleeds, one piece picked too deep.

Emily takes a deep breath. *Oh the shame.* 'Fine. I was having a bad day, at work. Nothing huge, some trouble with a student and so I thought I'd go down the pub and drown my sorrows.'

'What, and you bumped into Joe and then fucked him to make yourself feel better?'

'Nicole!' Emily's hand goes out to stop the vulgarity coming from Nicole's mouth as though she is stopping traffic. 'No.' She shudders.

Nicole's shoulders lower a fraction and Emily carries on. 'Joe was there at the pub, with Grant. They came in after I'd opened my second bottle of wine and had done a shot of tequila.' She looks down at her feet, the embarrassment of the evening shrouding her like a heavy cloak.

'Go on.' Nicole's legs have stopped jangling now. Her hands are still.

'Obviously I was pissed and I started having a go at Grant, about you two at the funeral, which I now know, by the way, is not a thing. And then I threw up all over him, projectile vomited like the girl in *The Exorcist,* in the middle of the pub, with everyone staring at me. Fuck, I was so embarrassed.' She sits back down on the sofa, puts her head in her hands and swallows back the taste of vomit.

'Oh Emily.'

'Don't "Oh Emily" me. You know I hate being pitied.'

'I know. Sorry.' Nicole moves to lean back on the sofa, deflated.

'Anyway, the bar staff wouldn't let me carry on drinking even though I told them my stomach was empty and raring for more. Joe and Grant dragged me home and Grant stayed over – on the sofa before you say anything: there was no funny business. I don't remember Joe leaving. But I begged them not to tell you. Joe wanted to; he's a good man, Nic.'

'Why didn't you want me to know?'

'Oh I don't know.' She can't stop the sarcasm dripping from her words. 'You'd have given me a lecture or said my drinking is linked to Bex's death and I didn't want to hear the truth. Still don't for the record.' She holds up her finger to stop Nicole from berating her.

'Trust me, I'm not one to criticise anyone else right now.' Nicole throws the packet of cigarettes on the table and looks resigned.

Emily wonders what Nicole means. They sit in silence for a bit, Emily waiting for Nicole to be the first to speak.

'Sorry I thought you'd slept with my husband,' Nicole says a few minutes later.

'Sorry I thought you'd slept with my ex-husband.' They look at each other and burst out laughing.

'We're fucking idiots. You know that, right?' Emily shakes her head and gulps back more wine before refilling their glasses. 'How long have we known each other?'

'Too long. And we've never had secrets before.'

Emily thinks of the journal in her bedside drawer. Some secrets have been held too long to be revealed now. Nicole was upset enough with her on the day of Bex's accident. If she knew Emily had taken the journal from Bex's bedroom on top of everything else she'd done then she isn't sure their friendship will survive.

'So what's going on at work?' Nicole asks.

'Oh no, we're not doing that. You were outside smoking and full of rage, which means you need to talk. This can't only be about you thinking I'd slept with Joe.' *Screw being patient and waiting for Nicole to come clean,* Emily thought.

'Nothing, just the stuff about you and Joe.' Nicole wafts her hand about before taking a large sip of her wine and Emily knows she's lying. There's more. Emily will happily bet money on the fact.

Without saying a word she refills Nicole's glass and waits.

'Have you been on Facebook recently?' Nicole asks.

'No. Why?'

Nicole gets her phone out of her bag and unlocks it.

Emily holds out her hand.

'What the–' Emily's heart skips a beat. Thoughts race around her head. 'Why has Mel's mum posted this now?'

'I don't know, but it's weird, right? That's why I was here the other night. I saw she'd posted and came round to talk to you about it. Then I saw Joe and left.'

'Who knows why she's chosen to post this. Maybe, like me, she was having a bad day and drank too much and posted without thinking? Maybe the status means nothing. Bex dying has messed with everyone's heads.'

Emily thinks about the text on her phone. She can't tell Nicole about the message because then she'd have to tell her about all of the stealing she's done recently. Nicole already disapproves of Emily's questionable behaviour.

'You're right. Hopefully the post means nothing. No one's commented either; so that's a good sign. If she thinks no one cares then maybe she'll stop?'

'I hope so.'

Emily feels uncomfortable, as though all her secrets are growing and pushing all of her organs out of place.

She isn't sure how much longer she can keep them contained.

TWENTY-EIGHT
NICOLE – 2022

Joe gives Nicole a WTF look as she walks into her parents' lounge. Of course, the rain had started pouring down in the middle of their picnic and they'd all decamped back here, instead of going home, where they thought she was in bed with a migraine. Good job: if they had gone home they'd have discovered she wasn't there.

After clearing things up with Emily, Nicole thought she'd better pretend her migraine had passed and show up to celebrate her dad's birthday, although her foul mood hadn't entirely disappeared.

She's sprayed herself with Emily's perfume to hide the smell of cigarettes, and cleaned her teeth with Emily's toothbrush to disguise the fact that she's been drinking wine mid-afternoon.

Earlier, she'd toyed with telling Emily about the weird texts as well as the Bex's Army Facebook post, but then decided she'd have to own up to all of her dodgy actions of late and she wasn't in the mood for Emily's reaction. No doubt Emily would punch the air and revel at how Nicole wasn't perfect after all, and then expect a medal for suspecting this all along. Besides, Nicole isn't going to call anyone else up on their misdemeanours anymore, she'd decided she's dished out enough karma, and that she is bloody lucky she hasn't been caught doing so. The fear of ending up like Uncle Tom is the gift that keeps on giving.

'Put the kettle on, love,' her mother says, her shitty parenting bang on the money again.

'Why don't you make me a cuppa?' Nicole asks, her eyebrows raised. 'I'm getting over a migraine. Maybe someone wants to look after me for a change.' She watches Joe tense in the background.

Then she settles herself down in the chair next to the window and stares out of the clean glass, ignoring her mum's sharp intake of breath. She might not be behaving in the slightly illegal manner she has been recently, but she will start standing up for herself and not be such a doormat around her family.

'What is up with you?' Joe looks furious, his cheeks have a red glow to them Nicole isn't sure she's seen before. But even he's going to have to suck her new attitude up, she thinks.

'Nothing,' she says.

'Are you kidding me? You stropped off earlier, and now this, being rude to your mum?'

'Don't you think she's the rude one, demanding a cup of tea as soon as I walk in?'

'She's always done that though. You've never complained before. What's changed?'

'Maybe *I've* changed.'

Joe leans back and runs his fingers through his hair, an exasperated look on his face. Not for the first time Nicole wonders why he loves her. Does he love how she never complains? Or how she always makes dinner without asking for a hand? Quietly gets on with the housework? Maybe he loves her for looking after him in the exact same way his mother did when she was alive. He might not like this new Nicole though.

The one who no longer gives a toss. And she surprises herself by realising she doesn't care.

'Hope you all ate a lot for lunch, because I'm not doing dinner tonight. I'm on strike,' she says, picking a bit of fluff off her jumper.

'You're on strike? What are you, twelve?'

'I'll tell you what I am, Joe, I'm pissed off.' She speaks as though hissing. 'You and the twins... Where are the twins by the way? Never mind. You *all* take me for granted. No one ever says thank you. No one ever buys me a little gift to show I'm appreciated. You sit there at dinner-time and wait for me to produce a delicious meal as though I'm your bloody personal chef without even ever offering to cook for me for once. I'm sick of being treated that way.'

'But I thought you liked cooking?'

Nicole laughs at this. 'How convenient for you.'

'Is this to do with you and Emily?' he asks and she knows he is desperate not to be at fault or be the reason why she's behaving this way.

'Partly I guess. But no. Mostly this is to do with me, and how unhappy I am. Not that anyone would ever notice.'

She's about to continue when her mum walks back in with a tray of tea, the cosy on top she'd knitted when Nicole was a baby withering from the heat of the pot.

'I made chamomile,' her mum says. 'Thought the herbs might help with the tail-end of your migraine.' She smiles at Nicole as if to say, *See, I can be nice,* and then sits down in her usual spot. 'What do you think brought your headache on? Have you been stressed lately? Maybe it's the menopause. Awful headaches I had when that was all going on.'

Joe splutters, never comfortable talking about anything period-related.

'Maybe, Mum. I feel a bit better now anyway.'

'You need to get some HRT. Lifesaver.'

Nicole wants to ask what her mum means and then stops herself. She probably doesn't want to know and can't handle any more drama right now. Trust her mum to try and make this about herself.

'Where are Dad and the twins?' She pours the tea before the liquid overstews. Then curses herself for not letting someone else pour her a cup for a change.

'In the garden. They've been on those devices all day and your father thought they could do with some culture. He's showing them the plants.'

Nicole looks out the window, but she can't see them. The sky is dark, the sun behind thick clouds, a grey sheen signalling it'll be dusk soon.

'Bet they're loving that,' she says, not able to keep the sarcasm out of her voice. She glances at her mum who looks like she's tasted something unpleasant.

'They did grumble a bit but once they get into it I think they'll maybe want to start doing up your garden.' Her mum smiles, revealing a speck of something caught in between her front teeth.

'Our garden is fine.'

'There's not a lot of colour, is there?'

'Maybe that's how we like it.'

'What on earth has got into you, Nicole?' Her mum looks horrified, hand on her chest as though Nicole's comments will cause her to have a heart attack or funny turn.

'Nothing, Mum. My head is still a bit sore I guess.'

'Hmmm.' Her mum is unconvinced.

Joe remains mute, sipping his tea every two seconds and then grimacing. He hates chamomile, but won't say anything.

Again, Nicole looks out of the window and into the garden. 'How long have they been out there?'

'Oh quite a while. They must be really interested.' Her mum looks smug and Nicole is irritated.

Something doesn't sit right, Nicole thinks. They'd been here for at least a couple of hours before she even arrived, and she knows her children – they can't stay away from their phones for long no matter how interested in horticulture they might pretend to be. 'Have either of you heard or seen them?' She's on the edge of her seat now, scanning every inch of the garden behind the window.

'No,' her mum says.

'Joe?'

'Don't think so.' He shrugs.

'You don't think so? You haven't seen the children for over two hours and you don't think to check they're okay? Do you ever do any parenting?'

Without waiting for him to answer her rhetorical question, she jumps up from her seat and heads out into the back garden, not entirely sure what is making her so unsettled.

'Dad?' she calls, but doesn't get a reply. Her mum and dad's garden is long and thin, stretching away from the back of the house. They've worked hard out here since they retired and walking down to the end is like walking along a secret pathway with bushes and flowers decorating either side. The pathway flourishes with chrysanthemums, pansies and sedums. Names of flowers she only knows because her mum has tried to get her to grow them on many an occasion.

'Dad, are you here?' She continues along the cobbled pathway, and then she sees his feet in their worn brown shoes, peeking out from a bush ahead and to her right. He's unconscious.

'Dad.' *Where the hell are the kids?* Nicole prays they got bored of gardening and left him before he fell ill, and not after he'd passed out in some hideous echo of that day on the beach.

She rushes over to her dad. His eyes are closed and he is lying half in and half out the bush. She screams for Joe and her mum as she tries to drag her dad out onto the grass. He mumbles and she's relieved he hasn't carked it. Yet. She is furious. Her poor, poor dad.

Joe appears at her side.

'Where's Mum?' she asks. 'Call an ambulance.'

'She's doing it. What happened?'

'I don't know. I just found him here. God knows how long he's been like this. Where the hell are the twins? Why didn't you check on them?' She can't breathe. Anger and anxiety swirl inside her and grab onto any ounce of oxygen she has, making everything tingle.

Without speaking, Joe helps her to put her dad into the recovery position and then they look around for the boys before spotting the open gate at the same time. At the end of the garden, the small wooden gate her parents usually keep locked, bashes in the breeze.

'The little shits.' Nicole stands. 'Get Dad a blanket.' Fuelled by fury she marches to the end of the garden and slams the gate open fully.

A little lane runs behind her parents' house with gates from the gardens of the houses next to and opposite theirs peppering the brick wall lining either side of a stony passageway.

They're not there. But two empty Monster cans she knows they'll have left behind rest by her feet. She balls her fists and clenches her teeth. If they left him unconscious she doesn't know what she'll do. They'd never admit to doing so, she thinks. And of course, she has no way of proving what they did either way. The day of the accident rears its head again. She can see the other side, how everyone would feel if they knew the truth.

Back in the garden Joe is bent over her dad and her mum hovers beside them, whimpering.

Now isn't the time to kick off, she thinks, even though she wants to. She'll be taking all devices away and cancelling the wifi for the foreseeable future as well as grounding their sorry asses for several months. As for Joe, she doesn't know what to do. She's angry with him for not checking on the boys, but most of all she's angry with herself all over again. This is all her doing. Her fault. She's enabled them all for too long because she needed to be in control and toe the line.

But what's worse is the belief that this is her fault. She hasn't conformed lately, and now her dad is sick.

'Back to following the rules,' she mutters. 'With bells on.'

TWENTY-NINE
NICOLE – 1997

'Gardening gives me time to think,' her mum said, pulling on her flowery gloves. 'Although, most people say having your fingers in dirt does the opposite and makes you think of nothing except the mud.'

Nicole nods, not listening.

'Today–' her mum picks up the secateurs '–I think we need to think in light of what has happened to her poor family. Come on.'

Nicole rubbed away the knot in her stomach. Her mum had said over and over again how glad she was Nicole wasn't caught up in anything to do with Bex's accident.

'My good little girl, always,' she'd said, patting her on the head.

Nicole got up from the sofa and followed her mum outside. Sighing, she knelt down and pushed her hand further into the soil and buried the daffodil bulb her mum had passed to her.

'I should've planted these several weeks ago,' her mum said. 'But hopefully they'll still take and flower in the spring. Or maybe the squirrels will pilfer them again and the garden will remain bare and colourless like last year. Such a shame.'

Nicole didn't care. Bex had been at the forefront of her thoughts, of course she had. Her and Emily hadn't even been able to mention her name, or visit her in the hospital. The guilt was eating her from the inside out. At one point she'd even thought about visiting Uncle Tom in prison and asking him how he coped with feeling guilty for the hurt he's caused others. But then she reminded herself he didn't feel guilty, otherwise he'd change.

'I saw the mother of your friend from school the other day, in the supermarket. After the horrible accident on the beach.'

Nicole swallowed hard. Something stings in her throat. Not a lump, more like a cut. She swallows again and winces.

'That poor girl. Awful. Simply dreadful thing to happen to anyone. I can't get the haunted expression her mum wore out of my mind.'

Her mum doesn't notice Nicole's distress, too lost in her own memory, somehow making the tragedy about her. She hands Nicole another bulb and points to the back of the flowerbed. 'Without her seeing me, I watched her pick up six rolls of toilet paper, then stop, put them back and pick up a pack of two instead, pausing there and biting her lip. And then I understood, she was still shopping for her daughter as though life was normal and the accident hadn't happened, and with every item she chose she was reminded about how her daughter wasn't at home anymore.

'Putting three apples in the basket instead of four. Choosing only one tube of toothpaste. No extra tampons. Even the mundane act of shopping would never be the same for this woman again and the realisation broke my heart. I'd wondered if there was a favourite meal she'd no longer cook for her daughter. Or if there was a bar of chocolate that would forever remain on the shop shelf instead of being put in the basket ready to be eaten by a teenager with PMS. I'd had to stop next to the clingfilm and take a moment to be grateful my Nicole, you, wouldn't misbehave like that, and go to the beach alone. Such a good girl.'

If only you knew, Nicole thinks.

Nicole had been doing her best to support Bex's family. Going with them to church to pray every Sunday, even though she hadn't been once since her christening. She knows her mum had heard her arguing with Emily about it too. They'd caught her listening outside Nicole's bedroom thanks to the creaky floorboard and had stopped talking before her mum could hear what they were saying to each other.

Emily wasn't going to church. But then Emily had only ever pleased herself.

A bird Nicole didn't know the name of landed on the soil not far from where she knelt. The bird hopped about and then dug its beak at the ground, pecking as though a worm was there ready to be nipped and caught, but then the bird flitted off again empty-beaked.

'Shall I cook your favourite meal tonight?' her mum asks. 'You might like to help me.'

Nicole nods, then wished she had more backbone. But Nicole being a good girl was for the best, had always been for the best, she knew that. It's who she was now. Being the daughter who never disappointed had huge advantages. But she was worried about what that behaviour meant for her future. Did her mum want her to stay close to home? To look after her parents as they aged? They'd expect her to do the right thing whether she wanted to or not.

She always did.

THIRTY
EMILY – 2022

Emily isn't sure why she's here, but here she is.

Waves break in the distance, rolling in, the crests looking like giant white spliffs. As the sea reaches her feet the cold water then retreats. Her eyes sting as the wind whips the salty air around her. The skin on her face is tight, the breeze drying, as though she's had a mini facelift. She inhales deeply, the sea sucking the stress from her as she exhales.

She couldn't sleep last night. Thoughts and images whirred around and around her head and every time she closed her eyes they were jolted open again. The beach was the only place she could think of to come, and she'd been drawn here as if by a magnet.

The sun hasn't fully risen yet. A few hardened early morning surfers bob about on the waves, too far into the distance to see the tears falling down her face. No one is walking their dog – it's too early for even those who like to be up at the crack of dawn. This is when she likes the beach the best. Without teenagers blaring their music and smoking, or dogs sniffing her in places she does not want to be sniffed. With no tourists littering the sand.

The beach was like this before the storm swept in, on the day they came here all those years ago.

On that day, the hardcore surfers had nipped in and out and were back home by the time she, Nicole and Bex had arrived. Nicole hadn't wanted to go at all, had told them again and again she knew the day would end in disaster, but Emily and Bex had forced her.

Things between Emily and Nicole had been strained since Bex had started at the school – threesomes in female friendships rarely ran smoothly – but Emily had been excited by Bex's carefree attitude. There'd been a side to her Emily had wanted to emulate. Dangerous even. Nicole had been dependable and loyal and yes, they'd had fun sometimes, but when Bex came into her life Emily felt a buzz of electricity inside her as though she was reigniting and coming alive again.

She'd known Nicole had hated seeing her change. But, Nicole being Nicole, she hadn't spoken up. She'd simply let Emily be who she wanted to be even if allowing that hurt her.

On that day Emily had been so annoyed with Nicole's Little Miss Perfect act she'd wanted to drop her and be alone with Bex. And then everything had gone wrong anyway.

Emily shakes the memories away and focuses on the horizon. Two shades of blue, the sea and the sky, separated by grey clouds full of rain.

The journal she'd retrieved from her parents' old house burns a hole in her bag. She shouldn't have taken it from Bex's bedroom all those years ago, and even then after she had, she should've given the damn thing straight to Bex's parents.

Even Nicole doesn't know about the journal or the truth of how the events unfolded that day. It's as though Emily is holding onto the journal as a way of holding onto guilt she knows she doesn't deserve to let go of. Nicole blames her for the accident, but she doesn't know the truth, or about how Emily blames herself too.

From the depths of her back pocket her phone buzzes. Nicole again. Emily rejects the call just as she had done last night. She's had eleven missed calls now and knows she should answer, but if Nicole is going to give her bad news – why else would someone call so relentlessly? – then she'd rather not know. She can't handle the extra stress. They'd rekindled their friendship. They are good. That is enough for now.

Besides, last night Emily had received another threatening text, this time with an ultimatum, and she'd turned her phone off until this morning, missing the first seven of Nicole's calls.

> Own up, or I will tell everyone the truth.

Emily didn't even know what she was meant to own up to, as there were endless possibilities. She hasn't stolen anything else, even though her fingers have itched to take several items over the last month, so the message can't be about that, she thinks, wiping a stray strand of hair from her face. She gave the watch back.

Then, out of the corner of her eye she sees movement. Another person stood staring out to sea the same as her. A woman. For a moment she can't breathe, the presence of this woman suffocating her, taking away her space as though she owns the beach and did not give permission for Emily to use the area today.

The woman is walking towards her now and Emily wants to move, to get out of the way, but her feet have sunk into the sand and she is frozen. She's been this way ever since her parents died. Fight or flight means nothing to her. She freezes every single time. The woman walking towards her is familiar, but Emily can't quite place her. The cropped brown hair, the curved shoulders. Then, all of a sudden, Emily is thrown back to the memorial, then further, back to school.

No. That can't be her. But as the woman comes closer Emily realises it is her. Mel's mum. Angela. Now Emily wants to take flight.

'You,' Angela shouts, her finger pointing at Emily like a witch casting a spell.

'Hi, Mrs–' Crap, she can't remember her last name. Her mind has gone blank.

'I want a word with you.' Angela marches closer as fast as the sinking, wet sand will allow.

'I can't stop, I'm afraid.' Emily moves backwards, but she trips over her own feet and lands on her bottom in the sand. Angela towers over her. Wetness seeps into Emily's jeans and knickers.

'I saw you at the memorial, wanted to talk about Mel, but when I looked again you'd gone,' Angela spits. 'I needed to talk to you, to someone who knew her at school.'

'I had to be somewhere, I'm sorry.' Emily scrambles backwards on her bum and tries to stand. She wonders why Angela wanted to talk to her about Mel, but more than anything she wishes right now to be the kind of person who owns her mistakes and apologises instead of behaving like a politician, trying to twist out of her lies.

Angela looks out to sea. Her shoulders slump. 'I try to not be upset she chose Mel out of all of you,' she says. 'Mel was fine before Bex started meddling with her, messing with her head, making her think she actually liked her.'

Emily genuinely doesn't know what Angela is referring to. Emily had never been friends with Mel at school, ever, and as far as she knew neither had Nicole or Bex.

Emily stands now and brushes sand from the back of her body. Her damp jeans stick to her backside. 'I'm sorry, but I don't understand. I barely spoke to Mel at school. I had no idea she and Bex were friends.'

'Lies,' Angela shouts.

Emily cannot work out why this is happening now. They left school decades ago. Emily can only think Bex's death may have triggered her somehow and this *Incredible Hulk* act is the result. Emily needs to get away. 'I'm so sorry, really I am.' She puts her hands up.

'No you're not; none of you are. No one cares.' Then Angela crumbles. Her curved shoulders shudder and her hand flies to her mouth.

Emily doesn't know what to say. She wants to cry too. She reaches out a hand and places it on the back of Angela's shoulders and then is surprised as the woman turns and sinks into her. Emily doesn't know what else to do other than wrap her arms around Angela and stare out to sea as she sobs into her shoulder.

When she finally pulls away she apologises. 'Bex dying brought everything back.' She wipes the tears from her cheeks. 'How everything went wrong for Mel back then and I couldn't stop it. Our relationship was never the same after they'd met, her and Bex. Mel started lying to me. She'd never done that before.'

'I'm sorry.' Emily isn't sure why she's sorry, but the apology feels like the right thing to do.

But her mind is buzzing. Bex and Mel were friends, and yet no one knew about it. And with Bex there was always an agenda.

What other secrets are left buried from back then?

THIRTY-ONE
NICOLE – 2022

Her dad is going to be okay – he had a TIA – but Nicole isn't sure she will be.

Joe has refused to discipline the twins for disappearing, saying the trauma of their granddad being in hospital is punishment enough, and no one can prove they left him alone and unconscious anyway. Nicole is fuming because of his rubbish parenting.

How dare he decide on his own what the twins need when if he'd paid more attention, her dad wouldn't have been out in the garden on his own for so long.

Her dad is lucky, the doctors have said, that Nicole found him when she did. She dreads to think what might've happened if she hadn't sucked in her emotions again and gone round to her parents' house. Would he still be lying out there now? With Joe and her mum happily nattering away in the lounge without a thought for anyone else?

Emily is pissing her off too as she is still ignoring all of Nicole's texts and calls. Nicole is confused as she thought they'd sorted everything out, but clearly not.

Emily is so bloody fake sometimes and Nicole's fed up of

not knowing where she stands. Only now is she beginning to realise she's never felt secure in their relationship. She's always the one to contact Emily, do what Emily wants to do. She spends too much of her time worrying about what Emily thinks about her. Why should her opinion matter? *My God, Emily behaves appallingly sometimes and I still like her. Don't I?*

Isn't that what friendship is? Or maybe in Emily's case she keeps Nicole close so she can keep an eye on her, keep control of her, and make sure she keeps her filthy little mouth shut.

Nicole throws the last of the clean cutlery into the drawers, the dishwasher now empty. She cannot be bothered to reload the shelves with the pile of dirty dishes mounting on the side. Maybe if she leaves them there for long enough someone else might think to clear up.

She wants to go and do anything but be a mum and wife, but she doesn't know where she wants to go or what she wants to do, so she puts on her trainers, shoves her phone and wallet in her bag and heads out the front door. Walking is good for your mental health, and so in the absence of anything better to do, she decides to give pounding the streets a go.

No one is around and at first Nicole is grateful, and then for a split second she feels vulnerable in the way all women do when they are walking alone, day or night. Joe regularly goes running down the cycle path near to their home and doesn't understand why she doesn't feel safe doing the same even though she's explained the fear to him in explicit terms.

All of a sudden she slips, curling her nose at the stench coming from the pavement.

'Gross.' She looks down at her trainer, covered in dog poo. And then she spies the owner of the dog marching around the corner. As though on autopilot she gets a carrier bag out of her handbag and scoops up the poo, warm in her hands like the fire burning inside her chest. She ties the top of the bag and follows the dog and his owner, holding the bag of poo away from her body so the foul stench can't reach her nostrils.

A short little man with bandy legs waddles ahead of her; being pulled along by his dog who is tugging so hard on the lead he chokes and has to stop every few steps to catch his breath. Nicole is covered by a calm rage. She doesn't care how far she has to walk; she will follow this man home.

He doesn't turn to look at her and nor does his dog. They want to leave the scene of the crime as quickly as they can, no doubt. Nicole smirks. He thinks he's gotten away with not picking up his dog's mess, she knows.

There has been a dollop of dog poo in the same spot every day for weeks now and Nicole's frustration and anger at the irresponsibility of the owner has been bubbling up inside like the dog's shit needing to come out.

She doesn't have a dog because she doesn't want to have to clean up after anyone or anything else. Bex's family had a dog and her parents used to leave him in the garden for hours and hours on end, barking and howling every time an ambulance with its siren on went past. Whenever they went out into Bex's garden to play they had to dodge the poos the dog had left scattered about, which her parents refused to pick up.

Nicole can remember wanting to shout at Bex's parents that if they didn't want to properly look after their dog then they shouldn't have bought one in the first place.

She bites the inside of her cheeks in frustration and carries on, the little man still unaware he has a stalker behind him carrying a bag full of his dog's poo. *Ignorant twat,* Nicole thinks.

She has a spring in her step, she feels alive with rage as though it's been swelling inside of her since the day she was born. She feels as though she's been misjudged all of her life and has fallen into step with those judgements, never thinking to question them or fight back. Too afraid no one would like her if she did.

Now, she no longer cares if they do.

Her teachers used to tell her parents she was an absolute pleasure to teach. They'd explain how she was a shining example to her peers and highly emotionally intelligent. She remembers her maths teacher, Mrs Cooper, on the last meeting before she took her GCSEs, not long before Uncle Tom went to prison for the fifth time.

'You do have an exceptionally mature daughter, you know,' Mrs Cooper had said in her slow way of speaking, every pause punctuated with a sharp intake of breath. 'Always helping her friends, showing them how they should behave and leading by example.'

Her parents had beamed, but Nicole had shrunk a little. That parents' evening was the first time she can consciously remember not wanting to be liked for what she did and instead wanting to be loved for who she was. But not long after that, the accident had happened and any chance she had of making this desire a reality drowned alongside Bex.

The little man leads her past a small row of shops. He pauses outside the charity shop and Nicole holds back. *Would the type of man who lets his dog crap everywhere also give to charity?* she wonders, fully aware of how judgemental she is being. Besides, he doesn't have a binbag full of clothes with him or anything else to donate that she can see. But then he pulls a small, black box out of his pocket. Pausing, he holds the box to his chest and his shoulders slump. Nicole is frozen. She wants to know what is in the box causing him so much grief. Surely if the contents are jewellery of any value he'll be the kind of man to pawn or sell them, not donate the lot to charity.

But he does neither. Instead, he places the box back in his pocket and carries on before stopping again. He pulls what looks like a wrapper or empty crisp packet out of his other trouser pocket and throws the rubbish on the ground, then walks off, his dog grunting and choking as before.

Right, thinks Nicole. She stops to pick up the discarded wrapper and places it in a nearby bin as she passes.

She doesn't have to follow him much further. A couple of roads down he turns right and marches up to what she assumes is his front door, and lets himself in.

Nicole looks around her. She's alone. No one around who might catch her, although to any unsuspecting person she'll look as though she's merely posting an innocuous parcel into his letterbox, not a bag full of dog crap.

Pushing out the extra air in the bag and holding her breath against the smell, she shoves the bundle into his letterbox, then rings the doorbell, and runs away like a teenager taking part in a dare.

Maybe you'll pick up your dog's poo next time, she thinks as she strides down the road. *And if not, then I know where you live.*

One last consequence, she thinks. *No more now.*

Hackles prick the back of her neck as though she is being watched, but she doesn't care. Holding her head high she marches down the road. Maybe walking is good for mental health after all.

THIRTY-TWO
EMILY – 2022

Inside the small café by the harbourside Emily spots an empty table for two in the far corner. A furry brown dog laps at a bowl of water placed by the door and Emily takes a deep breath. She can smell the coffee as well as the wet dog and her brain wakens at the thought of a cappuccino.

Hesitating for a second, she looks around the room some more. An old man at the back reads a newspaper and she wonders if this is where he comes to escape and get some peace. An empty plate is on the table beside his elbows, the napkin scrunched and stained with brown sauce. His glasses are perched on the end of his nose and his face scrunches up so they don't fall off the end. Grant used to do the same on a Sunday morning when they'd read the papers together. She pushes the memory away, wishing she could smash the rose-tinted glasses she is looking through.

'Shall we sit there?' she asks Angela, whose arm is still wedged beneath hers as though they are walking down the aisle together. She smells of coconuts and for a second Emily remembers Mel smelling the same.

'This harbour is so beautiful.' Angela looks out of the

window, and then without waiting for a response loosens her arm from Emily's and walks over to the small table covered in a blue gingham tablecloth in the far corner.

Emily nods even though Angela has her back to her.

For years Emily has taken this view, this place, for granted. She remembers the first time she'd gone to the end of Cornwall with her parents before they'd moved here to be near the sea. The caravan they'd stayed in overlooked the beach and she felt like the large waves would crash through the front windows every time the tide was on its way in. She'd spent the entire time staring at the beach and the sea, watching the water inch forwards and backwards.

Now she has access to such a view anytime she wants and she's stopped looking. No, not simply looking, she's stopped appreciating the view because Bex has tainted the sea. Emily feels like apologising to the beach for taking no proper notice, for neglecting its beauty.

Emily walks over to the table too, realising all of a sudden she has no idea what she needs to order for Angela. 'What would you like?' she asks.

'Coffee, please.' Angela pats her pockets and scrunches her face. 'I didn't bring my wallet, I'm so sorry.'

'Don't be daft,' Emily says. 'I can pay.' This had been one of her and Grant's favourite things to do after a heavy night out together. Share a pot of tea for two, and eat gigantic slices of cake after devouring a fry-up. Comfort food at its finest. The smell of sausages alone brings the memory back with full force.

This bizarre situation, however, doesn't feel comforting at all.

Her stomach rumbles and she rubs her hand on her jumper. She can't remember the last time she ate anything. She leaves the queue and heads back towards Angela. 'Do you want some cake too?'

Angela shrugs. 'Up to you. Maybe.'

'Lemon drizzle then.' Emily joins the queue again, smaller than when she'd first stood waiting. She feels odd, as though her centre of gravity has been misplaced, not sure why she'd suggested going for coffee after Angela had stopped crying. The poor woman had been so angry with her on the beach before completely breaking down; Emily hadn't known what else to do other than treat her like one of her students having an episode and take her for a chat. Maybe fate has played a hand and they've bumped into each other for a reason. Except, Emily doesn't believe in fate.

After she has ordered, they sit opposite each other without speaking, picking at their cake and sipping at their drinks. She wracks her brain for questions to ask. The closeness they'd had when they'd embraced at the seashore is gone. Angela has closed herself off and Emily is worried the anger will return.

'What brought you to the beach today?' Emily asks.

'Today is her birthday.'

'I'm so sorry.' Emily has nothing else to give. Nothing else she can say.

For a second Angela stares at her full of intensity, her eyes wide and her lips tight, and Emily is terrified she's going to ask her what she is sorry for. Then she looks away and flicks a fleck of dirt off the table.

'Not your fault,' Angela says.

But it is, thinks Emily. She purses her lips, wanting to ask another question, to make some kind of conversation, but stops herself. She hasn't a clue what to say, or what she can do to make this better. Her heart is skipping beats in her chest. She can't change what happened. She can't take away this woman's pain. Mel made her own choices back then too.

'I'm going to nip to the bathroom.' Emily feels as though someone has hold of her upper body in a vice. She needs a breather. Angela nods and sips her coffee. Her features have softened and Emily is relieved.

In the bathroom she looks at herself in the mirror. The wind has ruffled her hair. She looks feral. Flattening the stray strands with water she takes some deep breaths, expanding her diaphragm, which feels like an elastic band squeezing all air from her lungs. But the unsettled feeling remains as though she's drunk ten cups of coffee, and not simply taken a sip from one.

When she returns Angela is gone.

Emily stares at the café door as though Angela is going to walk back in at any moment, like she used to stare at the front door after Grant left, willing him to turn the handle and admit he'd made a mistake walking out in the first place. But there's no sign of her. Emily even goes back into the toilet to check she's not in there.

Walking over to the counter she waits for a pause in service. 'Excuse me. The woman I was with, did she say anything before she left?'

The waitress shakes her head. 'Not to me, no. Clare, did anyone leave a message just now?'

The young girl clearing tables shakes her head.

'Sorry,' the waitress says and faces the next customer.

How strange, thinks Emily, even more out of sorts now, feeling as though she's been stood up and not understanding why. But then part of her is relieved she doesn't have to talk, or lie, to Angela anymore. But no, she wants to know why Angela wanted to talk to her at the memorial. She suspects it's more than simply indulging herself in conversations about her daughter.

Emily leaves the coffee and cake on the table and rushes out through the café door, bumping into someone as she does. She doesn't apologise.

Looking left and right she wonders how much of a head start Angela has got on her, and where she's heading. And then the fight goes out of her. She doesn't need to defend herself or indulge a woman who has no idea Emily was even there on the beach the day of the accident, alongside Mel.

Mel was the one they hadn't accounted on being there that day. The girl at school who was the most desperate to be liked; the one they'd all ignored because including her wasn't cool. Or so she and Nicole had thought.

Emily goes back to her table in the café and stares out of the window – past the fairy lights and people brave enough to sit outside in the wind – at the rough sea. None of them were meant to be there on the beach. But they were. So far the fallout has lasted a lifetime.

And Emily is sick of it.

THIRTY-THREE
MEL – 1997

This was all new to Mel. The first time she'd had a friend, if that's what you could call Bex. Mel still didn't fully trust her. Couldn't believe she liked her for real and wasn't simply using her. As far as Mel could tell, Bex hadn't fallen out with Nicole and Emily either, so the whole situation was even more confusing. But then again, she was having so much fun she didn't care.

Bex was coming around for dinner later. Her mum was cooking a fish pie this time. The house stank like the rotten end of a beach where all the seaweed gets stuck between the rocks. Every time Bex had come round before they'd not done much. Bex would sit on the floor and Mel on the edge of the bed and they'd sing along to the charts on the radio and record their favourite songs without the DJ talking over them. Bex might crimp her hair for her. Or they might do each other's make-up. They'd chat about how dreamy Michael was, and plan how to make him fall in love with Bex.

A couple of weeks ago they'd made face masks out of all the beauty products Mel's mum had, which wasn't many, but they added hair gel and they shouldn't have, because the skin on her cheeks had tingled and burned bright red for two whole days.

Emily had laughed at her, called her 'tomato face' in front of the whole dining hall and Mel had run out leaving her lunch behind. Her stomach had rumbled all afternoon in her classes and by the end of the day she'd felt dizzy and sick.

But then Bex had said she was sorry for not checking she was okay, that she didn't want Nicole and Emily to know how close they were because they'd be even more jealous and mean, and Mel had forgiven her.

'Mel?' her mum calls up the stairs. 'Bex's on the phone.'

Mel tripped over her rug as she ran downstairs to take the call. Bex didn't normally ring and fear swirled in Mel's stomach at the thought she was calling to cancel.

'Hi.' She took the handset from her mum. 'Is everything okay?' Biting her bottom lip she twiddled with the curly phone cable and twisted the plastic around her middle finger one loop at a time.

'Yep.' Bex's voice was crackly on the line. 'I didn't catch you at school to check you were still okay with me coming round later. I've got an important question I need to ask you.'

'Of course you can come round. Mum's got dinner on already.' The swirl of fear melted into excitement. Bex had a question to ask her! *Maybe she wants me to come to her house for a change,* Mel thought. Or maybe she wanted Mel to sit with her at lunch tomorrow and not worry about what Emily and Nicole thought of their friendship.

'Brilliant,' Bex said. 'See you later. I'll leave in about half an hour, okay?'

'Cool.'

'I hope you'll say yes.'

The line clicked dead and Mel clutched at her stomach to stop the butterflies flitting about inside. *Bex really does like me,*

Mel thought. She was only hanging around with Emily and Nicole to look more popular at a new school, maybe. She didn't like them after all and now she wanted to find her true friends. People who were more like her.

'Everything all right, love?' Her mum appeared in the kitchen doorway and wiped her hands on a tea towel that was once white.

'Yes. More than all right, Mum. Bex will be here by five, okay?'

Her mum frowned for a second and Mel couldn't think why. Then she watched as her mum regained her composure and smiled as though a camera was pointing at her and she was being photographed for *Vogue*. 'Great. I'll have dinner ready for six. Hope she likes fish.'

'Maybe open a window.' Mel holds her nose. 'Fish pie tastes great, but smells rank.'

Her mum laughed and Mel walked back upstairs one careful step at a time. With each step a voice in her head spoke. *Bex. Has. A. Question. To. Ask. You. She. Likes. You. She's. Your. Friend. She. Hopes. You. Say. Yes.*

By the time she reached the landing her cheeks ached from smiling.

THIRTY-FOUR
NICOLE – 2022

Right, Nicole thinks, *here we go.* She would rather be doing so many different things now, but seeing as she'd received another horrible text she had no choice. This is the only other idea she's had to stop the message sender from harassing her.

She nearly told Joe this morning, but the shame of owning up to her actions of late was too much, and so she kept quiet. This way she can stop the situation from escalating.

Her knock isn't loud enough at first and so she sucks in a deep breath and plucks up the courage to rap harder. There'd been no more dog poo in the spot by her house since she was last here, and so part of her feels like she has no reason to be here, that her actions were justified and the message got across. But still, the patterns and beliefs she has held for years have reared their ugly heads and she cannot ignore her poor behaviour.

One more time, she thinks, *one more attempt to let the man with the dog know someone is on his doorstep.* This time she hears movement from within the house and Nicole swears her heart is about to beat out of her chest as she waits for the door to open.

She doesn't have to wait for long.

Own up, or I will. You have until Friday, the last message had said and this time she believes whoever is sending them.

'Can I help you?' The man she'd followed home not long ago looks frail. And she can see no sign of the dog, then realises there was no bark when she bashed against the glass on the front door.

'Hi, yes. You don't know me, but I know you.'

He looks puzzled, and rightly so, thinks Nicole. 'I followed you home, the other day, after your dog had left his mess on a pavement near my house.' She pauses, waits for a reaction. But can't see even a hint of recollection in his face.

'Okay,' he says and huffs a bit. Nicole is scared he might keel over in front of her.

'And I got angry.' She wants to spit everything out now. 'I picked up the poo and put it through your letterbox. I'm so sorry.'

'You did what? When?' He sounds surprised not angry.

'Not long ago.' Nicole is struggling to understand why he can't recall dog poo being posted through his letterbox. Then worries he can't remember anything.

'Haven't walked Maggie for a while, you see,' he says. 'Probably not since that day, thinking about it. My last time. Not been well, you see. My neighbour's been taking her out. Gone with her again now she has. Reckon the day you're talking about might've been when she started coming and helping out, yeah that's right. She let herself in and took him out that evening.'

'Right,' Nicole hesitates, 'so maybe she picked up the bag of poo and didn't say anything so you weren't upset?'

He looks into the distance as if he is recalling a piece of information he can't quite grasp. 'Maybe.' He shrugs. 'I certainly didn't see anything by the door. Or smell anything either.' Then he chuckles.

'Okay, but, I'm still sorry.'

'Fine, love. No bother.'

'Right. I'll go then shall I?' She backs away from him.

'All right, thanks for popping by.' And he shuts the door.

Nicole stands there as she hears him shuffle away, back to wherever he sits and rests while the dog is out with the neighbour. Now she feels even more guilty that someone who wasn't involved in the dog mess had to throw the bag of poo away. She imagines the neighbour letting herself in and then opening the bag to see what the contents were. Nicole grimaces. Maybe she should wait until the neighbour brings the dog home and then apologise to her, but Nicole doesn't want to.

She can always keep the apology up her sleeve for later as an added bonus.

Now, she'll move on to the next one.

The drive to her twins' school doesn't take long. The traffic is waiting in the wings to cause havoc later. She's not rehearsed this apology because she's not exactly sure who she needs to apologise to. Walking up to the reception, she pulls an envelope out of her bag. Inside, on a small piece of card, is her name, phone number and insurance details.

'Hi,' Nicole says, but the receptionist doesn't look up. 'Hello.' She tries again, then taps on the Perspex screen separating them when the receptionist still fails to acknowledge her presence. 'Excuse me, I need to leave this card with you.'

The receptionist sighs and turns to face Nicole, her hand out to accept the envelope.

'The other day I hit the wing mirror off a black car parked on the yellow zigzag lines outside. My insurance details are written in here to hand to the owner.'

The receptionist looks from Nicole to the envelope and back to Nicole again, speechless.

Give me strength, Nicole thinks, exhausted by the day so far.

She only wants to put things right, to turn the hand of karma back in her favour, to keep the threatening messenger from outing her, but everything appears to be conspiring against her.

'You are joking, aren't you?' The receptionist is stifling a laugh, Nicole can tell.

'No I'm not. I want to apologise somehow, but I've no idea who owns the car or how to get hold of the driver, but I figure since they were parked – illegally by the way – outside of the school then maybe the car belongs to one of the parents here.'

The receptionist looks thoughtful. She turns the envelope in her hand and then places it on her desk. 'No one has been in about damage to their car, but if anyone does then I shall pass your apology and details on.'

'Thank you.' That'll have to do. Nicole cannot sit here in reception waiting for the owner to return.

She walks back to her car and rests her head on the steering wheel. Two down, one to go. This one is going to hurt the most, she predicts. The woman who drives the car she threw soil over isn't pleasant and Nicole is scared of her. But she knows, if she wants to keep her dignity and reputation intact, she needs to 'own up' as the messages have demanded.

The traffic slows her journey to the primary school down, and she is torn between feeling glad she isn't there yet, and frustrated as the added time is heightening her anxiety.

Outside of the primary school, her heart sinks when she sees the car parked across a driveway as usual. The owners of the driveway she is blocking must be out, otherwise Nicole has no doubt they would be voicing their annoyance.

Closing her eyes she tries to summon up as much confidence as she can muster. Then she gets out of her car and walks over to the woman who she knows is about to hate her.

For the third time that day Nicole knocks to get the attention of someone.

The woman, who is sat in the driver's seat, engine running even though the school isn't due to finish for another fifteen minutes, winds the window halfway down. 'What?'

'Hi, my name's Nicole and the other day I threw soil over your windscreen. I wanted to say I'm sorry.'

The woman shifts in her seat. 'That was you?' She looks Nicole up and down.

'Yes. I was annoyed by the way you'd parked and felt like you needed to be taught a lesson. But like I said, I'm sorry.' Her hands are shaking.

The woman cackles. 'You do not look like you've got a reckless bone in your body. Fair play.'

Fair play? 'Do you need any money for the cleaning costs or anything?'

'Honey, I sprayed the screenwash and put the wipers on. We're all good.'

Nicole doesn't know what to say. Turns out she doesn't need to think of anything as the woman dismisses her with a wave and rolls the window up.

Heaving a sigh of relief Nicole goes back to her car and gets her phone out. Then she types out a message to the unknown sender.

> I've done it. Owned up to everything. This ends now.

Shaking, she throws her phone onto the passenger seat. And then screams into her scarf. She didn't dish out karma to anyone else. There cannot possibly be anyone else she needs to apologise to.

Relieved the whole thing is over and she can get back to normal – with a visit to the doctor to discuss her hormones in the near future maybe – Nicole drives home. She'll cook a nice cottage pie for dinner. Maybe do an extra portion or two and take them round to her parents or her sister. In fact, she's not seen her for ages; they should come over for dinner.

She and Joe can share a bottle of wine tonight. She's been too harsh on him recently too. He must feel awful about what happened with her dad and she's made everything worse. She can feel her body calming and rebalancing.

Pulling into her drive a sense of ease washes over her like a wave.

And then her phone pings.

> Nice try. But you're not even close. Friday.

She screams into the space around her in the car and throws her phone onto the back seat.

They can't mean what she thinks they mean. They can't. Because if they are inferring what she thinks they are, then only one person can be sending these messages, because only one other person knows the truth.

Emily.

Or was someone else on the beach too?

THIRTY-FIVE
EMILY – 2022

Anna is in the staff room and for a second Emily considers not going in. She has pretty much avoided her colleague since she stole the lighter from her bag, apart from staff meetings where they don't get any time to chat anyway.

But Emily knows she cannot avoid her forever, and has been looking for an opportunity to give the lighter back; maybe now is the perfect time.

'Hey stranger, how are you?' Anna greets her with a warm smile.

'Not too bad thanks, nice half term?' Any conversation in the staff room after a holiday is the same. Emily stifles a yawn.

'Yeah, didn't get up to much. Had a stinking cold. You?'

'Didn't do much either. Managed to avoid the cold that's doing the rounds though.'

'Lucky you. It's nasty. Was in bed for two days straight. Was actually quite nice: John had to do all the childcare and I got a proper rest.'

'Lucky him.' They laugh.

Emily pulls a mug from the cupboard above the sink, and makes herself a coffee. A wash of guilt spreads over her, her ears burning as though Anna knows and is waiting to confront her about the lighter.

She adds two sugars into her coffee for good measure, not sure of what that says about how she is feeling. It's only the start of term and she normally saves the sugar rush for when she is crawling on her last legs towards the next break.

'Just need to nip to the loo.' Anna dashes from her seat. 'Can you watch my bag?'

'Of course.' Emily blows over her hot, sugary coffee and waits for the door to close behind Anna. Then, without hesitating she takes the lighter from her own bag, and walks over to Anna's. *Too obvious?* she then wonders. Anna might suspect her as she is the only person who was here when the lighter went missing, and then when it was returned. But then she has an idea.

Reaching down to the bottom of Anna's bag she pulls hard at one of the seams until the material comes loose, and then pushes the lighter into the lining. A waft of hand sanitiser floats out of the bag and she worries she's nudged the lid off a bottle. But she has no time to check.

When Anna returns Emily is stood where she had been when Anna left, blowing her hot, sugary coffee.

'That's better,' Anna says, tucking her blouse into the back of her trousers. 'I was desperate. My bladder has got used to being able to go at any time during the holiday.'

Emily chuckles in solidarity, but her heart pounds in her chest and she feels nauseous. The rush of giving back without getting caught is greater than the theft in the first place, she is discovering.

'I've got the dreaded year elevens next.' Anna rolls her eyes. 'That's if they turn up.'

'I only had half my class this morning. I think some students might still be away. I know one flight back from somewhere, Spain maybe, was cancelled.'

'Nice to be stuck abroad, I always think, if only I could afford a foreign holiday.'

'We need to do the lottery.'

'Ha, yes! I'd never work again!' Anna laughs so hard she spills her tea. 'Guess this is why they like us to use travel mugs with lids.'

Emily's body twitches and her coffee toys with spilling over the edge of the mug too. She can't believe she's gotten away with putting the lighter back unscathed, but now her fingers itch for the next theft.

No, she thinks. *Not again. Stealing solves nothing. You need to get your kicks elsewhere.*

As the bell goes to mark the end of break the staff-room door opens and the headteacher smiles as he spies Emily. 'Ah, just the person. Can I have a word?'

'I'll leave you to it.' Anna grabs her bag.

'Won't take long,' the headteacher says.

Emily doesn't move. Her brain whirs with thoughts of what this impromptu meeting might be about. A parent complaint? Her recent assessments, which were lower than they usually are for this time of year? He only ever wants to talk to her about negative things.

Chloe?

A bead of sweat drips down the small of her back.

'We had an unusual message left on our answerphone over the holidays.'

Emily's stomach drops. *Oh please, no.* The texts. Whoever is sending them has left a message at her work. Then a fireball explodes inside her. *How fucking dare they?* 'Okay.' She raises her eyebrows in the hope her headteacher thinks she's as baffled as he is.

'We can't do a lot about the message, and we've no way of working out where the call came from, but they said to talk to you about what you'd done. That you'd know what they are referring to and the time had come for you to own up.'

Emily shrugs. 'How strange. Got to be a prank call, right? You know what students can be like. Especially around Halloween.'

'So you've no idea what they could be referring to?'

'Absolutely not.'

The headteacher scratches the stubble on his chin. He's younger than she is, Emily thinks. But she never wanted to climb the career ladder or be a headteacher. She would be awful at the job for starters.

'Very odd indeed,' he says.

'What did the voice sound like? Male or female?' Emily is hungry for information, but needs to stay calm in front of him. The person leaving these messages needs to be stopped before her whole life is ruined. Adrenaline courses through her as though her body is preparing for a race. Or a fight.

'Hard to tell, the voice was distorted. Maybe you're right and the caller is a student; they're so good at using technology these days. Some silly dare maybe.'

'Definitely.' Emily is pretty sure she knows which student as well.

'I should talk about pranks and dares in an assembly sometime, about how dangerous they can be for all involved. No egg throwing or tricks on Halloween for starters.'

'Good idea.' Emily isn't listening. She's trying to work out what class Chloe is in now. 'All right if I go? I've got a free period and loads of marking to do.'

'Yes, yes. Thanks for chatting with me. They could've picked any teacher. Sorry they chose you.'

'Don't worry about it. I've had worse happen.'

He laughs, but frowns as though he would like to know more.

Emily pours the rest of her coffee down the sink and heads to her classroom. She reaches into her bag for her phone and opens up the string of threatening text messages. She types.

> You've gone one step too far. I know this is you, Chloe, and you need to stop right now.

Then she places her phone on the desk and attempts to do some marking. Her brain keeps flitting to Chloe's smirking face and she clenches her jaw.

Every now and again if she stops to think about it, Emily hates how her life is a series of events happening to her, instead of ones she's set in motion.

She's exhausted. But also, she wants to take charge. Needs to have control over everything happening to her. This job isn't enough, her house isn't her dream home, her friends... What friends? Nothing is the way she'd choose. Not having children is the one thing she's been able to control, and for this she's grateful. But for so long she pictured sailing around the world with Grant when they retired. Or travelling around Europe with Nicole and writing a blog about the best spas, having tested every single one.

But she's no money. And no hope.

Her phone beeps and she hesitates to pick it up, as though the metal will shock her when she does.

> Who's Chloe? Don't distract me. You have until Friday.

Emily puts her head in her hands and groans.

THIRTY-SIX
NICOLE – 2022

'I think I'm having a mental breakdown.' Nicole is sat opposite Grant in his kitchen, her hands wrapped around a hot mug of tea. 'I don't even recognise myself anymore.'

She has nowhere else to go, no one else she can turn to. *Emily be damned,* she thinks. She needs a friend.

Bryony is still away on holiday, her flight back cancelled and so she's booked to stay away another week to escape her in-laws, and her dogs who are staying with them.

Grant is Nicole's only option.

'Nicole, grief can do weird things to you.' He reaches over to place a hand on hers and she grabs hold of the tips of his fingers. 'We're all struggling since Bex died. We're all feeling guilty.'

She wants to tell him the truth so much. About the wing mirror, the soil, the dog poo, but mostly, how she was on the beach back then too. She's reached a point now where she isn't sure why she and Emily have never told anyone. The police were never going to arrest them. Nothing they'd done was technically illegal. They didn't grab Bex's head and hold her face under the water. In fact, they'd tried to stop her going for a swim.

Thinking about the facts now, Nicole doesn't know why she's always been scared about owning up to being on the beach too. They did a bad thing, no denying that, but their actions weren't illegal. Is she simply worried about how opinions of her might change if people know the truth? And then she laughs out loud and Grant looks confused.

Nail on head stuff. Of course she knows why she's worried about revealing the truth – she's scared people will think she's a bad person for what happened and the part she played. And she doesn't want to be punished.

'Sorry.' She takes her hand away from his. 'I remembered something funny. See, I'm losing my mind. I can't even grieve for Bex appropriately.'

He leans back, a frown on his face. 'Look,' he says, as though he's her father about to discipline her, 'the day Bex decided to go swimming,' he pauses before adding, 'by herself,' then he pauses again and coughs. 'It was a dark day for all of us. Part of me wishes she'd died then. I've hated the whole thing being dragged out for years and years afterwards. She'd had no quality of life after the accident, couldn't talk or walk or anything. Her condition was cruel. As though she was being permanently punished for making one bad decision, while the rest of us got to continue our lives, whether we wanted to or not.'

'Grant.' She puts her hands up to stop him.

'Let me finish.' He is stern and Nicole realises he's waited a long time to be able to open up like this. And so she looks down and lets him continue. 'You and Emily... I know Bex's accident hit you both hard too. I think what happened brought up some stuff for Emily to do with her parents as well, about how they died. When we were married she was always so closed off, as though she didn't think anyone was allowed to love her. Or, cheesy though it sounds, that everyone she loves gets hurt. I dunno. She feels so emotionally stunted, if that doesn't sound too harsh. Never feeling tough emotions, or taking responsibility for anything in case those emotions bubble to the surface and she can't control them.'

'She's not like that with me,' Nicole says. 'But I see where you're coming from. She has this part of her I can never reach, you know?'

'I really do.' His shoulders slump. He looks resigned, as though he has more to say, but hasn't got the energy.

'So, back to my mental breakdown.' Nicole smirks at him. Her fingers are cold now he's let go.

He sighs and looks up at her, his lips pursed. 'Why do you think you're having a breakdown?' His glare is intense and she feels naked. For a second she wonders what he is implying.

She picks at the biscuit he's offered, scraping the inner cream off with one half and then spreading it back on with the other. 'I don't know, maybe because I am angry all of the time. I have a rage inside of me I can't control. Everything and everyone pisses me off.'

'Am I pissing you off?'

'Little bit.'

They smile at each other. Nicole doesn't know how honest she can be. She promised herself she'd never tell anyone about the dog shit incident. She is mortified. But saying that, there have still been no more little brown deposits so her actions did work and she feels happy. Plus she apologised. She can't do anything else.

'Look,' says Grant, 'the rage, being pissed off, this is probably all to do with grief for Bex. Like I said, her dying has brought a lot of stuff up for everyone. We're all a bit angry about what happened. Some more than others, but then some have more of a reason to be infuriated.'

'How are your parents doing?'

'They're a bit lost I think. Their lives were full of caring for

Bex and now they don't have to do that anymore it's like they've forgotten how to do anything else. I keep thinking they should book a holiday, separately of course, but it's too soon maybe.'

'Probably. But it's nice of you to suggest they each have a break and be ready for them to go.' They never remarried and Nicole has always wondered if Grant and Emily will be the same.

He sighs and smiles at her and Nicole blushes.

'What?' She folds her arms, closing herself off.

'You're always so damn nice and kind aren't you?' he says, but it's as though this is making him cross. 'I can always rely on you to be dependable.'

An emotion stirs inside her. That's when she realises – all everyone sees her as is safe and dependable, when in reality she is so much more and always has been. 'I'm not perfect. Don't you ever look back and count up all the things you've done wrong?' she asks. 'Because I do.'

'Bet your count is zero.' He laughs. 'Or is it?'

'What's that supposed to mean?' Her heart hammers in her chest.

'Come on, Nicole. You've *always* behaved, haven't you? You're not exactly spontaneous or bad. You never have been. Unless you have done something terrible you're ashamed of in the past? Now's the time to own up if you have.'

Nicole freezes. Those words, *own up*. 'Maybe I've never been given the chance to be spontaneous,' she whispers.

'Nah, you've not got spontaneity in you. Emily is always the one who tells you what to do and where to go, right? The leader. You simply do as you're told.' He's laughing, but none of what he is saying is funny. Nicole isn't sure how this has happened. The atmosphere in the room has changed as if someone has sprayed poison into the air.

Like a bull before a red flag, she clenches her teeth and

sniffs in. *Good old dependable, boring Nicole,* she thinks. No one she knows has their own moral compass because they all know she'll be the morally just one for them. They don't need to question their behaviours because she'll right their wrongs to keep the peace. They can mess up and know she'll understand and make everything better. Balance the scales.

Enough.

'I've got to go,' she tells Grant and stands, throwing the broken biscuit back onto the plate with the others.

'What? Is everything okay?' He looks shocked, and also a bit smug, but she hasn't got the energy to tell him what he's said to her has tipped her over the edge. 'Sorry.' He holds his hands up. 'I went too far.'

'I'm fine,' she snaps and throws on her coat.

'Nicole, don't go. I really am sorry.'

She pauses and stands with her bag in her hands. She could lose her temper now, she thinks. Shout at him. Scream at him for judging her and making her feel even more invisible in this world. She could tell him she was there the day of Bex's accident and about how she's been blaming herself ever since – that she isn't as holy as he thinks. Or she could smile and walk out. Maybe blame her hormones in the awful way people do whenever a woman behaves out of character. The old Nicole would do one of these things to keep the peace.

The new Nicole couldn't care less.

'Yes, you should be sorry,' she says, fully facing him. 'But I am not going to be the person to tell you why your comments and observations are wrong. You can work that out for yourself. You bloody well all can.'

She heads out the door, not waiting for a response.

She's too angry to cry. Too fuelled by rage to stop. Her brain has learnt that in order to survive she needs to be the good girl, but that's not who she is – or at least, not anymore – and she wants to be wild. She wants to wash away any doubt as to who she is and why she deserves to be loved by those closest to her for who she is, not how she behaves. Her mum cannot slap her into submission or terrify her about turning into Uncle Tom now.

I know, she thinks. *I know exactly what I need to do.*

She unlocks her car and gets in, a chill in the air following her. The sun is out and from inside she could be convinced spring is coming, but outside in the breeze she's in no doubt autumn is here. But the weather isn't going to stop Nicole doing what she needs to do.

But first, she needs Emily to come with her. This is something they need to do together.

THIRTY-SEVEN
EMILY – 2022

A new term always comes with new tension, Emily finds, often for the entire first week. The students didn't want to be back, aside from the few whose home lives are so troubled, school is their sanctuary. Everyone, even though today is Thursday, is still walking around with a fake smile plastered on as they say 'Morning' to whomever they pass in an artificial sing-song voice. And 'Good half term?' to those they haven't yet seen to ask this week.

Emily has perfected nodding and saying, 'Yes thanks, lovely,' even though her half term had been mostly non-eventful. 'I bumped into the mum of an old friend from school and the whole thing was super awkward,' isn't the best conversation starter.

'Morning, miss.' Chloe stands beside her with a friend, mischievous grins on their faces. This is the first time Emily has properly seen her since school started again, even though she knows Chloe has tried to find her most days this week. 'See anyone interesting over the half term?'

Emily wonders what Chloe means by this. She couldn't know about Mel's mum, could she? That would be odd.

Students never go to the café; it's too expensive and not 'sick' enough for them.

'Not particularly,' Emily replies, trying her best to look unphased. 'Did you?' She does not want Chloe to know she intimidates her a little bit. If she told anyone about the watch incident then Emily could lose her job. If the voicemail to the school was from her, Emily is walking on a very fine tightrope.

'No, I definitely didn't,' Chloe says and sniggers with her mate. 'Thought I saw you on the beach, with some old woman. Was it your mum?' She sniggers again.

Irritation rises inside Emily like a wave swelling. 'No, Chloe. She was not my mum. Just someone I used to know a long time ago.'

'When you were at school?'

'Yes.' Emily takes a deep breath. 'Maybe you two should get to class now.'

'Okay, miss.' Chloe winks at Emily. 'See you later then.'

Emily watches them as they saunter down the corridor. She never had such an amount of confidence at their age. Back then she worried too much what other people thought, although to the outside world she pretended not to care. She's grateful social media hadn't existed when she was a teenager as she's not sure she'd have survived in a world where every mistake you made was plastered all over the internet for everyone to see and judge.

But then her mistakes are catching up with her anyway.

She goes to her classroom grateful her first two periods are free of students as they always are on Thursday mornings. She usually sits at her desk with a strong coffee and browses social media, pretending to be planning her lessons for the next week. No one has caught her out yet.

She shuffles in her seat, uncomfortable from her encounter with Chloe in the hallway. Emily is certain there was no one else on the beach back then, no one who could've witnessed the bizarre turn of events and seen her and Mel's mum embrace by the sea. But then, maybe Chloe had been behind one of the large rocks at the far end. What she'd have been doing there so early in the morning Emily doesn't know either. She feels as though she is on the verge of understanding a distant truth that's been staring her in the face for months. But as she closes her eyes and tries to dig deeper the sensation disappears.

Then her phone pings.

> I see you've not owned up yet and so I'll have to ramp this up. You have until the end of the day. Go.

Emily stands and paces the room. Who the hell are these texts from and what the hell is she supposed to own up to? She *still* doesn't know. Frustration builds inside her like water in a kettle about to boil, she grabs a piece of paper and a pen and starts a list.

> *1) stealing Chloe's watch*
> *2) stealing my colleague's lighter*
> *3) stealing the food from Waitrose*
> *4) Bex*

She taps the pencil on her forehead and thinks. Chloe, the sender of the messages has to be Chloe. No one knows about the other stuff – all of which she's returned apart from the pizza from Waitrose – and no one knows about Bex other than Nicole. But these messages can't be from Nicole, can they? She refuses to believe they are. She types back, her hands shaking:

> Who is this?

The reply is instant:

> If you don't own up you'll soon find out.

> Nicole?

But no one replies this time. Her phone remains silent and she throws it into her bag. This is ridiculous. She's going round in circles and is fed up of the whole thing. She's watched TV shows with stuff like this before and has always thought the scenario implausible. People don't go out and buy burner phones for this type of shit, she's always thought.

But clearly, they do.

She scratches her head until her hair is ruffled. Then she huffs out her breath and pulls herself together. Unless the person on the end of these texts is more specific, Emily isn't going to own up to anything.

She decides to text Nicole back now. She can't believe she's left replying for so long. They've never gone this many days without communicating before. Guilt rises in her gut. Nicole has been desperate to get hold of her as well. But before she can send the message she gets a call through on her classroom phone, something that only happens if the receptionist or head need to get hold of her very quickly.

As she picks up, a commotion outside her classroom door distracts her. A muffled scraping sound, as though someone is crawling along the floor and the sound of laughter makes her get out of her chair to investigate.

'Nicole, what the hell?'

Nicole is on all fours outside Emily's classroom, in hysterics. 'Emily, I've been looking for you everywhere!'

'And now you've found me. Get the fuck up.' Emily grabs

her friend's shoulder and yanks her up. 'What the hell are you playing at?'

'Sorry,' the receptionist says from the end of the corridor. 'I tried to call you to let you know she was here, but she barged past me saying she knew where your classroom was and it was an emergency.'

'Thank you.' Emily wants to slap some sense into Nicole, but instead grabs hold of Nicole's arm and guides her into her classroom. 'I can look after things from here. Please don't tell anyone.'

The receptionist frowns, but then nods and walks away.

'We're going for a swim,' Nicole says. Her face is suddenly serious, the frown line between her eyebrows a deep valley.

'Are you drunk?'

'Maybe. Why, does that surprise you? Good little Nicole getting pissed in the middle of the day?'

'It's not even mid-morning, Nicole.'

'Even better!'

Emily does not have time for this. If her headteacher catches Nicole here then he is going to become even more suspicious, and maybe take the voicemail seriously. She grabs Nicole's elbow and drags her into her classroom. Nicole stinks of booze, and cigarettes.

'Have you been smoking again?'

'Yep. Bloody disgusting. But also totally lush.' Nicole laughs, clutching her stomach and trying to catch her breath. 'You know what, Emily?'

'What?'

'I am so sick of everyone thinking I am boring.'

'No one thinks that.'

'Yes they do. You all do. Joe, my parents, Grant, even you. Everyone thinks I am this good little woman who can never do anything wrong, but I am so fed up of that being the only reason why people like me, you know?'

Emily grits her teeth. Why the hell has Nicole chosen the first week of term to go insane?

'Nicole, I'm not sure what's happened, but that's not why we like you.'

'Go on then, tell me why. Maybe you only like me because you can boss me around and tell me what to do. That's what Grant says.'

Emily knows she hesitates for too long before answering.

'See,' Nicole shouts. 'I knew it. I'll show you all.' Then she stumbles to the classroom door.

'What's that supposed to mean?'

'You'll find out. Anyway if you don't want to come swimming that's fine, but I'm going.'

'Swimming? Where? What are you on about?'

'The sea. I'm going to wash this guilt away.' She wipes her hands over her body and flicks her fingers beside her as though flicking off dirt. 'Every single last ounce of the guilt. I am so fed up of pleasing everyone else when no one ever pleases me.' She points her finger into her chest and then looks sad as though she pressed too hard.

'Nicole, the weather is freezing. You'll get hypothermia. You cannot be serious.'

'Well, Mr McEnroe, I am serious.' Then she sticks her tongue out at Emily and stomps out in a strop.

Emily doesn't know what to do. How did Nicole even get here? Did she drive? And why the hell has she decided going swimming in the sea will wash away any guilt she feels about Bex? She's bonkers.

And really fucking annoying.

Emily grabs her bag and rushes to follow Nicole, but as she

gets to the front of the school she's just in time to see her friend's car swerving down the road.

'Fuck fuck fuck.' She's meant to be teaching in an hour, but she can't leave Nicole to drunkenly drive to the beach and go swimming in this state. For a second she thinks about phoning Joe, but knows he won't be able to get out of work to help; nor will Nicole thank her for telling on her to her husband. And he cannot know the truth as to why she has lost the plot.

Emily nips into the school office and shouts to the receptionist that she has to go; an emergency and she needs to find cover for her classes today. The headteacher is going to be fuming, but Emily doesn't have a choice. If she doesn't go after her, Nicole may very well end up killing someone else.

THIRTY-EIGHT
MEL – 1997

October half term was always when the lifeguards stopped patrolling the beach in their red uniforms. But that didn't mean they stopped coming here altogether. Mel watched one of the regulars, Davey she thought his name was, head onto the beach with his dog. He was walking back home, and she was relieved. They didn't need witnesses yet.

This time of year was strange. The sea was at its warmest after being heated up slowly over spring and summer and she knew people thought diving in was safe if the sun was out and they felt a little warmth. But the water was still freezing and rip tides could be a bugger at this time of year. Her mum had drummed that into her since she was a little girl. People who didn't know what they were doing often got into trouble.

Which is why she thinks Davey found himself walking down here several times a day with his dog during October. She'd seen him save a little boy one October too; if he'd walked by a few minutes later the outcome wouldn't have been the same. Mel had been frozen on the sand, unable to move or scream or do anything.

She looked across the empty beach. A storm was predicted

and so she assumed people had got up and walked their dogs before lunch or had a quick surf. The sand was peppered with footprints from humans and animals, snaking across in all directions ready to be washed away by the tide and rain. The sky was still a light blue, for now, but she could smell the air changing. Clouds were beginning to form and she knew they would turn into dark-grey masses later. You learned these things when you grew up by the sea; you could tell when the weather was about to change, often before the forecasters did. You could sense the shift.

A loud shriek from further up the beach caught her attention. There they were, walking across the sand. They looked harmless enough and definitely didn't look as though they were thinking about going in the water, but still she was glad Davey was too far away now to see or hear the three of them arrive. He could've ruined everything.

She watched them settle themselves down on the sand at the back of the beach. She imagined their body spray overtook the scent of the salty sea air.

She moved closer, the strong wind blowing their giggles over for her to hear. The three of them laughed, Nicole more reserved than the other two. She looked like she didn't want to be here at all, wrapping her coat around her, her face scrunched into a scowl. Mel smirked.

Storm clouds were gathering in the distance like thick smoke from a fire. Mel didn't want to be out here too long. She hated getting wet and cold.

She shivered, nervous, biting her fingernails and twiddling her hair.

Exactly as she'd been told, Mel didn't move from behind the rocks. Her instructions were to stay hidden, hovering at the edge of the beach, watching them. Waiting.

For now.

THIRTY-NINE
NICOLE – 2022

Nicole is warm from the alcohol, but the wind nips at her exposed body parts and she shivers. She won't change her mind though. She *will* go for a swim. Like being baptised, she thinks. Dunked underwater, her soul cleansed and reborn.

She can't park the car properly so leaves it here – half on the kerb and half off – and does not care. There aren't very many cars here anyway. She hadn't wanted to leave her car in the car park, too obvious if anyone comes looking for her; she does not want to be stopped, and so chooses here, parked down one of the side roads leading to the beach. She holds her keys above her head and clicks the lock button, her indicators flashing at her.

She doesn't think anyone will come looking for her, and that's fine. Emily is at work; thank goodness no one had caught Nicole there. Joe is too, and the twins are at school. They won't start looking for her until their dinner doesn't appear as if by magic in front of them later.

Shame fills her. She doesn't like her children, she realises with a jolt. She loves them yes; but likes them, no. This makes her want to cry, but she bites her bottom lip and stumbles on. They are the way they are because of her. Their selfishness and self-absorption is no one's fault but her own. All her. Without meaning to, she's made a mess of everything.

No cars drive past as she crosses the road to the walkway down to the beach by the car park. No dog walkers or surfers are on the sand or in the sea. She has the beach to herself. She blinks away the tears, takes off her shoes and strides forwards towards the sea.

The waves are calm today as though they are ready for her, she thinks. Grey clouds sweep across the sky casting shadows over the sea. She takes a deep breath in and wipes the hair from her face, wishing she'd thought to bring a hairband.

She did remember the vodka though and takes the bottle from her bag before necking another huge gulp. Then she retches. Vodka always did make her sick, but is the one drink she knows will get her pissed enough to do this. And boy does she need to do this.

'Come on!' she shouts towards the sea to propel herself forwards. Doubt is already creeping in. She is sobering up and unsure as to why she thought this would be a good idea.

To cleanse yourself, a voice in her head says. *You can't keep living like this. Get in there. Wash the old you away and come out stronger. Be spontaneous. Shock everyone.*

'Yes,' she shouts. 'To the new me.'

She toys with the idea of taking her clothes off and going skinny-dipping, but then thinks she will be too cold and so she decides to keep them on, instead only removing her shoes and socks. She won't be in the water for long; that way they won't get too heavy and drag her down. In and out. A quick dunk – like a baptism. She takes another swig from the vodka bottle and smiles as the liquid burns her throat.

Then she stands at the edge of the sea. The tide is on its way in. The waves nip at her toes and she shivers before stepping in deeper. Inch by inch. She's moving too slowly.

Maybe she needs to run in and out, before the icy water shocks her.

The waves gently lap at her shins. Already she feels clean. No seaweed. No jellyfish. The water is clear and as she looks down she sees a shell swirl in the current. Forwards and backwards. Pushed towards the shore and then pulled away. Not fighting the current. She stands there mesmerised, her stare transfixed on the brown-and-white shell blithely accepting its fate. Should she accept hers? She is going round in circles.

Gritting her teeth she steps in even deeper, the water up to her thighs. The cold takes her breath away. Her hands are clenched into fists, her arms tight by her body, elbows out wide. With every wave she rises onto tiptoes and scrunches up her face as the water soaks into her jeans and cools her further. She can no longer feel her toes, but doesn't want to look down to see if they've gone blue yet. Her teeth chatter.

She wishes she'd brought the vodka in with her instead of leaving the bottle on the beach by her socks and shoes.

Was Bex this cold, she wonders? Did she not want to appear vulnerable in front of her and Emily and so strode in with fake confidence? She was so skinny by then too, there would've been nothing to protect her and keep her warm. Nicole can visualise that day now, as though she is following Bex further into the depths of the ocean. She can see her blonde hair catch the sea at the ends. She remembers Bex's shoulders disappearing under the dark-blue water. How her head bobbed up and down. The cold must've zapped her strength and so when the storm arrived and the waves grew she didn't have the energy to swim back. And then the fatal wave came and bashed her against the rocks.

Nicole shakes her head. Scrunches her eyes closed to rid the image of Bex from her memory.

'It wasn't my fault!' Nicole screams into the sky. '*You* chose to go swimming, not me. I tried to stop you. I did. Why didn't you listen? Why were you so determined?'

A shout from behind her brings Nicole back to the present. She turns, the water buffeting her back and splashing over her head. A burst of sea goes into her left ear and she tips her head in an attempt to clear the water from inside. Her hearing is muffled.

Squinting, she can see someone on the shore. She wipes the salty water from her eyes.

Emily.

She has come to find her. But Nicole isn't done, not yet. She turns back to face the horizon and ignores Emily's calls.

'I'm sorry,' she shouts again. 'I refuse to live like this anymore. I will not feel guilty all the time. I'm done blaming myself for your accident.'

A current from deep down in the sea knocks her off balance and she falls in completely. Her lungs feel as though someone has wrapped ten thousand elastic bands around them. She cannot breathe. Her chest won't expand. No air can get in.

Splashing and scrambling about she struggles to land her feet firmly on the sand below. The water isn't going to claim her today; she won't let that happen. Her body isn't turning blue and bloated. The sea is meant to inject her with fresh life, not steal her soul, shallow breath by shallow breath.

Emily is waving her arms at the water's edge.

Nicole waves back. 'I'm coming,' she calls, but her words are carried away by the wind.

Emily starts to undress.

No, Nicole thinks. *You'll stain the water, you'll spoil what I came here to do, don't get in.* She will not allow Emily to steal her thunder yet again.

'I'm coming,' she calls again and holds her hands up to stop Emily. 'Wait.' But another wave knocks her off her feet and she finds herself underwater. When did the sea get so strong? A ripple of fear passes over her. She can't even get this right. She's pathetic. For a second she is like the brown-and-white shell, succumbing to her fate and not fighting the current pulling and pushing her. She's so tired of life. Exhausted by living for everyone else and not actually living for herself. She wanted to go back to college and retrain. She didn't want to get to eighty having only ever been a mother, and not a very good one either. She won't let this end now.

Nicole lands her feet on the sand below and surges upwards only to be knocked over again. At least she isn't near the rocks; that had been Bex's mistake. She pushes herself upright again and again and uses her arms and hands to reach for the shore. But she's tiring.

Then all of a sudden she feels a hand in hers, pulling hard. The sea roars around them as they struggle together to stand and swim to dry land. Both of her hands are held by another now, then a strong arm reaches under her shoulder, another around the small of her back.

'What the fuck are you playing at, you daft cow?'

Emily. Oh thank you, Emily. Nicole laughs, an intense burst of energy surging through her as they emerge from the waves. She clutches her stomach and rolls onto the sand, gasping for breath and coughing. Then the laughter turns to tears and she finds herself sobbing, curled up into the foetal position. Grains of sand stick to her face as she lies there.

'Get undressed,' Emily instructs.

'No, I'm too cold to get naked.' Nicole shivers all over. 'Get me my vodka instead.'

'You can have a drink when you're dry. Now take your clothes off or I will rip them from you myself.'

Nicole can hear fear in Emily's trembling voice.

'Fine.' She tries to undo the zip on her jeans but she cannot get a grip, her fingers have stopped working. 'I can't. Too cold. You.'

'For fuck's sake.' Emily works quickly and Nicole is grateful all over again. Emily has also brought a towel and some fresh clothes, Nicole wonders when she'd had time to get these. Or maybe they were already in the back of her car.

After a few minutes they sit, huddled together on the sand.

'Drink this.' Emily hands Nicole a flask.

'Is this vodka?'

'No it fucking isn't. It's the tea I made for myself before leaving for work this morning, and then forgot and left the flask in the car. Drink.'

The tea warms her mouth and throat and Nicole wraps her hands around the hot metal flask.

They sit in silence. The waves roar in front of them, the tide on the turn. Emily rubs Nicole's back and arms to warm her up. The towel and an extra coat have been thrown over her shoulders, and a blanket covers her lap. Nicole's shivers become fainter and soon some warmth spreads across her chest.

Then, after what feels like hours to Nicole, Emily speaks. 'I need to tell you something.'

FORTY
EMILY – 2022

Emily feels unsteady even though she is sat down. They are so close not a single bit of air passes between her and Nicole's bodies; wound tight together as they have been since childhood. Mostly.

'Go on then, what is this thing you have to tell me?' Nicole asks, her teeth still chattering even though the pink is back in her cheeks.

Emily picks up on an edge to Nicole's voice. She doesn't know what the hell has gotten into her. Never before has Emily seen Nicole so close to breaking point. She's Nicole. She is meant to be dependable, steady, like a lighthouse on a rock. Immovable. She might not always be happy, but she is always predictable. This new weird Nicole freaks Emily out.

'Don't be like that,' Emily says in a soft voice. 'I need your help not your criticism.'

'What a surprise, someone else needs me to fix their problems, never mind I might have some problems too, you know.'

'You've clearly got problems.'

'Yup. You don't know the half of them.'

'Then tell me.'

'I thought you wanted to tell me your problems.'

'Oh for goodness' sake, Nicole. What *is* the matter with you?'

Nicole shudders and Emily realises she's crying again. She holds her tighter and rests her head on top of Nicole's and they once again sit in silence. Then all of a sudden Nicole pulls away and sits up straight.

'Go on,' Nicole demands. 'Tell me what's wrong. You go first.'

Without pausing Emily gets to the point. 'I'm in trouble. But I have no idea who with or what for.'

'You're not making any sense.'

'I know. Sorry. Look, at this.' Emily pulls her phone out of her pocket and shows Nicole the text messages.

Nicole's hand goes to her mouth. 'Em, wait. You're not going to believe this, look.' She shows Emily her phone and the messages she got too.

'What the fuck?' Emily runs her hands through her hair. 'These are identical. Who the fuck is doing this?' Emily can now dismiss the idea that the warning messages have come from Chloe. Nicole doesn't even know Chloe.

'Who did you think yours were from?' Nicole asks.

'This student at school. We've had a few issues recently and I thought she knew stuff about me and was trying to blackmail me.'

'What issues?'

'Doesn't matter.'

'Think it does.'

'Really doesn't. Drop this, please.' Emily's heart thuds in her chest. Her jaw aches.

'Whatever.' Nicole sighs.

'We need to find out who is sending them, right? Any ideas?'

'Has to be someone who knows us both.'

'Right.'

They pause.

'This is embarrassing, but for one horrible moment I thought they were from you. I haven't a clue. The only people we both know are Joe and Grant and Bryony, oh and my parents. Can't be any of them though, surely. My dad doesn't even have a mobile.'

'I thought they might be from you too at one point. Fuck, we've got so bad at communicating with each other. What about Bex's parents?'

'But why would they?'

And then they stare at each other. Their eyes are wide.

'No,' Emily says. 'No. These messages can't be anything to do with Bex, can they?'

A strangled scream nestled in her chest since the day of Bex's accident, and not dislodged since, wants to be released. Emily thinks of Bex's journal. The secrets the pages hold. Secrets even Nicole doesn't know. Emily knows she should've told her, but back then she had liked having information Nicole didn't for once. She'd felt some kind of sick loyalty to Bex. As a teenager Emily thought Nicole had everything she didn't. Emily can remember hating Nicole for having parents who were still alive. No one else knows about the contents of the journal and so the real truth about Bex's accident can't be what they are both being targeted for.

'Maybe someone saw us on the beach with her. Maybe that's what they mean?' Nicole says as though this is the only explanation.

'Don't be crazy. There was no one there. *No one* was there. No one. We checked.'

'We didn't. Not really. We were in such a hurry, remember, we ran away, needed to get off the beach before we were caught by anyone. We were terrified.'

'So you're saying there could've been someone else, behind the rocks or up by the car park?' Emily is beginning to hyperventilate. She's blocked that day out of her head. She isn't to blame. They aren't solely to blame. She has proof.

'The weather was awful too by then,' Nicole continues. 'I can't remember being able to see anything.'

'But why now? If this is to do with Bex, what the hell are they hoping to achieve?'

'I have no idea.' Nicole shrugs. 'People are weird.'

'Damn right they are.' Emily laughs and Nicole joins in. For a few blissful minutes Emily forgets everything that's going on and loses herself in their giggles. She can't remember the last time she felt so free.

Wind buffets them and the waves crawl ever closer. The sky above them is turning darker, as though it's watercolour paper and someone has flooded the fresh white page with purple paint.

Nicole's teeth chatter.

'Come on.' Emily stands and then pulls at Nicole's arm. 'We need to get you moving and warm.'

'Not home. Don't take me home, please.'

A look flashes in Nicole's eyes Emily hasn't seen before. She can't quite work out what is behind her expression. Not fear, but a darker emotion.

'Fine, you can come and shower at mine. I'll order us some food.'

Emily hands Nicole a mug of hot chocolate. She demanded wine, but Emily has pulled rank and said no chance. Nicole still has half a bottle of vodka inside her in need of diluting.

Before bringing them here, Emily had moved Nicole's car to a proper parking place so it won't get towed. She's promised to take Nicole back tomorrow to collect it; and has texted Joe to say she is staying the night. He didn't question why, which Emily thought odd.

'Nicole, what did Joe mean when he said he was glad you could talk to me about your dad and have a bit of time out?'

'Oh God, I haven't told you. Dad's in hospital. But he'll be fine.'

'I'm so sorry.'

'I rang you a million times. You didn't pick up.'

'Again, I'm sorry. I've been dealing with some stuff like I said, at work. I should've been a better friend.'

'Don't worry. He's going to be okay so it's not a big deal. Besides, sounds like I've not been the best friend recently either, so...'

Emily smiles. Strange how they've been pulling apart and keeping everything troubling them to themselves, instead of supporting each other as friends should. They've become so distant. Pushing the other away instead of reaching out. Until today, when Nicole's drunken cry for help couldn't be ignored by Emily, unlike the phone calls reaching out for support when her dad was ill. Maybe she is the one who's been pulling away, Emily realises with a jolt. Not wanting to admit her failings to anyone. She's an island with no port, nowhere to dock and settle. Surrounded by jagged rocks that will shatter any boat trying to get close.

Look at Grant.

'When's your dad coming out of hospital?' Emily asks.

'Tomorrow I reckon. I can call Mum and find out at some

point, when I can summon up the energy to speak to her.' An awkward silence cloaks the room. In the past Emily has balked whenever Nicole hasn't been too complimentary about her parents, and Nicole knows that.

'You can slag your mum off around me, you know,' Emily says. 'I'm a grown-up now. I can handle the fact you have a mum you don't particularly like while I don't have one at all.'

'You used to get so cross with Bex or me whenever we'd be mean about our parents.'

'I know.' She remembers the raw, burning shame she'd felt after shouting at them both, which she now knows was her grief forcing its way out of her.

'You said we should be grateful we had parents. I remember one day Bex challenged you on that opinion. Asked if the kids of parents who abused or ignored them should be grateful.'

'All right,' Emily snaps. 'That was a long time ago. I don't feel the same anymore, obviously.'

'Did you see Mel's mum updated her Facebook page again?' Nicole says, changing the subject.

'Yeah. Odd.'

'That's what I thought. You don't think...'

Nicole raises her eyebrows at Emily. 'Think what?'

'You know, she's involved with the messages?'

Emily yawns, a wave of tiredness washing over her. Her brain hurts. 'I don't know what to think anymore, Nicole. I thought this was all done. And I had no idea Bex dying would trigger this weirdness in everyone. She's practically been dead for years anyway.'

'Em!'

'She has. No point denying the fact. Surely we should be relieved she's finally gone and isn't suffering anymore. For everyone.'

Nicole rubs her eyes with the heels of her hands and groans.

She looks broken, Emily thinks, *like a rag doll left out in the rain. And then stomped on.*

'I can't discuss this with you, Em. We feel very differently about Bex.'

Emily sucks in a lungful of air. She knows her opinion on Bex is controversial. She and Grant used to argue about how she felt all the time when she'd refused to visit. She found supporting him when he was grieving for a living person difficult. He used to say the reason she didn't understand is because she is an only child. But she understands grief. He could still see Bex, talk to her, touch her, smell her. She'd give anything to be able to do that with her parents.

'Okay, you're right. But we do need to work out who is sending these fucking messages. They said I had until the end of today, which is now coming up and then fuck knows what's going to happen if I don't do what they want.'

'Let's make a list,' Nicole says, her hands wrapped around her mug, her fingers back to their normal pink colour.

'Good idea.' Emily fetches a pen and paper and then sits on the sofa next to Nicole.

'Nice to be together again, isn't it?' Nicole says.

And Emily smiles.

FORTY-ONE
NICOLE – 2022

'I'm home,' Nicole calls out, ashamed for hoping no one will reply and she's got the house to herself. She hadn't slept well at Emily's and could do with sneaking back to bed for a couple of hours. She deliberately left coming home until she knew the boys would be at school and Joe at work, but he had mentioned working from home one day this week and she hoped he hadn't chosen today.

She'd had a nice time with Emily last night and had been feeling calmer; but then some wanker hadn't said thank you when she'd pulled in to let him pass on the way home and she can still feel the anger he'd reignited inside her. Maybe the fire never fully goes out inside a perimenopausal woman, she thinks. The flames are simply dampened every now and again; ready to burst back to life with the smallest of breezes. She probably shouldn't have stuck both of her middle fingers up at the driver as he drove past with his young daughter sitting in the back and staring out of the window though. Oh well. Too late now.

No one has replied to her initial call. She throws her shoes and coat off, leaves them in a lump at the bottom of the stairs and heads up to her bedroom. Not like her to not put everything in the correct place, but she's gone way beyond that now.

'You need a fecking job,' Emily had said to her last night and those words have buzzed around her head ever since. She definitely needs something. This life, the one she'd carefully carved out with Joe and the boys, isn't making her happy anymore.

Joe hasn't made the bed. She pauses for a second at the bedroom door and clenches her fists. Not because she is mad with Joe, but because she is mad with herself again. He's never made the bed because she always has. The same goes for cooking dinner. Presents for everyone are always organised by her. Birthdays. Christmas. Anniversary cards. She's surprised he even wipes his own ass.

And all because she needed to control everything. Too scared of the alternative. Trying to protect everyone. To keep them happy. To keep them in order. To stop bad things happening. Never once did she consider how miserable this made her. Or how miserable her behaviour made everyone else too. Joe had tried to cook in the past, but all she'd done was criticise him. *That's not how I cook chicken, I wouldn't carve like that, you've left the kitchen in such a state.* No wonder he'd stopped trying.

She climbs under the duvet mostly clothed and she doesn't worry that sand between her toes will make the space between her body and the duvet grainy.

Groaning, she puts the pillow over her face and screams into the fluff inside.

She's made a total mess of everything.

And has no idea how to fix it.

Nicole wakes to the sound of cutlery being put in a drawer and for a second she is disoriented and wonders where she is.

Joe. In the kitchen and emptying the dishwasher. One of her stupid directives – the dishwasher needs to be emptied straight away. How Joe hadn't left her already she doesn't know. Sighing, she throws off the duvet and goes downstairs.

'Hey.' She flattens her bed hair as she walks into the kitchen.

Joe looks at her and smiles, with an edge of pity, she thinks. She knows what his head tilt means. 'Thought you were at work.'

'Had a meeting this morning then came home. Need to get on with some stuff without everyone in the office bothering me.'

Nicole doesn't know what Joe does for work. A job with computers maybe, and security for a big company, she thinks. His job title is always changing. She should ask him really, but now isn't the time. 'Oh fair enough. The boys will be back soon. I feel like I haven't seen them properly since they ran out on Dad.'

'Nic.' He sighs. And then stops. 'I've got a couple of pizzas in the fridge I can do for their dinner if you like?'

'Great. Thanks.' The twins are closer to him right now, and not her. She's made peace with it.

He grabs a cloth and wipes around after restacking the dishwasher. Nicole sits at the breakfast bar and wonders when things got so awkward between them. 'Might pop up and see Dad then, if that's okay?' she says. 'He's coming home from the hospital later.'

'Of course. Have you not been today already?'

'Nope. He wasn't being discharged until lunchtime at the earliest and so I thought I'd wait until he's home. That's when Mum might need a hand.'

She's not sure, but she thinks she catches Joe rolling his eyes. 'What?' she asks.

'What?' He looks at her, eyes wide.

'You rolled your eyes when I said about Mum needing a hand.'

'No I didn't.'

'Yes you did.'

He scrunches the cloth in his hand and leans onto the work surface. 'Fine, but I was rolling them because of your mum, not you.'

She picks at a crumb in front of her, not saying anything. They never talk about this stuff. Too scared to appear to be slagging her parents off, she's always kept her mouth closed, even around Joe.

'What about her?'

'She takes advantage of you.' He holds his hands up in mock surrender as though expecting an onslaught.

'I know,' Nicole says. 'She always has, but only because I let her.'

'Yeah, wasn't going to mention that, but you do and your behaviour drives me insane.'

'Then why haven't you said anything before?'

'Because you won't hear a bad word said against her. Or your dad. Even when they're saying bad things about each other. Or your Uncle Tom.' His voice is raised now and Nicole wonders how long he's been keeping this all in.

She wants to cry. Bit by bit over the last few weeks she's been worn down by her life. Joe's aunt had always said her forties were her best years, but so far Nicole's have been her worst.

'So are you saying I shouldn't go round?'

'No, that's not what I'm saying. Of course you want to see your dad. But maybe when you do go round, don't stay and cook them both dinner and then vacuum and clean the bathroom too, yeah?'

Nicole leans forward, her head in her hands. She digs her nails into her scalp and takes a deep breath. 'What is wrong with me?' she asks, not wanting an answer.

'I'm not sure where to start.'

She looks up at him and is about to lose her temper when she sees his smirk.

'Joke, sorry, poor timing.'

She picks up the tea towel beside her and throws it at him. 'Not. Funny.'

'Look, go and see your parents and then when you get back we'll have a nice dinner and chat about everything. How does that sound?'

'Sounds good,' she says and when he moves to hug her, she lets him.

She and Emily hadn't got very far in their detective search for the mystery texter last night. Maybe she'll talk to Joe later about the messages and see what he makes of everything. Time is running out.

Maybe she'll finally tell someone the whole truth.

No one answers the door at her parents' house and she has no way of knowing if they are in and ignoring her, or out, as they always park their car in the garage and not on the drive for all to see.

'Mum,' she shouts through the letterbox. 'Dad.'

But still no answer.

She has a spare key to their house on her key ring and lets herself in. The house is immaculate and the fridge full. Nicole wonders what task her mum would ask her to do if she were here, and questions whether her mum asks her simply because she can. No dirty dishes stand in the sink or dishwasher. A fresh toilet roll is ready to be used in the bathroom alongside fluffy towels and the grouting surrounding the shower and bath has not one single spot of mould.

No wonder I like order, she thinks. But also, this is not how the house ever is when Nicole has come over as planned. Then she realises – if her mum knows Nicole's coming then she saves stuff up. The cheek! Nicole feels like a fool.

She heads back downstairs and plans on sitting in the lounge with a cup of tea, waiting for them to get back, when an open notepad on the telephone table grabs her attention.

A single phone number is written on the flowered paper with a name beside.

Angela.

Mel's mum.
Shit.

FORTY-TWO
EMILY – 2022

'Nicole, slow down. You found what?' Emily puts the cans of cider back on the shop shelf and heads away from the booze aisle.

'On the notepad at my mum and dad's house, next to the phone, is a phone number and Mel's mum's name, Angela, is written next to it.'

Fuck. Emily can see why Nicole is freaking out. The room around her shrinks as though she is in a cage with the space between the metal bars surrounding her getting smaller and smaller. 'Okay, yes, I agree it is odd. But could be harmless. Nothing to do with us.'

'Bit of a coincidence though, right?'

'Right. So, are you going to ask your parents about it?'

'They're not back from the hospital yet, but yes I guess so?'

'Be cool, Nic.'

'I'm trying, I really am.'

'I saw her the other day, Angela, on the beach,' Emily finds herself telling Nicole. 'She was all over the place. Emotional, you know. Then I stupidly agreed to go for coffee with her. I went to the loo after I'd ordered and when I came out she'd vanished.'

'Why didn't you tell me this last night?'

'I don't know. I'm sorry. Been questioning myself a lot lately, which as you know isn't like me. Felt like I'd fucked up somehow with her.'

'Jeez Em, I think we've known each other long enough for you to be able to tell me when you've messed up.'

Emily hangs her head in shame. Everything feels ridiculous now. 'I know. Look, meeting her was nothing. She was angry at first and then wouldn't stop crying. To be honest, the whole encounter was all a bit fucking awkward.'

'I can imagine. Okay, that's them! They're back. I'll ring you later.' Nicole ends the call.

Emily looks around to discover she's wandered to the tampon aisle and picks up a pack. She bloody hates periods. Doesn't understand why women who don't want children have to suffer bleeding for one week out of four, or in her case now, three. Or maybe five. She wishes there was a switch she could flick and turn her damn menstrual cycle off. Or somehow suck every child-bearing organ out of her body.

She's forgotten what she came in here for, her mind instead filled with thoughts of Chloe, Mel's mum and Bex. How her past is doing such a terrific job of catching up with her when she has done everything she possibly can to keep that from happening is a mystery. And one that makes her angry.

If her aunt was still alive Emily might've spoken to her about everything. They'd been close and her aunt had never judged her or her actions.

Nicole is too close to everything and has such a different opinion on the events that Emily can't be fully honest with her. Plus, if she finds out Emily has been keeping Bex's journal a secret from her for all these years their friendship would be done. And without Nicole, Emily has no one.

She's lonely. She thought life would be easier on her own. Up until now she believed that if you didn't care for people then you couldn't cry when you lost them. But maybe caring for someone would be worth the risk. She cannot carry on living like this for another thirty or forty years. The thought makes her want to jump in front of a moving train.

But she has no idea what do to do change her situation. Or herself.

Without realising she finds herself back in the booze aisle. She picks up the cans of cider again and puts them in her basket. Then she heads to the ready meal aisle and picks up a curry. Anyone trained in the area might diagnose her as depressed. Emily calls her attitude 'no longer giving a fuck'.

She pays in full for all of her items and then heads home.

Back in her flat she shoves the ready meal in the microwave and opens one of the cans of cider, not bothering with a glass. She grabs Bex's journal from her bag and thumbs the cover on the table. She can recall the contents of the page she knows would seal her fate word for word, wondering why Bex had committed this truth to paper. Sitting down at the table she takes a gulp of the cider and opens the journal to one of the pages she has focused on so many times. Then she reads.

Dear Diary,

I'm not writing to you today. Today, I need to leave a message for my parents.

To Mum and Dad,

This is all your fault. Well done. Maybe you'll notice me now.

Love Bex.

Emily exhales slowly through her teeth and takes another swig from the bottle. Bex's parents have never said anything that has made Emily think they blame themselves for Bex's accident or if they knew why Bex had gone swimming alone. Why would they? Nor has Grant. In fact, none of them has ever spoken about what their family is like behind closed doors.

But then, no family ever does, she thinks. *We all keep our truths hidden, even more so now social media is here to ensure we only preserve the very best of our existences. Our photos like pickles in a jar.*

Emily had always envied Bex her family – her rich dad and glamorous mum, their amazing house and her lovely, caring older brother – she'd had none of those things and naively thought any family was a good one and better than having no family.

She looks around her kitchen. Until Bex died Emily was okay on her own, she really was. Emily knew she hadn't wanted children from an early age and if society didn't make her feel like shit about it then she wouldn't even have thought about her decision twice.

The same goes for marriage if she digs deep. Whether she'd feel like this if her parents were still alive she doesn't know, but marrying Grant had been a mistake, that she does know. The problem is she's taken these beliefs and emotions all too far. She might not want marriage and children, but she wants company and companionship. She wants friends. But aside from Nicole, she has none.

Bex's journal glares at her. For a minute she thinks maybe she should go to see Grant and Bex's parents and hand it over. But then, why would they need to feel even worse than they do already? She doesn't open the journal again. She doesn't need to read that entry, or the other one, again.

Those entries are the reason she stole the journal in the first place. Knowing Bex would've written about what happened, she couldn't help herself. Why she kept it at her childhood home she isn't sure. Almost as though when she left the house, she had to leave her past there too, in order to properly move on.

The microwave beeps and she gets up to fish out a fork from the cutlery drawer. She'll eat the curry straight from the container. Prepare herself a wholesome salad tomorrow to make up for the E-numbers and additives now.

As she spoons the second mouthful towards her, the ringtone on her phone goes. A number she doesn't recognise. The kind of number often alerting her to some scam or dodgy call. But today, she places her fork back down and answers because she wants to know who is on the other end.

'Hello?'

'Time's up. Own up. Tell everyone what you did.'

The voice sounds familiar, but Emily cannot place it. It's muffled, changed somehow, but belongs to someone she knows, she is sure – the pauses between the words when they speak, the inflection at the end – she knows this person.

'Who is this?'

'Someone who knows everything about you and what you did. Someone who wants you to pay for what you didn't do. Because you never take responsibility for anything, do you.'

'Go fuck yourself.'

'Bad move, Emily.'

'For fuck's sake, this isn't a two-star rated movie. This is a joke.'

'I promise you; this is no joke. Do you want to lose your job?'

A muffled sound on the end of the line as though the caller has put their hand over the receiver distracts her for a second and gives her time to pause and think.

'I'm not playing this game.' The voice, the owner, Emily feels as though if she keeps them talking then she'll recall who is behind all of this. The answer dangles in front of her like a carrot on a stick, if only she could grasp onto it.

'This is no game, Emily. Someone died and it was your fault. If you'd only told the truth sooner, I may have been able to understand, to forgive. You have twenty-four more hours. Or else.'

The line goes dead. She looks at her phone and bites her lower lip.

They've taken a risk calling her, gambling on their voice not being recognised.

But the intonation, the accent, Emily had recognised. The patterns of the words are familiar to her. If only she could work out how.

FORTY-THREE
NICOLE – 2022

'Hey Mum, Dad, where've you been?'

Nicole's mum frowns and the knot in Nicole's stomach tightens.

'Here, let me help you with your bag,' she says and regrets offering. After over forty years Nicole knows she isn't going to change in an instant, much as she'd like to. She needs to accept that.

Still her mum and dad haven't even said hello to her. They huff and puff in through the door and then her dad sits on the bottom of the stairs and struggles to take his shoes off.

'Is everything okay?' Nicole asks, concerned they've seen the doctor in the hospital and got some bad news. Maybe her dad isn't recovering as well as he should be. Maybe they've found another problem. Of course, if this is the case, she'll blame herself and her dubious actions of late, the apologies not affecting her own karma.

'Of course,' her mum snaps back. 'We're fine.' Then a pause and a puzzled look on her face. 'Why are you here? We didn't have plans.'

'Sorry, didn't realise I needed an invite to visit my own parents on the day my dad gets out of hospital. I'll go.'

'Oh don't be like that,' her mum huffs. 'You're always so dramatic.'

Nicole steels herself. 'In fact, Mum, I think you'll find I'm always anything but dramatic. I've been nothing but the perfect daughter, helping every single time you ask me to do a chore, which, by the way, is all the bloody time. I never shout or argue back, I simply nod and do whatever you've ordered me to. Married the first man who asked. Perfect exam results. No teenage pregnancy. No drug taking. No prison. Nothing. I'm the least dramatic person I know.' *Until now*, she thinks.

Her mum raises her eyebrows and looks shocked.

Good, thinks Nicole. Her skin fizzes as though an electric current is running through her body. Her dad is silent and she feels a bit bad she's chosen the day he's discharged from hospital to be a drama queen.

'I thought I'd pop round to see how Dad is and if you needed any help. But the house is immaculate so obviously you don't, and clearly you would rather I wasn't here so I'll push off and only come back when I've formally been invited. Does that suit you?'

She isn't sure, but she thinks her dad smirked.

'You're being ridiculous, Nicole.' Her mum shakes her head.

She looks old all of a sudden, Nicole thinks, as though the past twenty years have caught up with her overnight. She never did handle stress well.

'Go and put the kettle on and snap yourself out of whatever weird mood you're in.'

'I will not.'

'I beg your pardon.'

'Why don't *you* go and put the kettle on in *your* house like you would for any other guest. Or do you make everyone who doesn't live here prepare their own drinks?'

Her mum's face is turning red and this makes Nicole feel elated and ashamed. Maybe she should've acted out sooner, as a teenager like most people, but better late than never.

'I think you'd better leave and come back when you're feeling a bit more like yourself.'

'That's the thing, Mum. I've never felt more like myself. This *is* me. But I've shut myself away for years – too busy pleasing everyone else and ignoring my feelings and I'm not behaving that way anymore.'

'Nicole,' says her dad, 'I don't mean to be rude, but I really need a wee, and besides, I'm not sure my heart is up to this belated teenage strop. May I be excused?'

'Yes, Dad. You go.' She's cross with him for never standing up to her mum, but she can't change him now. 'But before you do, did you write this down?' She shows him the pad with Mel's mum's name and number written on the flowery paper.

'Not a clue.'

'Then you're excused.'

Nicole and her mum stand in silence while her dad shuffles between them and locks himself in the downstairs loo. Still within earshot, Nicole notes.

'Mum?'

'Let's put the kettle on, shall we?'

'No. I haven't got time for a cup of tea or a deep and meaningful chat right now. When did Angela call and what did she call for?'

Her mum's shoulders slump and she looks sad. No, more than sad, uncomfortable, as though she itches all over, shifting from one foot to the other. 'She wanted to get hold of you. She didn't say why.'

'Did you ask?'

'Not as such.'

'Mum!'

'The whole conversation was very awkward. I wanted her off the phone as quickly as possible. So I took her number and said I'd pass it on to you.'

'What? You told her I'd call her? Why the hell would you do that?'

'Like I said, I wanted her off the phone. I don't understand what I did wrong.'

'Right. As usual you were only thinking about yourself and how good little Nicole always does as she's told. Not for a second did you even think that if you were finding the conversation awkward then I sure as heck would too.'

'Are you drunk?'

'No, I'm not drunk, Mum. I'm pissed off.'

Her mum grimaces. She looks smaller stood in front of Nicole, as though the wind has gone out of her sails and she's deflated. Maybe her mum doesn't know who she is when she's not bossing Nicole around.

Nicole looks at the paper in her hand and the phone number and already she knows what she's going to do. She clenches her teeth, angry with herself once again as well as with her mother and the whole damn world for being such a mess.

'I'm going to go,' she says. 'Tell Dad I said bye. I'll pop round again tomorrow.'

No farewell hug. No invitation for Sunday dinner.

Nicole closes the door and walks down the path to her car with tears in her eyes. Changing herself is one thing. Expecting others to handle the change is quite another.

On the drive home she turns her music up loud and gives way to no one. She ignores the beeps and laughs at the fingers she knows are being flicked in her direction. When someone steps out into the road as she's rounding a corner and ambles across as though they've all the time in the world she beeps her horn and nearly wets herself giggling when they jump and put their hand to their heart in shock. She wafts them along with her hand and speeds down the road.

No one is in when she gets home. She checks her phone, which has been on silent in her handbag. Three missed calls from Joe and a text.

> We've gone out for dinner.

For a second she feels guilty, but shrugs the sensation off. No guilt. They can feed themselves. She isn't sure why they didn't have the pizza Joe said he'd put in the fridge. She's done nothing wrong. And then she wonders when she last did the food shopping, and can't remember.

Opening up the fridge reveals she last shopped some time ago. Apart from the pizzas, one egg on the top shelf and some wilting broccoli, the fridge is bare. She ignores all of the open jars of chutney and tartare sauce and mustard lining the top shelf that are used once and then discarded.

Toast for her dinner then.

At the breakfast bar she pulls out the piece of paper from her parents' house. Smoothing the creases on the worktop in front of her she wishes she had the strength to tear the number up and throw the scraps away. Nothing good can come of a conversation with Mel's mum. Not now. Not ever.

But still she pulls her mobile out of her back pocket and enters the number, then saves it. For a brief moment she thinks about texting Emily to ask her opinion again, but she knows nothing has changed and Emily will still tell her not to call Angela under any circumstances, even though this might be Nicole's final chance to make things right. To put things straight and move on with her life free from guilt.

Without hesitating she presses the green call button and holds the phone to her ear, wishing she had a shot of vodka she could neck.

The call goes to voicemail. Angela is obviously one of those people who doesn't answer calls from unknown numbers. Sensible woman.

'Hi, this is Nicole, Mel's friend from school. My mum gave me your number and said you wanted me to call, so I'm calling.' She hesitates. 'This is my number so please ring back when you can.'

Then she hangs up and takes in a huge gulp of air as though she's been suffocated and the pillow over her face has been removed.

She stares at her phone for a bit, thinking maybe Angela is listening to her message and will call back any second, but her phone remains silent.

Without making any toast she heads into the lounge and pulls out old photo albums lining the shelves in one alcove. There haven't been any new albums made for years. She and Joe keep everything saved in their phones. But here on the shelves are photo albums dating back to her childhood. When her mum and dad had wanted to relegate them to the loft she'd taken them home instead, often overcome with nostalgia and a longing to go back to the past.

Without hesitation she opens up the 1997 album. Her sixteenth birthday photos are at the start of the album. She laughs at her hair, her clothes. She'd thought she'd looked incredible, and maybe she had at the time, but sixteen-year-old girls now would not think so. One ponytail, crimped, erupts from the very top of her head. And she is wearing the baggiest clothes. In fact, she thinks the jumper might've been stolen from her brother. And her jeans are pulled tight with a belt around her tiny waist. She remembers them digging in, but not caring.

Back then she could eat whatever she wanted and not put on a single pound. Back then this stood in her favour as the opinion was that being skinny equalled being healthy. But she was anything but healthy.

She flicks over the page to the photos of her birthday party, although it wasn't a party because she didn't have enough friends to call the gathering that. Her, Emily and Bex are in the photo, stood by her front door, arms loosely wrapped around each other, smiling. They were about to go into town to spend her birthday money before coming back for pizza tea, movie watching and a sleepover on the lounge floor.

Nicole studies the photo. Bex's smile doesn't quite reach her eyes. And then a memory comes back. Bex had turned up late, her eyes red and raw and even though her and Emily had asked Bex what was wrong she'd said nothing was. Nicole remembers wanting to dig deeper, knowing Bex was lying, but not having the confidence to challenge her. She'd always been a little intimidated by Bex. This girl who'd breezed into their lives without a care in the world.

But looking back now, the cracks in Bex are obvious. Her hair isn't brushed in the photo. A dark stain stands out on the shoulder of her jumper.

How had she and Emily not seen the clues as to how unhappy she'd been?

FORTY-FOUR
BEX – 1997

Bex stands in front of the mirror and twists from side to side to see what she looks like from behind, but can't quite twist enough. Her dad had said earlier that her ass was so fat she could block out the sun and she wanted to know if the trousers she was wearing were the culprit, or if her actual backside was the problem.

Her dad always laughed afterwards as though the fact that he was making a joke took away the insult behind his cruel words.

She didn't want to go to Nicole's birthday thing later. Looking over at her unmade bed she sighed and fought back the tears. Hiding under her duvet and ignoring the world was what she wanted to do. Her parents weren't even here today, they wouldn't notice if she went out or not. Nor would they care. They didn't even notice her most of the time.

She was not asking for much, just a little bit of their attention. Grant got attention all the time. Golden boy Grant with his A-grades and football trophies. Sometimes Bex thought her dad only had another child after Grant because her mum had coaxed him into the pregnancy. He was happy with his boy, his son. Had never wanted a daughter with hormones and needs he didn't know how to meet.

But then her mum wasn't much better. Too busy drinking herself stupid and ignoring her dad's darker side.

A plan had been formulating in Bex's head for a while now. A plan that would make them sit up and take notice. Make Michael notice. Make everyone notice. Even Nicole and Emily. They'd welcomed her into their little friendship group, but she still felt like the fifth wheel and besides, Emily had let her down recently too. Mel was helping, but there was a reason for that. Bex was making it happen.

Bex noticed a stain on the corner of her jumper, but didn't care. She wasn't sure what the mark was from. Ketchup maybe. That was right. Grant had made her sausages and chips for dinner last night and the bottle had exploded when she tapped the base.

They'd laughed and for a second she'd been happy and grateful for her family.

She flopped onto the bed, leant over and fished out her journal, hidden under her mattress. She'd poured her heart into this journal over the last few months, confident no one would ever find it and discover the truth of what went on inside her head.

Until afterwards, maybe, but by then nothing would matter. She'd have the attention she craved.

Picking up a pen she started to write today's entry even though it was only ten o'clock in the morning.

Dear Diary,
I have to go to Nicole's party later, but I don't want to. Michael won't be there so what's the point? I don't know why she's calling the thing a party; only

three of us are going. I tried to make her invite Mel too, but she wouldn't. Emily called her a boring fat cow, which to be fair she is a bit, but that's only a good thing for what I need her for.

Anyway, I saw Michael yesterday walking to school and I swear for a second he looked at me right in the eyes and smiled. He's so good-looking.

That reminds me, stupid Sam phoned again yesterday. I don't know who gave him my number, probably Emily for a joke, but it's not funny. She's still mad Grant dumped her. Sam and I didn't talk for long because there was nothing to talk about. Wish I hadn't got off with him at the party to try and make Michael jealous. But he'd been paying me so many compliments so I kinda thought I should.

Right, better go to this stupid party. Going to give Nicole some perfume I got from Mum and Dad for Christmas. I sprayed it and my room now stinks of wee so she can have the bottle. Will write again later, need to plan the thing a bit more and writing everything down helps.

See ya x

She slammed the journal shut and tucked the book back between her mattress and the bedframe.

I'll show them, she thought. *I'll show them all.*

FORTY-FIVE
EMILY – 2022

Emily is trying her hardest not to fart but for some reason downward dog does this to her every time. Work has been challenging yet again today and she had a choice between going to the pub or coming here. The sensible side of her brain was in control then and so here she is.

She can see Bryony through her legs and clenches her teeth. Bryony is never someone Emily relishes seeing, but this yoga class is cheap and good and run by someone she doesn't want to punch in the face every time they instruct her to come back to the breath, so she has to risk bumping into Bryony.

Chloe hadn't said anything to Emily today at school, but she'd hovered outside her classroom throughout her lunch-break and made Emily tense. She had needed the toilet but had crossed her legs and stayed put at her desk. Normally this kind of thing wouldn't throw her off so much; she's had tricky students in the past and surely if Chloe is going to tell someone about the watch she'd have done so by now. And she has no proof anyway. But her behaviour, her words, they all unnerve Emily and so she's decided avoidance is best for now. Do. Not. Engage.

They move into a few sun salutations and then as always at the end of the session lie on their backs in corpse pose – the ultimate pose for relaxation – but Emily hates lying on her back because the position reminds her of how she had imagined her parents' bodies lying in their coffins when she was a child.

She refuses to put her hands on her stomach as instructed as she knows that's how their hands were placed. Her aunt had told her after she'd been to see them at the funeral parlour. Had said they'd looked as though they were sleeping peacefully. Emily remembers running to the toilet and being sick. There was nothing peaceful about any of it, from their deaths to their burials.

'Now breathe into your calves,' the instructor is saying in a voice Emily can't imagine she speaks in normally, too soft and songlike. Emily tries to focus. For years after their deaths she'd have flashbacks. Bright lights would trigger her and she'd be back there in the moment.

Now, she breathes in deeply and tries to remain in this moment. But she can feel herself being pulled back in time. The sound of a siren outside propels her further back until she is there, staring at the broken cars mangled together in the Cornish lane. Hearing the eerie silence for the few minutes afterwards before one of the men from the other car stumbles out and shouts for help, before the farmer from a nearby house comes to their aid, says he's called an ambulance. No one saw her there, in the field, behind the large metal gate. She'd thought about staying silent forever because then she didn't have to deal with the truth of what was to come.

Then a torch had shone in her face. She'd blinked the light away. Had wanted to run. Couldn't.

'Imagine the breath in your lower back and hips. Feel the air cleansing you.'

Emily feels dirty inside as though a fire had raged through

her body and left her charred. She imagines her breath as water flowing down her spine, pulling at the charcoal lining her muscles, running in her veins and loosening every bit. Then she pictures the black debris flowing out of her mouth as smoke.

Not your fault, a voice whispers inside her head, one fighting to be heard. One she works hard to push down over and over again, but not now, not today. Instead, she chooses to indulge the voice and live life as though she believes those words for a second, as she lies here pretending to be dead in order to relax.

And she can breathe. Her body is lighter. But she aches as the tension leaves her alongside all of the guilt and the pain she's been carrying.

'Now focus on your head; hold the breath there and notice how you feel.'

Fuck. She's crying. Tears leak from her eyes and fall down her cheeks and onto her yoga mat. She can't move; if she wipes them away she will draw attention to herself. The instructor will see, ask her to stay behind after class. Emily's seen her do that before with other people taking part, but not to her. Emily hardly ever allows herself to cry, even in private, the feeling too raw and vulnerable. She pushes her tongue to the top of her mouth and even though her eyes are closed, looks up in an attempt to stop the tears. But they keep coming.

The instructor's feet are so close to her head she's concerned she's about to be trodden on. *Please don't let her see my tears,* she pleads to no one in particular. *Please, please, please.* She breathes deeply into her stomach and out of her pursed lips, as instructed. But the feet beside her don't move.

'Wriggle your fingers and toes, and open your eyes.'

Emily rolls away from the instructor and uses her vest top to wipe her wet cheeks. Then she feels a hand on her shoulders, a touch so soft she could've imagined the sensation, and she looks up. The instructor smiles, and indicates with a nod of her head that Emily should stay behind today. And before she says no, as the rejection she wants to give hovers over her lips, she catches Bryony coming over and changes her mind. She will stay if only to avoid that awful woman.

As though the instructor knows this, she walks over and without any effort glides with Bryony to the door of the hall, showing her out before she can even reach Emily. This small act makes Emily want to cry all over again.

Soon the hall empties and only the two of them are left.

Emily doesn't know what to say, how to start, but finds she doesn't need to. Her instructor hands her a steaming mug of herbal tea and a biscuit. The smell from the tea is intoxicating; cinnamon, cloves and another scent she can't place.

The instructor holds up a pretty, pricy-looking box of teabags. The mix is designed to calm and soothe. Then she winks at her. 'And that's an oat biscuit with a hint of turmeric. It's healing.'

'Thank you.'

'My pleasure. I'm not going to pry, I never do, but sometimes I find the people I teach need a bit longer in this safe space before they leave.'

'I wouldn't know where to start even if you did pry,' Emily says, half wishing the woman would dig deeper so she can let everything inside out.

'That's what they all say.'

'How come you're so calm?' Emily blurts out. 'Sorry, that's a silly question.'

'Not at all. I've had to do a lot of practice to get here, trust me. I've not always been so serene.'

'I don't think I've ever been serene.' Emily lets out a half-hearted laugh, but it's true.

'Life doesn't offer many chances to be that way by default;

we all have to work on being calm and dealing with everything our lives throw at us.'

'How do you move on though? How do you let go of everything?'

The instructor stands opposite Emily and bites her bottom lip in thought. She looks around the room as though searching for the answer, or the right thing to say. 'I don't think we do ever truly move on. We can't change the past, but we can change our response to everything that's happened.'

'I think I killed my parents.' There, she's said it. She's told someone her worst fear.

A breeze sweeps through the hall and chills Emily's skin. They sit together and she tells the instructor everything, letting herself cry as she does. The herbal tea in her hands cools, but the soothing scent remains and clouds them in comfort. No judgement comes from the instructor. She listens, gently prompting when Emily struggles to continue. And just as she'd been encouraged to do earlier in corpse pose, she feels cleansed. She doesn't mention Bex. One revelation is enough for today, she feels.

'I'm so sorry you had to go through such a trauma,' the instructor says.

Trauma, Emily thinks, *of course. Why have I not seen my parents' death in this way before?* She thought she'd caused the accident, that she'd been the perpetrator, not the victim.

'Has anyone ever worked through with you what would've happened if you hadn't begged to stop the car so you could go to the toilet?'

And there, like a loose thread on a jumper begging to be pulled, is a memory stored so deep she'd forgotten it existed.

Her aunt is beside her, at the site of the accident, but years later. They'd walked down the lane, hand in hand, and followed the winding road around bend after bend.

'Yes, oh my God, yes. I remember,' Emily says.

'Keep going,' says the instructor. 'Keep remembering.'

She closes her eyes and inhales. And everything comes flooding back.

'*Or maybe on this bend,*' she hears her aunt saying. '*Or this one.*'

'They'd have killed me too.' Emily's voice is a whisper. 'If I hadn't made my parents stop, I'd have died with them.'

The instructor smiles and rests a hand on hers and Emily lets this realisation, the one deep down she's always known, settle inside her, the truth.

Not your fault.

Finally, after far too many years, she fully believes those words.

Her phone beeps in her pocket and the magic is broken. She knows who is messaging and what the message will say.

Time's up.

FORTY-SIX
NICOLE – 2022

'Come on, Emily!' Nicole shouts up the stairs. Nicole should be cooking a roast at home right now. Joe is fuming she isn't. They had a brief chat about how she needs to be with Emily today, but she knows he doesn't understand why. He is so tired of trying to work out her recent change of character that agreeing to her going out with Emily is the easier option.

'I'm coming. Have you messaged her?'

'Yep, she said she'll get to the coffee shop for two. She's out walking the dogs now.'

'Dogs, more than one, fricking madness.'

Nicole agrees. A few years ago she and Joe toyed with the idea of getting a dog – she'd felt bereft she wasn't going to have any more children – but now they are relieved they'd never committed to the idea. She'd been delusional in thinking the boys would've ever walked a dog as well. The responsibility would've been all hers and she'd have ended up resenting everyone even more than she does already.

'You're sure this is all her, aren't you?' Nicole asks, not convinced herself. She knows Bryony can be a pain, but Nicole isn't sure she even knows about Bex's accident in enough detail to blackmail them like this. She has no idea what her motivation could be for doing so either.

'Pretty sure.' Emily puts on her coat.

'What does she stand to gain out of us owning up to being on the beach? And how would she even know?'

'Oh I don't know.'

Nicole notices Emily's head dip.

'What is it, Em?'

Emily puffs air out as though she is blowing up a balloon. 'There was that night, a while back, when we went out and got rat-arsed? Remember?'

Nicole pauses and thinks. 'When we went to the cocktail place in town?'

'Bingo.' Emily sits on the bottom stair and Nicole leans against the shelf above the radiator by the front door.

'Did anything happen?'

'I can't remember, that's the problem. I was so drunk I blacked out and have no memory of how I got home. Bryony texted the next day to say she'd taken me back in a taxi and to ask if I was all right.' Then Emily pauses and fiddles with a button on her coat.

'And?' *Spit the truth out,* thinks Nicole, again wondering why Emily has withheld some vital information from her.

'And then she messaged and said my secret was safe with her and she'd never tell a soul. But to this day I cannot remember what the secret I told her was.'

'Oh, Em.'

'Don't *Oh, Em* me. Just don't.'

'What am I meant to do? Are you sure that's the secret you told her?'

'I think so. How many secrets do you think I have?'

'More than I did yesterday, they keep coming don't they?'

To think every time Nicole has seen Bryony recently she might've known the truth about Bex is like a punch to the stomach. Nicole replays all of their conversations. The questioning from Bryony when she'd gone to her house about lies she might've told has taken on a different meaning. Had Bryony really known the truth even then? Nicole feels so foolish.

'Shall we go then?' Emily looks like she used to when she was in a teenage sulk, which, now Nicole thinks about those days, was quite a lot.

'If you're ready.'

'Ready as I'll ever be. I want this done with, you know?'

'I really do.' The messages hadn't worried Nicole as much as they could've done when she'd suspected they might be from Emily, but now she knows they aren't the whole thing frightens her a bit. She hates the thought of someone menacing knowing where she lives, and where Emily works. The whole thing is too close to home. Emily is right, they need this to be over.

They don't speak in the car. Nicole plays the radio and hums along so the silence doesn't engulf them. She isn't sure what they are going to say to Bryony when they get to the coffee shop. Starting such an awkward conversation is never easy. Bryony thinks they simply want to meet to discuss a Christmas party she's hosting. Nicole feels a pang of guilt that they don't even plan on attending the bash in question.

Glancing over at Emily she feels another pang of guilt, her body so wracked with the emotion she isn't sure where the bulk of it lies anymore. She's glad they are back to supporting each other and communicating like they used to, but a tiny speck of mistrust dances in front of her eyes like dust in sunlight. Emily has always been private, always a part of her she won't let anyone see, but Nicole is wondering how much of herself she's hidden.

'Where shall I park?'

Emily sighs. 'You might get lucky and find one on the road, if not then maybe the harbour car park?'

Nicole doesn't want to park near the beach. She shudders, thinking what might've happened if Emily hadn't come to her rescue the other day.

'What was that?' Emily laughs.

'Someone walked over my grave.'

'Probably me in the future. I'd find making you shiver funny.'

'You're such a good friend.'

They laugh, but then are quickly silent again, each lost in their own inner turmoil.

'Oh look, there's a space.' Emily points a little way down the road.

'Nice one, now I need to actually parallel park like a pro.'

'You got this.' Emily smirks.

Nicole has always been shit at parking and Emily knows it. A car horn behind them beeps and Nicole can feel a knot of frustration tightening in her stomach. She pulls in and out of the space again, distracted and positioned all wrong, and as she does the driver behind beeps his horn again, for a fraction longer than necessary.

'If he does that one more time,' Nicole says through gritted teeth, 'then I am going to get out and give him a piece of my mind.'

The road is narrow and cars have parked down both sides, making reversing into a space Nicole isn't sure is even big enough for her car, near impossible. But she does not want to go to the harbour car park by the beach.

'Deep breaths.' Emily places a hand on her shoulder. 'Ignore that twat.'

'I can't do this, the space is too damn small.' Nicole is about to lose her temper, or cry; she is unsure which might happen, maybe both.

'You can.' Emily's voice is gentle and Nicole listens and breathes. 'A little to the left, that's it, you're nearly in.'

After a few more manoeuvres in and out, Nicole switches off the engine, giving the silent finger to the beeping knob from behind as he passes by.

'He got to you, didn't he?' Emily looks straight at Nicole.

'Yes. I don't understand why he couldn't be supportive and patient and let me get on with parking in peace. Why did he have to make me feel like a complete muppet for not being able to park the first time? He was only inconvenienced for about three minutes.' Tears threaten to fall from her eyes and she blinks them away.

'Nicole, if you get annoyed by everyone like that you are going to explode. Twats are everywhere. Who cares? You know what I'd have done?'

'Got out and spat at him?'

'No. But I might've taken longer than you did to park, kept him waiting, but without letting him know he'd got to me. Why give him the satisfaction?'

Nicole knows Emily is right. Getting angry with these people who offend her doesn't make her feel any better. And they don't care. 'Fine, I'll try not to take stuff so personally in future.'

'Exactly, it's not about you.'

'Whatever.'

Emily undoes her seatbelt and goes to open the door. 'Okay, are you sure you're ready for this?'

'Yep. You're going to start the talking though, right?' They'd rehearsed who was going to say what several times at Emily's house before they'd left. Nicole had fluffed her lines even then because she'd been so nervous. Confrontation makes her want to vomit.

'I am going to play bad cop,' Emily says and salutes, 'and you good.'

The look at each other for a few seconds – their shared respect and happiness at being a team again not needing to be spoken out loud – and then get out of the car.

'Let's do this.'

FORTY-SEVEN
EMILY – 2022

They haven't chosen to meet at the harbour café, but instead a bigger, busier one a few streets back from the beach. Emily had pointed out that in a busy café no one will be able to hear them talk.

The door jangles as they walk in, but none of the customers look up from their tables.

'Doesn't look as though she's here yet.' Nicole scans the room. 'Shall we grab the table at the back?' A booth with two slim benches either side of a table is hidden away in the far right-hand corner.

'Perfect. You go and sit there and I'll get the drinks.'

Unlike with Angela, Emily knows what to order for Nicole. Only ever a tea drinker at home, she always has a cappuccino when she's out. It's one of the ways she treats herself, which in itself makes Emily laugh. Life is too short. Why Nicole doesn't have a cappuccino every day instead of denying herself, she doesn't know.

Whilst she is ordering Bryony walks in. The bell on the door alerts everyone to her arrival, and yet Nicole and Emily are the only ones who look. Bryony has dressed up for the occasion. She wears leather leggings under a fluffy pink jumper and a scarf so big Emily could sleep under there and hibernate for the winter. Her skin bears the faint hint of a tan from her recent holiday too, giving her a healthy glow. Bryony waves at Nicole and then walks over to Emily at the counter.

'I'll get these,' she says, a statement not to be challenged. 'Latte for me too.' Then she air kisses Emily on both cheeks. Bryony smells of the sickliest flowers, and Emily sneezes into her elbow as though she has got hay fever from smelling her.

'Bless you.' Bryony's smile is also sickly sweet. Her lips shine with a clear gloss, her eyes wide and framed by false lashes. For a second Emily feels a bit bad, luring her here under false pretences. And then she dismisses the emotion as quickly as it came.

She walks over and sits next to Nicole. Bryony will have to sit opposite them, as though she is being interviewed, or interrogated.

'She's in a ridiculously good mood.' Emily scrunches her nose, which is still itching from the perfume. 'And is wearing all the make-up.'

'I'm nervous.' Nicole picks at the skin around her nails again and Emily whacks her hand.

'Stop that. We're here because she's been threatening us. She's the one who should be nervous, not you.'

'We don't know that for sure. What if the messages aren't from her after all? What then?'

Emily shushes Nicole as Bryony joins them, placing a tray holding their drinks on the table and spilling each one a little.

'I've got some sugar.' She hands Emily her coffee and Nicole her cappuccino, before resting the tray on the floor against one of the benches. 'Really lovely to see you both at the same time. I can't remember the last time this happened.'

'I can.' Emily cannot be bothered with small talk. Her fingers fizz and she wraps them around her mug so Bryony cannot see them shaking. 'The night we all went out for cocktails.'

'Ah yes.' Bryony laughs. 'That was so much fun. We all drank way too much, didn't we?' Emily glares at her. She feels Nicole shift on the bench.

'I went home early,' Nicole says. 'But I had a lot of fun before I did.' Playing good cop well so far, Emily notes.

'Ah yes,' says Bryony. 'You'd had your allocated three drinks and then left.' Emily detects a hint of sarcasm in her voice.

'But you dropped me home, didn't you? We shared a taxi,' Emily says.

'Ah yes, that's right we did. We should make sure we pre-book some taxis for the Christmas party for people. Often difficult to find one around Christmastime.' Bryony gets a notebook out and starts writing a list. 'It's so kind of you both to help me plan this party. I'm a bit overwhelmed by everything already to be honest. I have so much to do.' She giggles like a school kid.

'Actually, Bryony.' Emily takes the pen from her hand and Bryony looks shocked, but doesn't grab it back. 'We wanted to talk about the cocktail night a bit more first.' Emily hopes Bryony can't detect the tremor in her voice. She's frustrated with herself. Normally she would have no trouble demanding answers or confronting people, but lately, with everything that's happened, she's lost her bravado.

'Okay,' says Bryony, frowning. 'I'm a little confused.'

'You texted me the day after that night. You said you'd keep my secret safe.'

'And I have.' She sits up tall, her cheeks flushing red. 'Of course I have.' She places her palms flat on the table.

'Are you sure? Look, I know this is odd, but you haven't been messaging me or Nicole about the secret, have you?'

Bryony's eyes flit from Nicole to Emily and back again as though she is watching a game of tennis. 'Why would I do that? And I haven't even told Nicole. You were adamant I mustn't. Begged me to keep this to myself, and I have. I haven't told a soul, I promise.'

Emily and Nicole look at each other. Emily is very confused now. Why would she beg Bryony not to tell Nicole? Maybe because she didn't want Nicole to know she'd betrayed their friendship and told someone else their secret?

'What was the secret Emily told you?' Nicole leans forward, no sign of the nerves she mentioned earlier.

'That's not my secret to tell.' Bryony looks down at the table and picks at a crumb.

'The thing is, Bryony.' Emily leans even closer over the table. 'I can't remember what I told you. And I need to know what I divulged. I can't say why, but Nicole and I, we have to know.'

They are all silent for a while. Emily wills Bryony to speak, to reveal the secret Emily was so desperate for no one else to know.

'Are you sure you want me to say? In front of Nicole?'

'Yes. We need to know.'

Bryony pauses and Emily swears if she doesn't speak soon, she'll grab her by her clothes, push her against the back of the booth and force the truth out of her.

'Okay then.' Bryony takes a deep breath in. 'If you're sure.'

'I'm sure.'

'Fine. You told me you're still in love with Grant. That you'd do anything to get him back.'

Emily leans back on the bench, against the hard wood of the

booth. The memory comes flooding back to her now. The tears, so many tears. Bryony, stinking of her awful flowery perfume, hugging her tight in the back seat of the taxi, patting her on the shoulder and saying, 'There, there. I won't tell a soul.'

Emily's cheeks flush red. Her heart pounds in her chest. She wants to cry at the shame. Nicole reaches out and squeezes her hand and the action makes her want to run away. She pulls her hand away and sips her coffee. Then she carefully places her mug down on the table.

'Sorry,' says Bryony. 'But you did make me tell.'

'Don't worry about it. I was drunk. We all say and do stupid things when we're drunk, right?' *All of us apart from Nicole,* Emily thinks. 'I didn't mean it.'

'Look, I'm going to go.' Bryony shuffles out from her seat. 'You two have obviously got some stuff you need to talk about. Why don't we arrange to do this another time?'

Emily and Nicole nod and Bryony wafts out, her movement releasing more of her scent and making Emily sneeze again.

'That was unexpected,' Nicole says. 'Are you okay?'

'I'm fine. We can talk about all of that later, not now, okay?' She sips her coffee again, her throat dry. 'So, not Bryony threatening us then?'

'No. Clearly not.'

Emily sighs and puts her head in her hands.

'Are you still convinced this is all about Bex?' Nicole's eyebrows are raised. She wipes the remnants of frothy milk from around the rim of her mug and licks her finger.

'I think so. I can't think of anything else involving us both.'

Nicole pauses. 'Then maybe we should go and see her parents?'

Bex's parents being involved has crossed Emily's mind, but she hasn't thought them capable of such deception. But if anyone is going to be devastated by knowing the truth, they will be. This doesn't feel like something they'd do though. Revenge and Bex's parents do not go hand in hand, she's sure.

'They'll be back from church now,' Emily says. 'Let's go.'

FORTY-EIGHT
NICOLE – 2022

'Hey Grant, are your mum and dad in?'

Nicole and Emily are stood on the doorstep of Bex's parents' house, fired up from their meeting with Bryony and ready for a confrontation.

Grant is here again, and whilst she understands why he's always here these days – the estrangement from his parents, as well as their divorce, put on hold by their grief – she is frustrated as his presence makes being direct with everyone a bit harder. And after the revelation of Emily confessing her love for him to Bryony, she knows Emily must feel awkward too. Emily bristles beside her. He smells of cigarettes and Nicole is thrown back to the days where they'd all hang out at the beach and pretend to enjoy smoking, before addiction set in and having a fag became a need.

'They're in the lounge, I was about to leave and go home, why?'

'We need to talk to them. It's important.' Nicole tries to give him one of Emily's teacher death stares and fails. Then she smiles sweetly with puppy dog eyes.

'For fuck's sake, let us in.' Emily pushes past him. Again

Nicole is thrown back in time to a place where Emily's teenage strops were expected and ignored. Grant rolls his eyes and steps back to let Nicole in, arm outstretched and leading the way. He knows better than to stop Emily when she is in one of these moods.

The house hasn't changed, but looks dated, as though time has stood still for the last twenty-five years. Faded wallpaper lines the hallway and travels up the stairs, edges lifting where the seams meet. A coat stand looms to the right and overflows with coats. A mirror with gold edges is hung on the wall next to it, as though the entrance is a changing room giving people the opportunity to analyse their coat choice before leaving the house. At the foot of the stairs is the sort of telephone table all people over the age of fifty are keen on keeping hold of, even though the landline only rings in most houses when someone has died.

Nicole follows Emily through to the lounge. She's already placed herself in the seat she used to curl up in when Bex's parents were out and they would watch a film they weren't supposed to. Looking at her now Nicole can clearly see it's teenager, not adult Emily who sits there chewing her hair. She recalls the teenager who appeared to be confident and strong, but was a mess inside. Nicole should've done more, said more, but then if she had Emily would've simply snapped at her and denied there was an issue. Just as Bex had done.

'We need to talk to you, about Bex,' Emily says and Nicole places herself on the armrest of the chair Emily is in.

Mr Williams puts his newspaper down and gives his wife a look Nicole can't interpret. Puzzled, as though he is trying to solve the newspaper's crossword puzzle. 'Okay. We're listening.'

He's definitely puzzled, Nicole thinks. Maybe they are barking up the wrong tree again.

Nicole dives in and speaks before Emily accuses them

outright. 'This is hard to say, but we've been getting some messages, unpleasant messages, and we're trying to work out who might've sent them.'

'What kind of messages?' Sylvia removes her glasses as though this will make her able to focus better on what is being said.

'Fucking rude ones,' Emily snaps and they all wince. Nicole nudges her with her elbow.

'They are accusing us of doing a bad thing,' Nicole continues, trying to keep her tone neutral. 'Except we're not sure what.'

'Why on earth do you think my parents would know anything about these messages?' Grant speaks up, his voice thick with emotion, and Nicole realises they haven't thought this through. If they tell everyone what they think the messages are about then they have to admit they were with Bex on the beach on the day of her accident. What they did before she went for a swim. And after.

'We're exploring all avenues right now,' says Emily and Nicole stifles a random giggle, thinking she sounds like a detective. 'The messages are telling us to own up or they will take action. Is there anything you think we need to own up to?'

Direct, thinks Nicole, *but also clever.*

'I'm so confused.' Sylvia shakes her head. 'Do you mean to do with Bex? With her accident?'

'Maybe.' Nicole shifts on the edge of the chair, her left buttock aching. And then she panics, not sure where this is headed.

'I mean, we were her friends, we should've noticed somehow, and raised the alarm sooner,' Emily says before anyone can accuse them of anything else.

She's a good liar, thinks Nicole. She always has been. No twitch of the eye or smirk. No wobble in her voice or hesitation.

'Why are you bringing all of this up again now?' Sylvia asks, her voice wobbling as though she is about to cry. And Nicole doesn't know the answer. She doesn't understand why she and Emily are so bothered by the texts and reminds herself again they didn't do anything illegal. At least, nothing they can be punished for now. They've spent years punishing themselves anyway. In fact, owning up to everything might alleviate their guilt, finally. But, as she looks at Grant and his parents, she realises again they've been through enough already. They don't need to know what she and Emily did or didn't do.

'I guess the texts and messages have forced our hand,' Emily says, shrugging. 'This isn't us wanting to bring everything up again. We know you've all been through so much.'

Nicole can feel energy radiate from her body as though she has been in a sauna and is cooling off. She rubs her palms together and splays her fingers. For a second Nicole wonders if Emily has secrets she doesn't know about. Emily would normally shrug these messages off and say, fuck it. But for some reason they have affected her too and Nicole wants to know why.

'Mum and Dad know nothing about any texts, right?' Grant looks at his parents. 'And neither do I, so maybe it's best if you leave right now?' He has an edge to his voice and Nicole stands as though a teacher has told her off. Grant looks angry and emotional all mixed into one.

'Of course.' Nicole nudges Emily's shoulder beside her. 'Come on.' Wanting to leave, she nods towards the door, but Emily doesn't move.

'We really are sorry for what happened,' Emily says. 'I thought about Bex every single day since the accident.'

'You never visited,' Bex's dad whispers. The newspaper in his hands shakes.

For a minute everyone is silent. The clock on the

mantelpiece ticks and counts the seconds until someone speaks again. Nicole stands like a statue, afraid to move. Specks of dust dance before her eyes in the faint sunshine beaming through the window.

'I know I didn't. And I'm sorry for that too.' Emily's face is twisted and Nicole feels like she is having an out-of-body experience. Her best friend is behaving as though someone has possessed her. 'I couldn't see her like that, knowing we could've prevented her accident if only we'd noticed. I felt too guilty about what had happened. Staying away was easier. I wanted to remember her how she was before her accident.'

'Some of us didn't have that privilege,' Grant says.

Emily looks at Grant. His eyes burn through her and Nicole holds her breath.

'I know. I can't imagine what it's been like for you.'

'And for Bex, trapped in her broken body for years and years.' Sylvia lets out a sob. Nicole's insides churn. She picks at the skin around her thumbnail then sucks the blood.

Grant moves forward now and lifts Emily from the chair. With his arm linked in hers she doesn't fight him and Nicole follows them out of the room.

'This is low even for you,' Grant hisses.

'Grant.' She shrugs off his grip and stops in the centre of the hallway. 'Nicole and I are getting threatening messages. I think we have a right to find out who the fuck is sending them, don't you?'

'You should've texted me first and asked before barging round here; but this is just like you, isn't it. Act first think later. My poor parents do not deserve this. You didn't need to get them involved.'

Emily takes a step back. 'Fuck you,' she says and walks out.

Nicole pauses for a second, glaring at Grant before

following Emily. 'Emily, wait,' she calls and runs to catch her friend up.

'I fucking hate him.'

'I know, but he's rightly protective of his parents.'

Emily gives Nicole a death stare and Nicole scrunches up her eyes and rubs her temples. 'Sorry, I can't help but see where people are coming from even if they're being a dick,' Nicole says. 'It's a curse.'

Emily's shoulders lower and they smirk at each other. 'Where next?' says Emily. 'It's clearly not them and now we've started this I cannot stop until I know the truth.'

'I agree.' Nicole inhales deeply. 'But remind me why we want to find out who is doing this so badly? Who cares what we did back then? I don't give a rat's ass if everyone finds out now.'

'Because we don't want anyone to know what we did; our actions were unforgivable.'

'But why not? Bex is dead. What good will keeping the truth hidden do, other than continue to make us feel like crap?'

Nicole watches as Emily's whole demeanour changes.

'What aren't you telling me, Em?'

'Nothing.'

Nicole raises her eyebrows. 'Emily?'

'Honestly, nothing. You were there, you know what happened.'

Nicole isn't sure she believes her best friend, but doesn't have the energy to dig deeper right now. The people-pleasing side of her ruling once more, she relents. 'Right, so if we are still convinced the messages *are* to do with Bex, then we'll go and see Mel's mum next, right?' she says.

'Right.'

FORTY-NINE
EMILY - 2022

Even though Nicole is urging her to slow down, Emily can't control her speed and marches down the road, as though all of the years of internal pain and torture are trying to stamp themselves out of her one step at a time.

Grant has got to her. To think he once loved her makes her want to punch him in the face. The thought is absurd now. He hates her. Regrets all of their time together. Fact. A pain flashes across her chest and she places her palm there and inhales deeply.

Maybe the texts aren't about Bex. Maybe someone knows she's been stealing things again; but then why would Nicole be getting them too? Unless Nicole is lying? She's going round in circles. Her head feels as though it is about to explode.

'Show me your texts.' Emily stops walking and Nicole crashes into the back of her.

'What?'

'The texts you got, like mine, show me again.'

'Why?'

'Just do it.' Emily tries to grab Nicole's phone from her hands.

'Hey, what's happened?'
'How do I know it's not you sending them to me?'
'You've lost the plot now, Em.'
'Have I?'
'Yes. Here, look.' Nicole hands her the phone.

Emily looks at the texts, then gives the phone back and groans, pulling at her hair. 'I am sick of all of this,' Emily shouts. 'From the day Bex joined our school it's been one shitty thing after another and now she's dead and still we can't move on.'

'That's why I think we should own up to being there. Then it's done. No more secrets, right?'

Emily rolls her eyes at her. 'She was going to go swimming no matter what we did, there was a weird energy in her. What you did, what we did afterwards wouldn't have changed anything.'

'But it might've. We could've saved her. Should've–' Tears form in Nicole's eyes and she looks to the sky and blinks them away.

Emily puts her arm around her and Nicole allows herself to be comforted. They stand there, arms wrapped around each other, for several minutes. Cars drive by, some slow down to look, rubbernecking at anyone who might be in distress. Emily wonders if net curtains are twitching and the neighbours are texting their street WhatsApp group wondering what's happening outside their homes.

'I'm sorry I didn't trust you then,' Emily says.

'You're saying that word a lot today.'

'Haven't said sorry for about twenty-five years so guess I've got some catching up to do.'

'Stop trying to be funny. What's going on?'

Emily sighs and they start walking together side by side. 'I don't know. Stuff I guess, being brought up by Bex dying.' Emily has never told Nicole about going to her childhood home, never a word about the stealing either. Now isn't the time. 'Plus, a student at work has been giving me a hard time. Reminds me of what Bex was like back then, I guess. Do you remember what she was like to the teachers? They hated her.'

'Yeah, she did give off "spoilt bitch don't mess with me" vibes. She used to get us in so much trouble. We were the good pupils until she turned up.'

'You know, now I'm a teacher, those are the students I want to find out more about. There's usually a reason why they are playing up and trying to get attention.'

'But there wasn't a reason for Bex, was there? Although sometimes I wonder what we missed, you know?'

Emily keeps quiet. She hadn't missed the truth. And yet she still married into Bex's family. She'd married the brother of the girl she hadn't tried to save. She'd blamed Bex, not her parents.

'Are you saying everything wasn't as happy as things looked from the outside?'

'I don't know. You don't always know what goes on behind closed doors.'

They've walked a long way. Nicole's car is still parked outside Bex's parents' house. Chewing gum splodges are stuck to the pavement below and Emily feels ashamed for all of the times she's spat her gum out and not cared where the blob landed.

'We don't even know if Angela still lives here,' Nicole says as they round the corner onto the street where Mel lived when she was at school with them.

'Worth a try. If not, you've still got her phone number, haven't you?'

Nicole nods, with a frown etched on her face. Right then and there, Emily knows Nicole has already phoned Angela back. Of course she has. Nicole always does what other people ask of her, whether she wants to or not. Again shame washes over Emily as the years of pleasing herself and never considering anyone else's take on things catches up with her. She puts a pin in the thought, and links arms with Nicole.

Emily remembers the first time they walked together like this, side by side, attached at the elbows. Life had been lonely for Emily until Nicole had joined her at school and made her feel like maybe she didn't need to be by herself after all.

They'd invented games where they could lose themselves in their own imaginations, not caring that everyone else called them babies for doing so. They dreamed of being fairies, Emily always the autumn fairy with powerful magic to make the leaves turn the brightest of colours. They made up dance routines, pretended to be teachers, invented puzzles and mysteries needing solving wherever they went.

Emily had found Nicole a source of comfort growing up. Grateful her friend balanced out her selfishness and always did the right thing, enough for the both of them. Stealing a chocolate bar from someone's packed lunch didn't matter if Nicole then used her pocket money to buy the child a new one.

'Right, here we are,' says Nicole. 'Mel's house.'

They stand at the bottom of some steps leading up to a terraced house. Each step is cracked and weeds poke through as if planted there, making them look like a work of modern art. Emily only came here once when they were all at school together, on Halloween. Bex, Nicole and her hadn't been invited to any parties and so instead they'd dressed up and walked around the town trick-or-treating by themselves. They'd come here, to taunt Mel, and thrown eggs at the front door. Emily remembers that Halloween because Nicole tripped on the bottom step and put an extra hole in her already laddered witch's tights. Come to think of it, Emily can't remember Bex being there then.

'You go first then.' Nicole snaps her back to the present.

Emily isn't sure why, but she's nervous. Seeing Mel's mum on the beach the other day had unsettled her and then having her walk out of the café without saying a word had only added to that. Emily still doesn't understand why she left.

Nicole shoves her hand in the small of Emily's back, encouraging her to climb the steps.

'All right, I'm going.' Emily takes the steps two at a time and is a little out of breath by the time she reaches the top. She tries to take a full breath but can't, her lungs ejecting the air before they can fully inflate.

'Ring the bell then.' Nicole looks as nervous as Emily feels. She's gone a bit pale.

Emily pushes the bell, not one of these fancy camera ones most people have these days, but the same bell that had been there all of those years ago when eggshell had smashed into the plastic casing.

After the bells rings she can hear definite movement inside the house. A light switches on in the hallway. A call of, 'I'll go' rings out from a voice Emily recognises.

And then, as the door opens, the air is knocked out of her. 'Chloe!'

FIFTY
NICOLE – 1997

There was a chill in Nicole's bones the heat of the rum was not taking away. She took another gulp from the flask she'd brought to the beach, and winced as she swallowed. Her dad wouldn't notice she'd taken his alcohol, or that what Nicole had left in the bottle at home was now watered down so he wouldn't realise some of the liquid was missing. He didn't drink rum anymore anyway.

Bex had refused to drink any, which wasn't like her. Nicole thought she was in a strange mood today, all weird and preoccupied. Sometimes, Nicole wished her and Em could be alone like they used to be. Bex could be such a good-mood vacuum.

'How's your fit brother?' Emily asked Bex.

'He's sound.' Bex smirked. 'Got a job so is at work all the time.'

'Oh. Cool.' Emily's face dropped and for a second Nicole wondered if she was going to cry. Emily and Bex's brother had snogged last Christmas at a house party and Bex had not been happy about them making out, but then Grant had told Emily their kiss was a mistake after she came on to him again him at

New Year. Emily still thinks Bex forced Grant to end things with her. She cared about him more than she let on, Nicole reckoned.

'Anyone fancy a swim?' Bex's expression was wide and full of expectation.

'Are you joking?' Nicole asked, hoping she was. She didn't even want to be here on the sand, let alone in the sea. 'It's bloody freezing in there.'

'Nah, it'll be fine once we're in. Come on.' Bex got up and started to undress.

'But we don't have a towel or anything. You're bloody nuts.'

Emily didn't say anything. She was too busy pouring some of Nicole's dad's rum into Bex's coke while her back was turned and then holding her finger to her lips, instructing Nicole to stay quiet about what she'd done.

Emily winked at Nicole, as she kept Bex distracted. Nicole was torn. Since they were little, she was the one who'd toed the line and was uncomfortable she was allowing Emily to spike Bex's drink. But a small part of her was excited to listen to the devil on her shoulder instead of the angel for once.

'Look at the size of the waves.' Nicole pointed, averting Bex's gaze further away from Emily. 'You'll get swallowed whole.'

'I do this all the time.' Bex waved her hand and dismissed Nicole's concern. 'I'll be fine. Grant and I have been swimming in the sea since we were kids.'

'In October?'

'Why not? Swimming is good for you.'

'Bloody isn't.' Nicole had watched enough *Baywatch* to know hypothermia was a real possibility. 'You'll turn blue and seize up and I am not coming in to save you.'

'You won't need to. I'll be fine.'

'Here.' Emily handed Bex her drink. 'Have some of this before you get in. The caffeine will help keep you afloat.'

They all laughed. Emily and Nicole looked at each other with eyebrows raised as Bex downed the rest of her drink. Then she grimaced. 'Yuk, it's gone flat. Tastes weird too.'

'You're weird,' Emily said and they all laughed again. Bex shrugged and wiped her mouth with the back of her hand before running towards the waves. The smell of the seaweed beside them on the sand made Nicole turn up her nose.

'You're fucking crazy,' Emily shouted to Bex.

The roar of the waves drowned out any of the yelps coming from Bex as the cold hit her legs. Nicole could only imagine the sound as she watched her friend go in deeper. Her stomach twisted as they stood by the rocks and shivered as Bex stepped in further and further away from them, the waves now crashing against her back and spraying white froth into the air. A dark cloud rolled overhead and a herring gull called out as though alerting them all to the danger.

But they didn't hear the cry over the roar of the sea.

Or if they did, they chose to ignore the warning.

'Come on, come in!' Bex beckoned them with her arms, but Emily lit a cigarette, waving the white stick at Bex as an excuse not to swim.

'You going in?' Emily asked Nicole, who shivered at the thought.

'No, it's freezing in there. I don't know how she does it.'

Nicole had always been a delicate soul, and she was happy with that. Emily had tried over the years to toughen her up, but, aside from getting her to smoke, she'd failed. Nicole wasn't going to change for anyone.

'Are you gutted Grant's not around?' Nicole asked.

Emily's expression changed and she looked down at her feet. 'No, stupid fucker. I mean he's fit, but such a loser.'

Nicole watched as Emily blinked away tears and turned to face away from her for a second. Nicole hadn't properly snogged anyone yet, even though she'd had crushes on boys at school. Michael kept trying, kept asking her out, but she knew Bex liked him, so wouldn't go there. They all called her frigid and with good reason. She was. Nicole didn't want to know how snogging someone felt, only for them then to tell you the kiss was a mistake. She would happily wait to discover that hideous emotion.

'Em, I'm not sure you should've spiked Bex's drink. She's gone a hell of a way out.'

They stood on a rock at the edge of the sea. Bex's head was the size of a grape in the distance. Her arms were waving and Nicole couldn't tell if she was distressed or doing the front crawl.

'It was only a dash, plus she didn't drink much. Not as much as she has done before. Stop being such a bloody goody-two-shoes, Nic. We're rebelling today, remember? Bex wanted to go for a swim, we didn't make her.'

'Kinda think I should've stayed at the library. What if my parents have come looking for me and I get caught out?'

'So what? If they have then you'll get told off and grounded for a week. Fucking big deal.'

'Being grounded is a big deal.'

'It really isn't. Chill out will you, you're spoiling the fun.'

A sudden dark cloud hovered over the sun turning the sea a rich dark blue. Fat drops of rain fell and landed on their noses and foreheads. Emily's hair turned a darker shade of brown one drop at a time.

Emily pulled her hoodie out of her bag and held it above her head while Nicole scrabbled about to do the same. 'What about Bex?' she called.

'She's in the sea, therefore already wet.'

But as Nicole tried to look for Bex through the pellets of rain she struggled to find her grape-sized head. The rain peppered the sea making the surface look like shattered glass. There was no wind. The sand before them turned a dark shade of brown. Nicole shivered.

'I can't see her.' Nicole's eyes were wide, her heart hammered in her chest. 'Emily, where is she?'

'I don't know,' Emily snapped. 'She said she does this all the time, maybe she's swam to the other side of the beach and has got out and is walking back?'

'We need to call someone. We can't huddle here and wait. She's our friend. She could be in danger.'

'I don't even know where the nearest phone is. Look,' Emily pointed to the sky in the distance, 'the sky is brighter over there. This is a shower, when the rain stops we'll be able to see her again I'm sure.'

But Nicole wasn't convinced. Everything felt wrong, as though they were in the middle of a teenage horror film and a murder was about to take place.

'I don't like this, Em. Why did you have to put the rum in her drink?'

'Will you lighten up? There was no way enough rum to get her pissed.'

'But no one knows we're here. I mean no one, Em.' Nicole ran her hands through her hair, soaked through from the fresh rain. She could feel a panic attack coming on. Her palms were sweaty. Her mouth dry. 'I'm going to look for her.' She started to undress.

'Don't be an idiot, Nic. You'll fucking drown too.'

'I am not going to leave her out there on her own. I didn't even want to come today; you made me. And Bex's been odd as well.'

'Once again, we didn't make her go swimming, did we? That was all her idea.'

'We didn't try very hard to stop her.'

Nicole's skin pimpled as the cold wind and rain splattered against her. She'd seen this on *Baywatch* too, knew she couldn't go in wearing any clothes or they'd weigh her down. She'd have to dive below the surface and look for Bex in the depths of the salty water. She wasn't very good at holding her breath, but she had no choice.

Emily had started gathering up their things. She'd turned her back on Nicole as she'd undressed and Nicole grabbed her shoulder and spun her around.

'What are you doing?'

Emily's face was white, as though she had seen a ghost. She muttered, 'Not again' under her breath and Nicole couldn't understand what she meant.

'Please don't leave, Em. I might need you to help me resuscitate Bex.'

'You are being a drama queen now.' Emily's voice had no power to it, as though she was running out of battery. 'We'll go and get help. Find a phone box. Knock on a door. We'll get someone.'

Nicole nodded, but she stripped off her last sock, determined to save her friend. She stuffed her clothes in her bag so they didn't get wet and turned to face the sea.

'Who's that?' She frowned, pointing at a figure running towards the sea from the rocks they'd been stood on earlier.

Emily came to stand beside her and put her hand to her forehead as though this action would block out the rain and allow her to see better.

'I don't know.' Emily threw up her hands. 'But they look like they're about to do your job for you.'

Nicole and Emily headed towards the edge of the sea and

then, as they reached the place where the waves flowed further and further up the sand as though trying to reclaim the land, they watched Mel jump over the white rolls of water out to where Bex's body floated next to the rocks.

'What the fuck is Mel doing here?' Nicole said.

'I have no idea.'

Nicole is in a state of panic. She can't save them both. And she can't have Mel tell anyone they were involved in this – that her dad's rum had made Bex drown.

'We need to go.' Emily yanks Nicole's arm and drags her up the beach, grabbing their bags as they go.

Nicole remains mute. Her brain whirs. Mel will save Bex. She'll know what to do. They'll be okay. Mel will be a hero. She'll be happier at school, popular. Just what she's always wanted. No one needs to know she and Emily were here. Bex wouldn't say anything, she'd be too busy basking in the attention of nearly dying, and even if she did speak up, they'd deny everything.

Emily was right. They needed to go and they needed to go now. Get home before anyone suspected they'd been anywhere but where they said they'd be all afternoon. Spend some time looking in the mirror, practising their surprised faces for when they're told of the drama at school tomorrow.

If this was what happened when Nicole didn't stick to the rules, she didn't ever want to even so much as bend them again.

FIFTY-ONE
EMILY – 2022

The door slams in their faces.

'Who's Chloe?' Nicole asks.

Emily doesn't answer, but instead presses her finger on the doorbell and doesn't let go.

'Em.' Nicole pulls her hand away, but she knocks on the door instead.

Blood boils in Emily's veins and her cheeks burn red. Chloe. Of course the messages are from Chloe, she knows they are. But how on earth does Chloe know Mel's mum? About any of Emily and Nicole's past for that matter? Emily tries to catch her breath, but still her body is stopping her from filling her lungs and inhaling deeply.

'Emily,' Nicole shouts. 'Who is Chloe?'

Emily closes her eyes and leans her forehead against the door. It's over. If Chloe knows the truth, however she is connected, then Mel's mum must know too. That's why she wanted to speak to Nicole. Why she left the café. Why she was so angry on the beach. But why not simply tell everyone? Why the game-playing?

'She's a student from school. The one I told you about.'

'What's she doing here?'

'I've no idea.' Nicole bangs the door again. 'That's why I want her to open the door,' she shouts through the letterbox.

'Chill,' Nicole says. 'You'll get the sack.'

'You don't know the half of it.' Emily turns her back and slumps against the door. Of all the students whose watch she could've taken she had to choose Chloe. Emily feels like an idiot. Her gut twists and she grimaces with shame as if she's got the worst hangover ever and has recalled drunkenly coming on to her boss.

'I stole her watch,' Emily says. 'I took it at work and she knew I had, says she saw me, but I managed to put it back without her ever being able to prove anything. I told her no one would believe her story over mine. That's what I thought the messages were about at first, the threats. I thought she was messaging to force me to own up to the theft. I had no idea she knew Mel's mum. I don't even understand how she can.'

Nicole looks thoughtful and bites her bottom lip. Emily wants her to speak, to make this all okay in the way only Nicole can.

'Mel was an only child, right? So Chloe can't be her niece.'

'I think so. To be honest we never really paid her any attention. I knew nothing about her. We didn't care.'

'I didn't think we were bitches like the popular kids, but maybe we were.'

Emily shrugs. Bex was the bitch. Not them.

A shuffling from behind the door makes them stand back.

Angela pulls the front door open. She stands there looking sad and angry and confused, all at the same time. Deep purple shading sits under her eyes as though she's put eye shadow in the wrong place. 'You want to come in?' She glares at them both.

'Hi, yes. I'm Nicole,' Nicole says and goes to shake her hand.

'I know who you are.' Angela stands back to let them past.

Exactly like Bex's parents' house, Angela's home looks and feels as though it's still 1997 and Emily wonders if anyone ever decorates these days. The wallpaper is patterned with flowers, the ceiling covered in Artex. The carpet around the base of the stairs is worn and Emily imagines Mel jumping off the bottom stair and landing there over and over again. Until she didn't.

Angela shows them into the lounge, but doesn't offer them anything to drink or eat. Once again Emily pictures Mel in here, lounging on the sofa and watching *Baywatch,* or *Top of the Pops*.

Emily doesn't know where to sit, so she perches on the armrest next to Nicole. Chloe is in the armchair next to the fireplace. She looks nervous, thinks Emily. Maybe Angela doesn't know about the messages, about the threats after all.

'Why are you both here?' Angela says from the doorway, before seating herself on a footstool in front of the sofa.

'We, um, we...' Emily can't speak. Why are they here? Chloe's presence is a game-changer and Emily has lost all of her nerve now.

'We wanted to talk to you about Bex, and Mel.'

Angela's face darkens. 'Don't mention her name in this house.'

'Who, Bex?'

'We were such fools.' Angela looks as though she is about to cry and Emily for some uncontrollable reason wants to give her a hug. She knows how grief never goes away. Instead, the emotion waits, hidden out of sight, while you learn to live again, all the while knowing the pain can jump out and haunt you whenever it pleases.

'We're so sorry for what happened.' Nicole has her telephone voice on. The one she uses when she wants people to think she has her shit together.

'We had no idea she was on the beach. We weren't friends, we still don't know why she was there.'

'You don't know?' Chloe says, leaning forward on the chair. 'Really? You honestly don't know why she was there?'

'No. Not a clue. Why? Do you?'

Chloe and Angela look at each other and for a second Emily feels out of the loop. If they knew why she was there, why she jumped in to save Bex, then why are they only speaking up now?

'What do you know?' Emily says. Her palms are sweaty and she twiddles the ring on her right hand as the metal sticks to her skin. She cannot believe they are here, in the house of someone who died trying to save Bex. Someone they thought was insignificant. She swallows down vomit.

Angela takes a deep breath in. Then she smooths the fabric of her trousers. 'Bex and Mel, they were friends.'

'No they weren't,' Emily blurts out and then apologises.

'They were,' Angela continues. 'She came here for dinner. A lot. I could hear them laughing upstairs, listening to the latest tunes and dancing around.'

'We had no idea,' Nicole says. 'We thought Bex hated Mel. She used to say as much. Sorry. But she did.'

'It's true,' says Emily. 'We had no idea they were friends.'

'But that's the thing,' Angela says, her arms wide. 'I don't think they were. I think Bex used Mel.'

Emily shuffles forward on her seat. A realisation is dawning and she doesn't like the feeling. 'In what way?'

'We found some diaries of Mel's, very recently. Not long after Bex died. I had to clear out Mel's things, after all this time.' Again, Angela looks at Chloe and Emily wonders what the connection is. 'And they, well they were hard to read, but they showed us a different side to their friendship. Finding everything out about them messed with my head and I haven't known what to do, who to tell, so I've only told Chloe.'

She pauses.

'Bex got her involved.'

'What do you mean?' Emily's hands are tingling. She wants them to get to the point. 'Involved in what?'

'Bex's accident, the whole thing, she planned what would happen that day with Mel.'

The air in the room stills and Emily imagines a white feather would fall straight down to the floor like a stone. Nicole looks at her, frowning.

'Planned what exactly?' Nicole says and Emily is convinced her heart is about to jump out of her chest.

'Planned the accident. She was going to pretend to drown.'

'Wait there,' Chloe says, jumps up and leaves the room.

Emily's brain feels as though it's submerged in quicksand and she cannot see clearly, everything muddied and confused.

'Chloe is my niece, by the way,' Angela says. 'I know you must be wondering. She reminds me a lot of Mel. I've got a sister, much younger than me. I find having her around comforting and she doesn't mind.'

Chloe comes back in carrying a small notebook.

Mel's diary.

Chloe opens it and starts reading. 'The plan is final now. Bex will pretend to drown and I will save her. Then I will be popular. A hero. Not the loser I am now. And Bex's parents will finally notice her and she will be happy too. And Michael will realise he loves her, not Nicole. I am so excited for tomorrow. We'll show everyone.'

Emily's throat constricts. Nicole is crying next to her. Angela is staring at them as though she is processing everything. 'You really didn't know?' she says.

Emily can't speak. She is worried her voice will give away the emotion she is swallowing down.

'No,' Nicole says. 'We thought going to the beach was a fun, spontaneous thing to do.'

'You were there too?' Angela's lip curls and Nicole realises what she's done. Her head dips and she pulls a tissue out of her handbag and holds the crumpled material to her mouth.

'Yes,' Emily says. 'We were there.'

'You watched Mel drown? You didn't call for help?' Angela's voice is raised now and Emily is torn. They were victims in this too. They'd suffered for years; everyone had thought what happened was an accident, but the whole time Bex going into the sea was an attention-seeking prank.

Chloe moves closer to her aunt and places a hand on her knee, a small barely visible shake of her head in an attempt to say, stop.

'Did you send us some texts?' Emily is defiant. 'After you found the diary? Telling us to own up?' She will not be blamed for this. Her eyes flit between them both. Nicole stiffens next to her.

'Let's go,' Nicole says.

'No, I want to know.' Emily stands. 'Did you send us some messages?'

Chloe shakes her head. A look passes between her and Angela that Emily can't read. Guilt maybe.

'No, we never sent you those messages,' Chloe says, her cheeks flushing red. 'We didn't know until today you *were* there. But I think we might know who did.'

FIFTY-TWO
NICOLE – 2022

Emily hasn't said a word since they left the house. Nicole knows now is not the time to make her talk either. They walk, or rather march, down the road, Nicole's breath ragged from trying to keep up. Litter on the pavement is being kicked out of the way by Emily and Nicole has to fight every urge in her body to stop and pick every stray piece up.

Her head is crammed full of thoughts. She cannot imagine what is happening inside Emily's. The betrayal must feel insurmountable. The deception stings for Nicole too, but not quite in the same way.

Grant.

Grant has been sending them the threatening texts. Why he hasn't confronted her she doesn't understand. Why has he been fucking with them both? Revenge?

When Chloe told them back at the house Nicole had thought Emily was going to smash their belongings. Her face flooded red, her jaw and fists clenched. Emily had sat in silence while Nicole had asked all the questions. Why? How did they know? Did they encourage him? Angela couldn't speak, emotion pouring from her eyes, and so Chloe had told them everything.

Grant and Angela had got chatting to each other when she'd reached out after Bex had died, after the memorial, after she'd found the diary. She'd told Grant about its contents. He'd assumed Emily and Nicole were involved and also on the beach on the day of the accident, without actually knowing for real.

Angela hadn't wanted to believe it, but then, Grant knows Emily better than her. He knows how inseparable the three of them had been. Nicole can't believe this hasn't happened until now, but whilst Bex was alive Grant had hope. Maybe he hadn't wanted to delve further into the events of that day until grief consumed him and filled him with an obsession to understand why his sister had done something so out of character.

Chloe had explained how Angela had liked the fact that Grant was angry. A fury ignited in her too. The rage gave her someone to blame for Mel's death other than herself, the mother who hadn't noticed her daughter being coerced into making a terrible decision.

Nicole recalls the glare Grant had given Emily across the beach on the day of the memorial. The expression she hadn't been able to read. He was always going to feel more resentment towards Emily, Nicole thinks, given how close they once were. She wonders at what exact point Angela and Grant had had this conversation, how many times they'd met and spat hatred at each other about her and Emily. Right before the first threatening text she guesses. Chloe said Grant had wound Angela up, saying justice hadn't been done, that she and Emily needed to be punished for the part they'd played. But Angela couldn't do it, she wasn't ready to be involved on a hunch Grant had, not a fact.

And apparently Grant had simply said, 'Fine, then leave dishing out the consequences to me.'

Nicole's chest is beginning to burn. She needs Emily to slow down. Grant's house is miles away. They cannot possibly walk there. Nicole will not walk all the way there. Bile rises in her throat and she swallows it. 'Emily, wait. Slow down. Please.'

'I am going to fucking kill him.' Emily pauses for a second to glare at Nicole before continuing to march on.

'No you're not,' Nicole says. 'Stop. For goodness' sake, stop!'

Emily stands still in the middle of the pavement, her back to Nicole. Her head is bowed. Her shoulders slump. And then they shudder.

Oh God, thinks Nicole. Emily never cries and she's balling her eyes out twice in one day. Nicole wraps her arms around her friend, saying nothing. For the second time, they stand there for what feels like hours until Emily's shoulders still.

'Better?' Nicole says. Emily shakes her head, but a twitch at the corner of her lips tells Nicole she is at least a little bit calmer.

'We can't simply go marching around to his house.' Nicole puts her hands on Emily's shoulders and tells her. 'We have to think first. He's clearly angry with us.'

'But–' Emily starts and Nicole glares at her.

In as calm a voice as she can muster, she points out the facts. 'Emily, even if Bex planned a fake drowning, her plan went wrong. And they are right, even if it's only something Grant suspects; we *were* there. We could've called for help. We could've saved them and instead we ran away and only saved ourselves. He's right to be angry. We've lied for years.'

She can see Emily go to speak, and then change her mind.

'Ultimately,' Nicole continues, 'if Bex hadn't set the whole thing up then no one would've been injured or killed, but we have to finally tell the truth. I for one cannot stand the guilt anymore. I'm broken, me. I have been broken for years.'

Nicole doesn't want to even think about what Joe will say, or her parents. At the moment she is only worried about Emily. She will not let Emily self-destruct and blame herself for her parents' deaths too. They were not her fault at all, but Nicole knows how Emily's brain works.

'But–' Emily starts and then stops again.

'No buts, Em. We were young, stupid, and scared. But we were there. We should've called for help. We could've saved them both.'

'I know.' Emily's voice is a whisper. 'And I hate myself for running away.'

'Right, this is going to sound cheesy, but maybe we're looking for forgiveness in all the wrong places. Maybe we have to forgive ourselves. Everyone makes mistakes. People do horrible things every day. We thought keeping quiet was the right thing to do at the time, but keeping our mouths shut isn't the right thing to do now.'

'I have to see him.' Emily runs her fingers through her hair. 'I can't forgive myself until he has.'

Nicole sighs. 'Fine, but I am not marching all the way to his house. Let's go and get my car and drive. We'll talk to him together. Okay?'

'Okay.'

They turn back on themselves to where Nicole had parked her car earlier. Arm in arm, not saying a word, the closest Nicole has felt to Emily for a long time. Painful though the truth is to admit, she can see why Grant divorced her. If she hadn't known Emily since they were young then Nicole isn't sure they'd be friends now. There have been times when Nicole has wished they'd lost touch. That they hadn't been bound together by this twisted survivor's guilt. Not that their lives had been in danger back then. They hadn't survived an accident, but still they'd survived a shared trauma.

The car journey to Grant's house takes longer than expected thanks to a road closure and a build-up of traffic. Nicole is pleased as the extra time gives Emily even longer to calm down. They don't speak. Emily stares out of the window, stopping to wipe away a stray tear every now and again. Nicole feels as though she is in limbo. In a space where she is safe from judgement, but knowing it's coming. Then she realises she doesn't actually care what her parents think, and this makes her want to punch her fist in the air and scream, yes. She doesn't care if she disappoints them anymore. She is not a disappointment and if they make her feel that way, then screw them. With this sudden realisation she smiles. She doesn't need their approval. The sensation is liberating.

'What are you smiling at?' Emily asks and Nicole sucks her joy back in.

'Nothing.' She shrugs. 'Didn't realise I was.'

They pull up and park and then get out of the car. The house looms over them. With the sun setting it's the strange time of day where people have the lights on inside their houses, but are yet to shut their curtains. Nicole likes to go for a walk at twilight and sneak a peek into the windows of the people who live in her area. The lights are on in the lounge here and they can see Grant on the sofa, looking at his phone. *Or the burner phone he sent the messages from,* Nicole thinks, a sudden flare of anger sparking in her chest.

Emily marches up to the front door and bangs on the wood.

'Don't be too aggressive,' Nicole says, but knows Emily is too far gone for that. 'We're here to apologise as well as get answers, remember.'

Emily clenches and unclenches her fists and blows a breath out slowly.

Grant opens the door and doesn't smile.

'Can we come in?' Nicole asks before Emily kicks off.

'Be my guest.' He doesn't disguise the edge of sarcasm to his words.

In the lounge Emily paces next to the bay window and Nicole hesitates before sitting where she'd seen Grant looking at his phone though the window.

'You tell him,' Emily says, biting the skin around her nails. Nicole feels a strange sense of pride that her friend realises she shouldn't be the one to speak.

'We've come from Angela's house,' she starts and watches as a shadow crosses Grant's face. 'We know you're the one who has been sending us the threatening messages.'

He rubs at the stubble on his chin and for a second Nicole feels a little scared of him. He's hurting and it's their fault. He's right to want to dish out some karma out of his own. 'Okay.' He shifts forward in his chair. 'And you've come here to what, have a go at me about it? Do you even want to know why I sent them?'

'No.' Nicole shakes her head while Emily still paces. 'We came to apologise.' She gulps, her throat dry like sandpaper.

Grant looks shocked. He says nothing, then turns to face Emily. Her betrayal would always pack more of an unpleasant punch. 'Even you, Em?'

She roots her feet in the centre of the floor by the bay window and stares at him. Nicole can see flecks of blood where she's bitten the skin around her nails too deep, like she does too when she's stressed.

'Yes,' Emily says. 'I'm–' She pauses and looks at the floor before lifting her head up and standing tall. 'I'm sorry. We both are. We were there on the beach and we did nothing to save either Bex or Mel because we were too scared about what would happen to us. And I couldn't, not after my parents, I couldn't stay and watch someone else die in front of me and so yes, we ran and we're cowards, but we have fucking punished ourselves ever since. We do not need you to send us horrible messages to make us feel even worse than we do already.' She takes a deep inhale and paces again. 'Why didn't you talk to us? Why play games?'

Grant ignores these questions and Nicole can hear blood pulsating in her ears. Emily has a genuine reason for running, but what does she have? Somehow the fear of letting her parents down isn't enough.

'I'm sorry too,' she blurts out. 'I have no excuse. No reason why I ran.'

'Other than you've always been Emily's minion and done as you're told?' Grant laughs and it's like a punch to Nicole's gut. She's pathetic.

'That's not fair.' Emily walks around the sofa by the window.

'Isn't it?' Grant stands now too and Nicole feels out of place, as though this is about more than her and Emily's friendship.

'Spit it out then, Grant, go on. These texts, the threats, you clearly need to get everything off your chest.' As though to encourage the words to burst out of him, Emily pokes his chest. 'Why haven't you gone to the police?'

But Nicole knows why – what they did was immoral, but their actions weren't illegal.

'You killed my sister.'

'No we didn't. I know it's easier to blame us and not her, but the swim, trying to get your parents' attention, that was all her. Maybe you should've noticed how miserable she was instead of being so damn perfect and self-absorbed.'

'How dare you blame me. I wasn't even here then, I was away at uni, how could I have noticed? You are the two people who knew her best, who spent every single day with her.' Emily lurches forward and Nicole rises and stands in between them both.

Her voice shakes. 'Maybe we all should've noticed.'

The words pour cold water over the fire of their argument, and as quickly as the disagreement started it fizzles out.

Grant flops onto the sofa. He shakes his head. 'I haven't got the energy to fight, Em, not anymore.' He puts his head in his hands. 'We're all to blame. I wanted you to own your crap like I'm trying to own mine. I wanted to give you the opportunity to speak up, to show some remorse. I wanted to blame someone else instead of looking in the mirror. I thought, maybe, my actions would help you get over your parents, everything.' He sighs, then continues.

'There was no point in telling Mum and Dad; they don't ever want to talk about that day anyway. Knowing you were both there changes nothing for them. The fact is they weren't there. They were never there for her. Neither was I.' He shakes his head. 'I got angry after she died. Wanted to blame anyone but myself. I let her down. I ignored how unhappy she was. I ignored everything.'

Nicole's shoulders slump and he sobs. This is what happens when you stop communicating, she thinks. When you lie and lie and lie and the guilt eats you alive. They all let Bex down. And each other.

'Maybe we should go.' Nicole moves towards the door. 'We're all a bit raw and emotional and we need time to process everything. We are going to own up though, Grant. Tell everyone what we did, we promise. Your messages worked, you've got what you wanted.'

'We should have visited her more, Em. She didn't deserve to be ignored.' His shoulders slump.

Then, he gives them a small wave, which they take as their cue to leave. Nicole can tell Emily doesn't want to go, but now isn't the time to stay and have a heart-to-heart with Grant. Not while these revelations are all so fresh. It's clear Grant has his own feelings of guilt to process before he can even begin to understand Emily's motivation, or hers, for running away.

'Where next?' Emily says outside, and Nicole knows.

Joe.

FIFTY-THREE
EMILY – 2022

Grant's words reverberate around Emily's head. Is Nicole her minion? She knows that's how the teachers at school saw them, this uneven friendship that shouldn't have worked, but did. Bex saw through the cracks, maybe even Nicole did, but chose to ignore them. The people-pleasing side of Nicole's nature was pleased she had more people to please.

Emily has left Nicole to go and speak to Joe and her parents by herself. She said she couldn't face any more truths today, but they'd vowed to meet later for a stroll on the beach.

Emily has found herself walking to her parents' house, her childhood home. It's pitch black now but Mrs Smith hasn't shut the curtains yet, meaning Emily can walk past at a snail's pace and look in. As she does she sees the wallpaper with green and yellow flowers and is transported back. She can hear laughter – hers – as she opens presents on a birthday, stacked high on a chair in the far corner. Then she sees them, her parents, cuddling together on the sofa and looking down at her playing with her Barbie doll on the floor.

Life is cruel, she thinks. *And unfair.* There have been times where all she has wanted to do is sleep and not wake up unless they would be there. But stood here outside her family home she realises she's failed them. Wasted her life when they hadn't had the chance to live theirs. Not anymore. She survived for a reason. She believes that now.

As she watches, the curtains are closed, shutting out her past and firmly rooting her in the present.

'Goodbye,' she whispers and blows a kiss towards the house. As she walks away her phone vibrates in her pocket.

'Nicole,' she answers.

'I need a drink,' Nicole says and they laugh.

'I've got beer, see you at the beach, ten minutes.' Emily hangs up and heads to meet her friend.

The beach is different in the dark. Strings of fairy lights line the far edge by the car park and light up the concrete below, but beyond, as you walk further out towards the sea, only the moon lights the space around her. Tonight, the full moon hovers just above the horizon, dripping a line of silver across the sea. The wind is cold and Emily wishes she'd brought a hat or some gloves. Her breath catches in her chest as though her body doesn't want to inhale the chilly air.

Nicole drives in and parks her car, then comes up beside Emily. They link arms and Emily can't recall a time when she felt so at ease. She's never been comfortable with being touched by other people. Sometimes, when Grant would return from work and go to give her a kiss, she'd recoil. Or if he reached out to stroke her thigh as they sat on the sofa she'd huff and move his hand away. No wonder he gave up trying.

'Was it horrible?' Emily asks and Nicole laughs.

'Totally, but I'm fine, honestly.'

'Really?' Emily can't fully comprehend the change in Nicole. Normally the thought of having let someone down would send her into a spiral of self-loathing.

'Yes, really. I mean, Joe and I have got some stuff to work

through, but that's mainly stuff *I* have to work through. I'm sick of being taken for granted, but then I have allowed everyone to take me for granted for forever, and so there's no one to blame but me really.'

Emily bites down on what she was going to say. She knows she's one of the people who has taken Nicole for granted. But isn't that how some friendships work?

Then Emily grimaces. Bex took Mel for granted, her loyalty and how far she would go, even to put herself in danger for Bex, and look how that turned out for them.

'I'm sorry, Nicole.' They stop walking and face each other.

'What for?' Nicole looks surprised and Emily stands back.

'For being a rubbish friend. For not realising how lucky I am to have you.'

'Oh shut up. Don't be such an idiot.' Nicole bats the apology away with her hand, but Emily needs to say this.

'I mean it.' Emily steps closer again. She can smell a waft of Nicole's perfume, the one she's worn since school. Emily can't recall the name, realising she'd never cared enough to find out. 'You've always been there for me, and I don't think I've ever told you how grateful I am for that. No one else has stuck by me like you have.'

'Well, maybe now I don't give a shit about other people anymore I might not stick around.' Nicole chuckles.

Emily knows this is a joke, but the thought makes her want to cry. She's pushed everyone away in her life; she can't lose Nicole as well.

'Oh, Em. I'm joking. Don't look so sad.' Nicole reaches out, her arms wide and they hug, laughing and wiping away tears, and then carry on walking.

Waves lap at their feet as they meander too close to the incoming tide. They stop, right by the smattering of rocks where Bex ran into the sea and Emily pulls two bottles of beer from her rucksack, takes off the caps and hands one to Nicole. She gulps the cool liquid and wipes drips dribbling down her chin.

'I feel like I'm in some kind of cheesy movie.' Emily shakes her head. 'We're not going to go all mushy are we?'

'Nah, we did that. We're here to say we're sorry. To finally move on and forgive ourselves.'

Emily makes a retching face and Nicole whacks her on the arm.

Nicole turns towards the sea, the water dark and unforgiving. She holds up her bottle of beer towards the moon as though addressing a crowd of people and making a toast.

'To Bex and Mel, I'm so sorry. I'm sorry I didn't call for help. I'm sorry we let you down. I'm sorry you died.' Then she takes a swig before turning to look at Emily. She raises her eyebrows in encouragement.

'Go on.'

'Fine.' Emily steps forward. 'I'm sorry too,' she shouts, knowing she's apologising to herself as much as to them. 'For everything she said.' And she knows when she gets home she will destroy Bex's diary so the full truth is never discovered. One last secret hidden forever.

They stand there for several moments looking out towards the horizon. The wind whips around them and Emily shoves her free hand in her pocket and covers the one holding her beer with the end of her sleeve. Nicole sighs next to her. For years this place has haunted them. Emily knows healing will take more than shouting sorry into the breeze, but at least they've made a start.

She knows the road from here might be bumpy as they all adjust. Grief never fully vanishes and whilst tonight has been cathartic, Emily knows this isn't over. Everyone makes mistakes when they are young, but those mistakes don't often haunt you and affect you like this one had her and Nicole. Their whole lives, the way they are and how they behave all stem from that day on the beach. The choice they made to leave. The wrong choice.

But this time, they don't run away.

Instead, they link arms and walk home together.

Free.

FIFTY-FOUR
BEX – 1997

Dear Diary,
Emily doesn't want to be a part of my plan and I hate her for saying no. All that time wasted trying to get her onside. Weeks and weeks of trying to get close to her, to pull her away from pathetic Nicole, and all for nothing.

She knows I'm going to go ahead with my plan anyway, but says she doesn't care. She says she won't save me, even if I get into real trouble, she told me over and over again. She says she'll leave me to drown because that's what I deserve for being so ungrateful.

Screw her. I've written everything down in here, everything she said, her refusal to take part in my plan, all of it, and so when the 'accident' happens they'll find my journal and know the truth. They'll blame Emily for putting me in danger and then hate her for doing nothing to help. They'll finally understand why I needed their attention, why I did what I did, how desperate I was. How I was let down by my so-called friends. Emily will get her comeuppance, what goes around and all that.

Now I need a new plan. A new friend to 'save' me. Mel might be a good choice as she literally has no one else. Yes, maybe she's the one I should focus on now. She'll get where I'm coming from. Her dad is a loser too, walked out on her before she was one, and so she'll understand why I want to teach my shitty selfish parents a lesson. Not like Emily who thinks I should be grateful for simply having parents who are alive, no matter how vile they are. And then Michael will realise it's me he loves, the icing on the cake.

I'll show Emily. I'll show them all.

THE END

ACKNOWLEDGMENTS

Writing your second set of acknowledgments is very different to writing your first. With a debut novel there are often years of hard work and dedication, and an army of people supporting you on the way. With a second novel the army is still there, quietly championing you, reading your messy first draft, editing your synopsis, chatting over the phone or via text about a tricky plot point, holding your hand when you want to give up yet again.

I'm very lucky that for me the army is still strong...

Firstly, thanks as always to the wonderful Bloodhound Books, to Betsy Reavley, Fred Freeman, Tara Lyons and Abbie Rutherford. Huge thanks must go to my incredible editor Clare, who has worked hard to make this book the best it can be and also to my fab proofreader, Ian Skewis.

My beta readers, always my most trusted readers, also deserve huge thanks... Rae Tabram, Heather Fitt and Emily Koch. You all agreed this novel is better than the last, let's hope the readers think so too! As ever your insights and honest feedback were game-changers and helped make the novel what it is.

A massive thank you again to my CBC Writing Gang, always on the end of a WhatsApp or email for support and advice. You inspire me constantly!

Thank you to my family and my children for their never-ending belief. I think my children are more excited about publication day than me!

And finally, huge thanks to all of you who have supported me and gently encouraged me to sit at the table or on the sofa and tackle my edits with an endless supply of snacks, or who have asked me with genuine excitement (I hope!) about when this novel was going to be published, or who are part of the awesome crime-writing community. I cannot name you all... you know who you are!

Everyone, all of you, you all absolutely rock and I could not do this without you.

Thank you.

ALSO BY JEN FAULKNER

Keep Her Safe

A NOTE FROM THE PUBLISHER

Thank you for reading this book. If you enjoyed it please do consider leaving a review on Amazon to help others find it too.

We hate typos. All of our books have been rigorously edited and proofread, but sometimes mistakes do slip through. If you have spotted a typo, please do let us know and we can get it amended within hours.

info@bloodhoundbooks.com

Milton Keynes UK
Ingram Content Group UK Ltd.
UKHW010609100124
435784UK00004B/113